I0687591

WATER

*The Elemental Series,
Book Two*

by

Nicki Greenwood

This is a work of fiction. Names, characters, places, and incidents are either the product of the author's imagination or are used fictitiously, and any resemblance to actual persons living or dead, business establishments, events, or locales, is entirely coincidental.

Water: The Elemental Series, Book Two

COPYRIGHT © 2011 by Nicki Greenwood

Cover Art by *Kim Mendoza*

The Wild Rose Press
PO Box 706
Adams Basin, NY 14410-0706
Visit us at www.thewildrosepress.com

Publishing History
First Faery Rose Edition, 2011
Print ISBN 1-60154-978-4

Published in the United States of America

Morgan risked a look over her shoulder. "It's hard to cook a breakfast for eight with you...distracting me."

"Distracting you?" Trent rose from his seat and rounded the butcher block. Morgan spun back to her work and heard him come up behind her.

Right behind her.

She felt his body heat through the back of her blouse, though he hadn't touched her. His breath puffed across her neck where her ponytail left it bare. "I have lots better ways of distracting a person."

His husky voice skimmed her spine as if he'd run a fingertip down her back. Why, why, *why* had she said anything to him at all? Why hadn't she just kept her big mouth shut and let him sit there until breakfast was ready? Her body tingled all over—her gift, bouncing off her tenuous hold on it, and something much more primal, responding to his unspoken invitation. She started to hope that he'd quit this seesaw of flirt-hate with her, and stick to one...then thought better of it. She doubted she could handle any more "flirt" without doing something dumb. "I don't need a distraction."

"But you want one."

Praise for Nicki Greenwood, author of *EARTH*:

"Fresh, fast-paced and riotously colorful."
~*Michelle McAdam, author of SOMEWHERE LOVE*

~*~

"Nicki Greenwood has a way with words like no other...a tender romance...intriguing elements of paranormal...and a bit of mystery thrown in."
~*Kari Lee Townsend, author of LOVE LESSONS*

~*~

"Nicki Greenwood's *EARTH* takes us on the emotional adventure of a struggling rancher and gives new meaning to the words 'Power of Love.'"
~*Barbara Witek, author of EXTREME LOVE MAKEOVER*

~*~

"Very enjoyable"
~*Bitten By Books (4 Tombstones)*

Dedication

For my mother,
whose meatballs I still can't reproduce

For Chris,
gone too soon, but not forgotten

Chapter One

"Son of a…" Trent Williams dropped his wallet and cell phone in front of the paneled door of the Seaglass Inn's Clipper Room. By some miracle, he managed to save his bottle of Dom Pérignon from crashing to the floor beside them. He breathed a sigh of relief. The ancient owner of the inn wouldn't appreciate him staining her immaculately polished hardwood flooring.

At least not before he closed the deal on this place.

Normally a self-confirmed cheapskate, he'd booked a room just before the Nantucket high season, but spent an extravagant amount of his petty cash on the celebration bottle of Dom. Hell, he deserved it. Not every day a man had the chance to snap up such a soon-to-be-money-making jewel for a song. The old lady's husband had died a while back, and she said she just wanted someone to love the inn like they did.

He'd love it, all right. As soon as the cash started rolling in.

Smiling, he scooped up his wallet and phone, then inserted his keys in the lock only to find it already open. Odd. Maybe they'd left it unlocked because they knew he was coming.

He pushed open the door. Ah, that must be it. Mrs. Preble had already opened his private balcony doors. A crisp, mildly salty ocean breeze fluttered into the room past the long, sheer curtains. He suspected, based on the inn's lack of business lately, that she'd done it to air the room. The small space bore traces of that antique-shop scent he remembered from buying trips in his startup days, before he got big enough to be on the list at social events featuring strings of glitterati. He then graduated from antiques to entire properties. Better money in it...or so said his financier every quarter when he reviewed Trent's portfolio with goggle eyes.

Someone had set a stack of plushy towels on the end of the four-poster bed, and laid a basket of fruits, crackers, and cheeses on the nightstand. Nice.

He set the phone, wallet, and Dom on his dresser. Slipping off his tie, he went to the walk-in closet, then stopped. The door was open. Had someone been going through his things?

Someone still was. Shuffling and the sound of unzipping issued from within. Stalking forward, he found a woman wrapped in a large, fluffy white towel—and apparently *only* the towel, he noted with surprise—with her hand in his suitcase, which he'd left on top of the closet's dressing bureau. "What the hell are you doing?" he demanded.

She shrank back until she bumped up against the closet's far wall. Her long, cocoa-brown hair hung in sleek, wet tendrils, and desperation flashed in her eyes. "You can't buy this place," she begged him.

Trent gave her his never-fail smile, the one that softened the toughest hard-sell clients into buyouts that favored him by a landslide. "And why's that?"

"This is my home," she said. She clutched the front of the towel, and her cheeks colored with an intriguing hint of rose red.

He stared at all the damp, creamy skin not covered by her towel. Hell, if a gorgeous woman walked half-naked and unasked into his bedroom, what was he *expected* to do? "I'll tell you what," he said in his most charming tone. He indicated the bed. "Why don't you have a seat and tell me why you're snooping through my luggage?" With a smug grin, he held out his hand. "I'm Trent Williams."

"Morgan Clifton." She edged around him, out of the closet into the bedroom, but didn't release her grip on the towel to shake his hand. What a shame. Nor did she spare the big, cushy bed a single glance. She inched toward the door.

"Ah-ah," he said, slipping forward to block her escape. "How do I know you haven't stolen something?"

Her sea-blue eyes blazed. "I don't steal. And I don't rob people of the roof over their heads."

Only years of practice during unpleasant situations kept his smile pasted on his face. Time for less charm and more business. "I don't, either," he said. "I bought this inn. Do you mind telling me what you call sneaking into my room and looking through my stuff, if it isn't intent to steal?"

She made a break for the door again, and he cut her off. She bumped against his chest, all soft and curvy and shower-damp, and her long-lashed eyes widened.

He reined in the million distractions of her and took her by the hand. "Whoa, whoa. Don't be so hasty, Mrs.—Miss?—Clifton. I'd like to see if everything's still in my suitcase." He flexed his fingers around her long, slender ones, trying not to think too hard about why his thoughts zeroed in on her marital status. He felt no ring on her finger.

"I told you, I didn't steal anything," she insisted as he towed her back to the closet. "Where do you think I'd hide it?"

He grinned at that, allowing himself an enjoyable moment of imaginary hide-and-seek under that fluffy towel, but she was still talking.

"—I'm not, nor will I ever be, a corporate thieving vulture who preys on good people—"

"Do I look like that much of a jerk? Don't answer

that, I can guess what you'll say," he responded for her.

She stared hard enough to bore holes in him. He tried to ignore the look while he sifted through his belongings one-handed. "You can let go," she said, her tone sharp with clear disdain. "I'm not going to vanish."

"How do I know that?" he demanded as he examined the contents of his suitcase. He found the folder with his copy of the sale contract and opened it.

"I don't have much choice. I work here."

"Yeah? Doing what?" He skimmed the contract pages. He'd sent his office the original over a week ago, after a preliminary look at the deal points and a scrawled signature. His lawyer had reviewed it and done the hard work, then sent this copy back. Trent had been in such a rush to catch a flight to Atlantic City for a client meeting that he merely stuffed the contract in his bag—where it stayed, because right after Atlantic City was his appointment to come here. He'd figured on having plenty of time to look it over before talking with Mrs. Preble, so he boarded the plane to Nantucket without thinking much of it. Now, based on that guilty look on the intriguingly near-naked Miss Clifton's face, he wasn't so sure.

He made so many deals of this laughably simple nature that his signature had become a formality. Every tired, legalese-laden clause matched one he'd seen a hundred times.

Except that one. "'...sale of the property contingent upon acceptance of new employment...Morgan Clifton...'" Trent stopped reading. "What's this?"

Morgan's face flushed and she tugged her hand, but he kept a firm grip on it. "Did you alter my contract?" he demanded, removing the last vestiges of amusement from his voice.

"I didn't alter anything you wouldn't see," she shot back. "That's the same copy your lawyer sent back. The same thing he sent Agnes Preble. The same thing *you* already signed." This time, she did pull away to cross her arms over the towel. He noted the relief in her tone with growing suspicion. Her eyes still shot blazing blue daggers, a Greek warrior goddess at the head of an invading army. He half expected her to pull a spear on him.

She hunched her shoulders and backed away to the closet doorjamb.

Trent looked more carefully at the inserted, typewritten clause, buried in a dry dissertation on transfer of ownership. The inn wouldn't be his, free and clear, until he found this nosy, dripping-haired, fiery-eyed interference a new job. One *she* had to accept. "How dare you change this contract?"

"You had the chance to review it," she snapped. "No one snuck anything under your nose. Agnes would have let you take advantage of her and buy the inn for half its worth, and I'm not going to let you cheat her out of good money, and me out of a home—" Morgan stopped short and backed away.

"Hold on a second," Trent said, grabbing for her and missing. He rushed around her and blocked her at the door.

She sucked in a breath and stared up at him with an expression of insult, and something more that brought him screeching back to how little fabric she wore. Trent, who had cut his teeth on power lunches and corporate schmoozing, lost every other notion in his head. He stood there like a tongue-tied first-day intern and gaped at her.

"If you'll excuse me," she said with that maddening disdain. "I have to get dressed and work."

He remembered then that she'd never told him what she did for a living. "What would that be?" he asked when he could get his voice to work again.

"I'm the chef." She elbowed him aside and stormed out, then slammed the door behind her.

Damn. Trent scratched his head and wondered whether he shouldn't just order out for the rest of his stay. She'd probably poison his food.

****

Morgan stomped into the inn's small kitchen, dressed and ready to start lunch for Agnes, herself, and Trent, but in no mood to do so.

Stupid, stupid! She had dashed from the shower to his room on discovering that he'd arrived, intending to be sure he'd signed that damned contract and rendered it impossible to close the deal. When she saw his signature, she was so swept up in relief that she hadn't heard the door open. And there he was, in all his prosperous, professional, top-of-the-world smugness.

And there *she* was, in a too-small towel without even her dignity to deflect that self-satisfied smile on his face.

She ripped a spatula out of the utensil crock and slapped it on the butcher block counter with a crack. "Of all the heartless, boorish, and mean-spirited—"

"That's uncharitable of you, dear," said Agnes Preble from her seat across the counter. "Mister Williams is just doing what's best for his company. I'm sure I'll do fine on the proceeds from the sale."

Morgan blushed and took extra time finding pots and pans, though normally she could grab everything she needed for a meal in just a few minutes. The little kitchen might have enjoyed a remodel, but Agnes and her late husband hadn't had the means to expand, and its compact size suited Morgan. Here, she was her own mistress, and nothing she needed lay more than a few steps away. "You won't need to leave for a while yet," she said, crouching to poke through a base cabinet. "I've made—er, arrangements."

"What's that, sweetheart?" Agnes asked.

Sometimes she forgot Agnes could no longer hear so well. Drawing a bracing breath, Morgan stood up. "There's been a change in the contract...to allow us to stay on for a while. You don't have to leave, at least until the close of the season in late fall." *Or maybe after that,* Morgan thought with a jab of guilt, since she had left the clause open-ended. She blessed her luck that Mr. Williams's lawyer hadn't thought the new clause unusual enough to question it. Some god was watching out for her. She only hoped he stayed in a generous mood.

Agnes stopped stirring her tea. "Mister Williams agreed to our staying on a while? How nice. I told you he wasn't so terrible after all."

Sure. Except *he* hadn't been the one to insert that clause. It was his own fault if he didn't read things before he signed them, Morgan thought with a self-righteous frown. She set a panini press on the counter and began preparing the gourmet sandwiches before guilt could jab her again. "You're too forgiving, Agnes. You could have sold this inn for a much more comfortable price if you'd waited."

Setting her teacup down, Agnes said, "My old bones can't take much more of these New England winters." Her pale-blue eyes sharpened with an astuteness that made Morgan squirm. "I just worry about you."

"I'll be all right," Morgan lied, aching even now with the thought of leaving the inn and its every creaking floorboard. She laid a hand on the butcher block counter to stroke the work-polished wood. "Lots of places need a chef. There's a restaurant in Boston that keeps begging me to join them."

"I don't think you'll be happy in the city," Agnes said. "Sometimes I do wish I hadn't had to sell at all. I like hearing you sing while you cook in the mornings."

Melting, Morgan rounded the counter and hugged Agnes. She kissed the woman's tissue-soft cheek. "I'll come to visit and cook for you every morning while I'm there. With lots and lots of singing," she promised.

Agnes gave her another of those probing looks. "This man's going to be around quite a lot," she said. She lifted her teaspoon to swirl it through her cup again. "In and out of the rooms. Inspecting things. He's not going to find anything...unusual...about you, is he?"

"You didn't suspect anything until I broke down and told you, did you?"

The corners of Agnes's eyes crinkled. "I'm not such an old fuddy-duddy that I didn't think something was strange. A pretty girl like you, moving here all alone and never a date in two years?"

"It's easier," Morgan said briskly. She returned to the other side of the butcher block and began slicing cheese and peppers for the panini sandwiches. "Can you imagine a man trying to date me once he learns I'm an Elemental? He'd lose his mind, and then try to commit *me*."

"What about your foster brothers and sister? They have powers, too," Agnes pointed out. She selected a shortbread cookie from the plate on the counter and dipped it into her tea. "Kincade, for instance. He seems awfully happy, and he's married."

"Cade got lucky," Morgan murmured, thinking wistfully of Cade and Ally Murphy and their adorable redheaded baby girl. They'd visited last summer, but running their Montana ranch normally kept the little family at home—a task they seemed to relish. Hope Creek had become legendary among horsemen and cattle buyers since Morgan decided to leave the ranch and find her own future. Kincade, an earth Elemental, never wanted any other life than ranching and helping crops flourish with his gift.

Her little sister Elsa was busy working with storm chasers in the Midwest. Even Ethan seemed happy, roaming around the countryside and sending postcards, when he remembered there were such things.

As for Morgan, landlocked Montana had been a far cry from her dream home by the sea. A water Elemental, she drew strength and peace from the sounds and smells of the ocean.

And now Trent Williams wanted to tear that out from under her.

"He can poke his self-serving nose wherever he likes," she said with fresh anger. She picked up a bundle of spinach and began chopping it with rapid strokes of a gleaming chef's knife. She allowed a surge of amusement into her tone. "The most he'll find is excellent food and a vacation spot where, strangely, it never rains on the weekends." She batted her lashes in a gesture of exaggerated innocence.

Agnes chuckled with her. "Howard did love you for that. This old place was the belle of the Sound in its day, and you brought some of that back when you came." Tears sparkled in her eyes. "Whatever will I do without you?"

Morgan stifled an inner wail of sadness and pushed the plate of cookies toward Agnes. "You don't have to worry, and if I have my way, you won't have to for a long, long time."

Agnes gave Morgan a watery smile for several seconds. Finally, she seemed to shake herself out of it. "Oh, pffft," she said, waving her hand in the air. "Nothing ever stays the same but change. It could be good for all of us, dear. You'll see."

Morgan didn't see. Wouldn't see. Trent Williams

saw nothing in this place but dollar signs. She'd make him sorry he'd ever offered to buy the Seaglass Inn.

****

"You can't be serious, John. How could you miss that?" Trent groaned into his cell phone and plopped down at his room's tiny writing desk. The chair protested with an ear-grinding creak as he leaned back into it.

His lawyer gave an uncomfortable-sounding murmur. He and Trent had known each other since college, more friends than colleagues. John Lattimer could be counted on to bring over a carton of wings and a six-pack whenever the Sox were playing.

He was still going to get pounded.

Trent heard the rumble of a file drawer and the sound of shuffling paper. "Trent, you relocate employees all the time," John said. "It's good P.R. How was this different?"

"Did you happen to notice there's now a contingency clause that could lock this deal up for the next millennium? Come on, the woman's as ready to stay here as the building's foundation. I've got people looking to buy the appliances, the fixtures, the furniture. Hell, I could sell the architecture and hardwood for a mint. Can't you find me a loophole?"

"Not unless she or the old lady breaches the contract first. Rules are rules, and you signed this thing. You're the final approval, man."

"She breaches it first," Trent murmured, turning over and discarding ideas one after another in his head.

"What are you thinking?" his lawyer asked with that don't-involve-me tone. John could usually smell legal trouble a few countries away. Notwithstanding the present contingency-clause problem, Trent trusted no one else to handle his business interests.

He chose not to inform John of the plans taking shape in his head. The less his friend and lawyer knew about Trent's intentions with the maddening Miss Clifton, the better. He steered the subject away from her to ask, "I don't suppose you got an answer from my parents."

"They're not in Boston anymore. Sorry, bud. I had to relay your dinner invitation to the housekeeper, but it looks like they won't be back for a few weeks anyway. I ought to start charging you extra for this secretary work," John answered with an edge of mock annoyance.

"What are friends for?" Trent parried. "Find me an out, John, or I swear I'm going to start shopping Harvard Law for a new pal."

A knock at the door brought his attention up from the day planner on his desk. The door creaked open to reveal Morgan, clothed—*damn*—and holding a tray laden with a fat sandwich and a glass of iced tea. The chilly look in her dusky-lashed eyes scoured over him and punched holes in his train of thought. "See ya, John." He clapped the phone onto the desk and sat back in his chair. "Ma'am."

"Miss," she said in a cool, velvety voice. He swallowed a smile at discovering he'd guessed right about her lack of a husband.

She set the tray on the edge of his bed. "You didn't come down for lunch."

"Busy," he said, watching every move she made. Wisps of her hair escaped from their clip. He much preferred her hair down, he decided—tumbling forward with artless grace over her bare shoulders. Then he remembered how she'd insinuated herself uninvited into his business arrangements. "Should I be testing that drink for arsenic?"

Her eyes widened, and her cheeks took on a rewarding shade of pink. She drew up to her full height and glared down at him with the air of an offended goddess. "Even here, we have standards, Mister Williams. I don't like you, but it's my job to see you get the meals you're supposed to while you're a guest."

Insult flashed through him, but he clamped his mouth shut on a snide reply. By God, her haughtiness could give his father's cold shoulder a run for its money. Trent angled his head, considering his response. "Not from here, are you?" he asked at last, noting the western accent layering her words.

Her lashes fluttered. "No. Should it matter?"

"Where are you from?"

"Where are *you* from?" she shot back.

"Boston. Red Sox, baked beans. Best chowder in Massachusetts."

She huffed. "What do you know about food?"

"I eat. I have taste buds."

She gave him a long look, and her lips pulled into a smirk that did nothing to detract from their full, rose-pink allure. Moving to the door, she said, "Your lunch is getting cold."

He swung out of his creaky seat and hefted the sandwich from its tray, then took a big bite. Unable to resist teasing her, he spoke around the mouthful. "Wyoming?"

"Ha," she said over her shoulder. The door banged shut.

Trent grinned and sat back down to finish the sandwich. Williams, one, Clifton, one. Tie game. This could get interesting.

He took his time with the sandwich, enjoying the smoky tanginess of the peppers and cheese, balanced by mild chicken and spinach flavored with something almost woodsy. He ate at a lot of good restaurants with his clients, and he had to admit this woman knew how to put together an entrée.

What a shame he had to get her fired.

He washed the sandwich down with the tea, then gathered up the tray to return it to the kitchen. He'd have bet she wouldn't expect that, and wondered cheerfully if the idea of a man cleaning up after himself might give her an apoplexy.

He dropped the linen napkin on his tray and left the room. During his boyhood at his parents' home in Boston, a single fleck of dust was high crime. Trent had learned fast to keep things orderly. He flexed one hand, remembering being slapped with rulers until his knuckles throbbed and bled.

Dear old Mom.

When he reached the kitchen, he found Morgan bent over a cast-iron stove, examining something inside. He paused to admire the view: shapely legs, rounded hips, a slender back arched in a position that reminded him forcibly of things not at all related to cooking. Plastering a sly grin to his face, he dropped the tray on the butcher block counter with a bang.

She shot upright and whirled around with her one bare hand thrust out as if to—what, he didn't know, but it seemed she planned to fling something at him, though her hand was empty. "Don't *do* that," she snapped. "I have hot pans in here."

"I'm sorry," he lied. She made it too easy to tease her. Her flushed cheeks might have come from the oven's heat and not blind outrage—certainly not from things not at all related to cooking—but he admired them the way he'd admired her backside.

The scent of whatever was in the oven drifted across the kitchen, something sugary and irresistible, and his mouth watered. "Didn't you just cook breakfast?"

"This is for after lunch. It needs time to cool." She turned around long enough to pull the sweet-smelling something from the oven, then set it on the stove with a blue mitt covered in white-stitched

13

lighthouses.

His attention snapped to the food. Some kind of dessert, he guessed. Chocolate and berries and a crusty golden topping. Damn, he wanted to try it, whatever it was. "You spend a lot of time in here?"

"I *am* the chef," she said, not looking at him while she washed the few dishes in the sink. She adjusted the ties on the back of her apron, a ridiculous-looking thing that matched the oven mitt.

"Nice wardrobe," he said. He cracked his ladies'-man grin. "No offense, but the towel went better with your look of hauteur."

"These were a present. From Agnes."

Her ice-filled tone raked his nerve endings in a disturbing echo of his mother's warning voice. He backed down at once, shrugging against the fit of his dress shirt, until he found her watching him with those bottle-blue eyes. Slamming a mental wall up between them, he snapped, "I brought your tray back," then swiveled to evacuate the stifling-small kitchen.

The moment he'd freed himself of her stare, he snarled under his breath. He'd look day and night if it took that long to get rid of the woman. Chrissakes, everyone and their brother needed a chef. She could be a private cook for any of the insanely wealthy people who could afford vacation homes in Cape Cod. What made her want to remain in this sad-looking, rundown, past-its-heyday building?

He touched a bit of architectural woodwork on the doorway to the inn's roomy, covered beachfront porch, then slid his fingertips along the fluted grooves. Some fool had painted it a zillion years ago, but the Prebles had sanded it to return the wood to its natural beauty. They'd done some things right.

"Come sit," came a voice outside.

He squinted through the screen door. Unable to see anything but the wide beachfront facing the inn, he opened the door and leaned around the jamb.

Agnes sat on the porch in a white wicker rocking chair, bundled in a thick cable-knit sweater. She smiled. "It's nice out today. Not too windy. Come and sit."

"I have a lot to do. Calls to make—"

"You can spare a few minutes to talk about the inn, can't you?"

With an inward sigh, he pushed the door open, then let it swing shut behind him. He hated this part—the part where the owners got all sentimental about their property before they honored the deal and handed it off to him. He stuffed his hands in his pockets, ignoring the slight chill in the air, and thumped across the porch to lean against its closed railing. A huddle of shore birds chattered at the edge of the surf, looking like a knot of tiny, gray-suited businessmen in black bowler hats. Probably about to have a more successful meeting than he was. "How'd you know I was there when I couldn't see you?" he asked Agnes.

"That floorboard in front of the door creaks so loud it could wake even me. Didn't notice, did you?" He admitted he hadn't, and she chuckled. "She talks a lot, this old place. Been listening to her nigh on forty years." Agnes gave him a long, disquieting appraisal. "But I'm familiar company. It's time she started a conversation with someone new."

Trent stifled a grimace and tried to wrap his head around the image of a talking building without letting on he thought the old lady had gone batty. Never mind he'd just been eyeing the birds, wistfully imagining how much less complicated their conversation was. Never mind his intention to deconstruct the inn and start fresh—but he didn't want to hurt the old lady's feelings, either. He supposed that counted for some scruples. "When did Morgan start here?" he blurted. He cursed himself for an idiot as soon as the question left his mouth.

"Oh, it's been two years, give or take a bit. I had my hands full with a beach wedding, and she showed up on the doorstep like an answered prayer."

He pushed himself to ask the safest questions, the ones that would help him get Morgan out of the inn and out of his life. "How much experience does she have as a chef?"

"Just here, really," Agnes said, and his hopes sank. "Before that, she cooked for her family. Her brothers and sister will all tell you, Morgan's cooking is the best anywhere. She's got a...a talent, that young lady." Nodding, Agnes rocked the chair.

"Why'd she leave and come all the way here?"

"Just a will o' the wisp looking for a place to land, I guess." Agnes stopped rocking and gave him a smile. "Where's your family, Mister Williams?"

"They're away a lot," he said. "I only find out when I get a postcard." Anxious to get the topic away from himself, he added, "With a little digging, I should be able to relocate Morgan. Lots of inns around here, lots of restaurants. I have some friends in the business, and I can put feelers out."

"Relocate?"

Trent's homing-instinct business sense zoomed in on the confusion in the old woman's voice. "Didn't you see her employment clause in the contract?"

"I don't recall one. I had my lawyer look it over before he sent it to you, and he didn't mention anything about Morgan."

Too rich. The interfering chef had put a stop to the contract without her employer's knowledge. Suddenly, he didn't feel so bad about missing the change on his end. This could work to his advantage after all.

"I think you might want to talk to her, then," he said, relishing the moment. "See, I can't close the sale until she takes a new job. Which means, you won't get the money until she leaves. Your cook tampered with the contract language."

Agnes's eyebrows inched up. Smug vindication swept through him until she said, "You're not keeping Morgan?"

He stifled his surprise in a surly cloud of annoyance. Why wasn't the lady pissed off? He would be. He *was*.

Keep Morgan? God, no. Not even if she were the last A-list chef in New England. Angling for diplomacy, he said, "Like I mentioned, I have good connections. I can get her a new job on the mainland."

"Oh, I don't think she'll like the mainland. That girl's tied to the water." Agnes began rocking again without any indication that the inserted clause bothered her.

He wondered, with an inward groan, whether Agnes and the chef were in cahoots on this delay. Then he decided Agnes couldn't have known. He doubted she was capable of cheating at checkers, let alone business deals. The woman had a worse poker face than Chet, the office IT guy and world-class loser of their Friday night games.

Morgan, tied to the water? Ha. He'd met some sentimental fools over the years, but Miss Clifton was entirely too much. She wanted to be near the water. He wanted his money. Looked like neither of them would be very happy over the next few weeks.

Chapter Two

Morgan tossed in her bed that night until the blankets wrapped her into a human burrito. By the time her clock chimed three a.m., she gave up. Exasperated and restless, she untangled herself and stumbled out onto the braided rug.

Damn that man. She almost wanted to use her power in front of him and scare him back to Boston, but her loyalty to her foster family prevented it. Her brothers and sister had enough trouble without being thrust into the spotlight for their Elemental powers. Morgan hardly knew how Elsa managed to tame tornadoes without someone besides her team of Midwest storm chasers knowing how she did it.

Better Elsa than herself. An air Elemental, Elsa considered her power a gift to be used in helping others. Morgan much preferred to make use of her power in a quieter, smaller way—bringing good food and a peaceful atmosphere to the little bed-and-breakfast on Nantucket Sound.

Peace that Trent Williams had obliterated the moment he walked in on her rifling his suitcase. Morgan gave a soft growl and stalked across the room to her dresser for a pair of pants and a shirt. An hour or two of baking might soothe her nerves. Finished dressing, she pulled a brush through her long, tangled hair.

Trent Williams was a self-important, arrogant piece of work. The way he sauntered into her kitchen and banged the tray on the counter, then grinned as if that...*devastating* smile excused it. She thought back to that flash of even white teeth, that self-assured look in his light-brown eyes. Even the lazy, one-shoulder shrug that all but said *Come and get me*. He must think women were pre-programmed to worship him.

"Not this one," she assured herself.

But then he'd charged out of the kitchen like the inn was on fire. Puzzled, she slipped into a fluffy pair of wool socks. The kitchen floor could be chilly in the wee hours. She made her way downstairs, avoiding the creaky third step. Agnes needed her rest, and Trent—well, she could do without him until *after* she had some coffee. On second thought, she might need an intravenous drip of the stuff before she was able to stand him.

Instead of arriving at an empty kitchen, however, she found Trent poking through the cupboards. "May I ask what you're doing?"

"Coffee cups," he said without looking at her. As he spoke, the *glug-hiss* of her percolator reached her ears.

She spied it chugging merrily away on the counter beside the sink. "You're making a thirty-cup pot of coffee for yourself in the middle of the night?" she demanded. Insufferable! There went her peace and quiet. Not to mention the presumption of him helping himself to the contents of her kitchen before he owned it.

Finding the glassware cabinet, he withdrew a ceramic beer stein almost twice the size of her head. "It's morning," he said.

"It's three-thirty."

"Yep. In the morning."

"Don't you sleep?"

One tawny eyebrow quirked upward, and he slid a pointed look at her. "Don't you?"

With a soft huff, she edged around the counter to the refrigerator. She pointed to the beer stein. "Tell me you aren't drinking coffee out of that thing."

"Why not?"

"Coffee goes in coffee cups," she informed him. "You drink from that, and you'll be awake for the next three years."

"You take your caffeine your way, and I'll take it mine," he said, sitting at the counter. "You seem awfully concerned about my sleeping habits, for someone who also rolled out of bed this early."

She opened her mouth on a retort, then decided that she didn't have the patience to keep trading jabs with him. "I have work to do," she said, hoping he'd take the hint and go away.

He thumped the stein on the counter. "Don't mind me."

Hard not to, whispered a little voice in the back of her mind. That same contrary impulse kept her staring at him well after she'd decided it was too long. She had to admit, to much internal resentment, that Trent Williams was a scorching example of male magnetism. Darned shame about his own-the-world attitude.

He sat on the barstool with an air of idle curiosity. His gaze never left her. She jerked her attention elsewhere—*anywhere* else—and hurried around the kitchen, pulling pans and cookie sheets from their cupboards with no idea what to bake. Something. Whatever it took, as long as it kept her focus off the way he watched her.

The percolator chugged its last chug. She grabbed a cup and saucer for herself, and with a distaste-driven twist of her mouth, she reached for his beer stein. Their hands touched, and instead of letting go, Trent curled his fingers around hers and held her there. His hazel eyes burned.

Sizzle. Her normally well-behaved power leaped through her, setting her skin itching with pins-and-needles. She tried to stamp it back with every trick she knew. Counting backward. Reciting the Pledge of Allegiance. Distracting herself the way most people tried to distract themselves from sneezing.

But the distraction sitting at her counter eclipsed anything she could conjure. Her hand twitched in his. "Let go, please," she squeaked. Speaking took mountains of effort while her power pounded at her mental restraints.

He released her hand, but the look in his eyes held her there anyway. Self-assured. Focused. Convinced of his own mastery. Thoroughly arrogant—and yet she couldn't look away.

He smiled, and the spell dissolved. "Nevada."

"Hardly." Her voice came out as a dry whisper, and she seethed. How dared he try to intimidate her, here in *her* kitchen?

No. Not hers anymore. She whirled to the percolator, filled the stein, then pushed it at him along with the sugar bowl and milk. Finding her resolve, she said, "I'm sure you have a lot to do, and so do I. Have a nice morning."

"Testy, aren't you?"

"Ever had your home sold out from under you?"

"Just making an observation." He shrugged and spooned about half a cup of sugar into the stein.

Ick. She decided to start a soufflé for breakfast, and pulled a carton of eggs from the refrigerator. She felt his gaze on her back, patiently predatory, while she preheated and mixed and seasoned. Each passing minute brought an increasing and unaccustomed rush of nerves. Tension and awkwardness lay on the air like thick smoke. "If you don't mind," she said when she could no longer stand it, "I need all the counter space I can get, so I would like the kitchen to myself."

"I do mind," he said. "I'm supposed to relocate you. That means I need to learn what you do to find another place for you."

She slapped a whisk down on the butcher block.

21

"Do I look like a piece of unwanted furniture? Don't answer that," she mocked, "I can guess what you'll say."

"Touché." He grinned, and all traces of the businessman washed away just as easy as that.

Her cheeks heated. She stared until the oven timer beeped, indicating its readiness for the soufflé. Spinning around, she snatched the pan and shoved it into the oven. "I cook. Breakfast, lunch, dinner, dessert. Good food. People have been here to review it for magazines. Isn't that enough to work with?"

"Maybe I need firsthand knowledge."

She wiped down the butcher block, sweeping up a scatter of sugar beside his stein. "Your firsthand knowledge is getting all over my counter."

Trent pushed to his feet with the businessman look back in place. "We'll talk later, then." And he was gone.

When he left, she sucked in a breath, then let it out in a rush. The Kit-Kat clock on the wall ticked in the silence. Somewhere in the depths of the inn, the water pipes gave an irritable gurgle that echoed her unsettled thoughts. Grateful for solitude at last, she let the familiarity of her kitchen fill her.

Oh, what would she do without this place? Without the creaks of the settling inn and the soothing sigh of the ocean every night? She walked to the sink to rinse her sponge, then gazed out the window at the just-awakening garden behind the inn. She had planted that little patch of herbs in the concrete tub with her own hands. Rosemary and parsley, lavender and dill, every season coaxed lovingly to life in a cold frame and cloches, sheltered from the salty wind coming off the Sound by a stone wall.

Grief squeezed her heart at the very idea of leaving this place. Whether her reluctance was due to her gift with water, or her love of the sea had been there all along, she knew she couldn't—wouldn't—go back to life inland.

If that man thought he was getting her a job in some mainland greasy-spoon, he was in for a big shock.

She puttered around the kitchen, cleaning up the percolator and planning the day's menu until the timer beeped again. She removed the soufflé, set it on the stove to cool and set, then found a few other tasks to keep her busy. The radio murmured in the background about this spring's unusually warm weather. She hoped that meant the Seaglass Inn would change ownership on a high note, if it had to do so at all. As she swept the floor, she glanced out the window again.

Trent was in the garden, pacing, with a cell phone clamped to his ear. He looked miserable.

She couldn't stop the pang of concern that leaped to life in her belly, but she slapped a lid on it before it took root. Maybe one of his shameless business deals had fallen through. Served him right.

But as he ended the call and slid the phone into his shirt pocket, he stood over her herb garden with slumped shoulders. The posture reminded her forcibly of her brother Kincade before his wife Allyson had entered his life.

Lonely.

"I will not be sorry for that vulture," she said aloud. "I don't care *what* his problem is."

"Dear," said Agnes, "I hope you're not expecting the appliances to respond. I think maybe you've been in this kitchen too long."

Morgan whirled around. Agnes slid onto the barstool with a crinkle-eyed smile. Morgan returned it and stored the broom in a little closet off the kitchen. "Good morning."

"Our Mister Williams is an early riser, isn't he? I'm sorry I slept so long."

"It's only eight o'clock," said Morgan. "No one's going to check in until two, unless we get a walk-in guest. Are you hungry?"

"No, no. I'll just have tea. I need to make a trip into town today to mail some letters and pick up a can of whitewash for the fence."

"I'll do it," Morgan said.

"You ought to ask Mister Williams to go with you. He'll want the particulars of your job here."

Agnes sounded innocent, but Morgan fixed her with a gimlet glare. "Did you talk to him this morning?"

"He did mention needing to find you new employment yesterday," Agnes admitted. "I thought you might like to go to lunch, and have someone else cook for a change. Maybe see something besides the kitchen?"

"I like this kitchen, and I don't mind cooking," said Morgan. She set a teacup on the counter.

"All right, sweetheart, all right. I can take a hint." Agnes chuckled and spooned sugar into the cup. "You'll have to talk to him sooner or later, you know. Nice-looking fellow, isn't he?"

"He's all right, as long as he doesn't talk," Morgan said.

Better than all right. She'd been thinking of his self-assured smile and piercing hazel eyes all morning, in spite of every attempt to thrust him out of her head. He wore handsome like an Armani suit.

Too bad he had the personality of a piranha.

****

Trent twitched with the urge to hurl his cell phone into the ocean. Why did he even try anymore? His parents would never see how hard he worked, would never understand the effort that made him one of the country's most successful businessmen.

A man who'd been born into generations of old money, Leland Buckland Williams brooked no

24

whining. In any case, he was too busy for it, since he was twice Trent's net worth.

Trent never saw so much as a nickel of his father's money. Leland insisted that Trent make his own name and his own wealth, claiming a man couldn't appreciate what he hadn't earned. Trent often wondered why his father never applied those same principles to himself.

He'd hoped this inn might be different. His parents had grown up in Nantucket. Trent thought they might be pleased at his find.

So much for sentiment. As soon as the elder Williams found out about Trent's purchase—and grudgingly, the circumstances holding up its finalization—he exploded with reproaches and reprimands. Trent needed an additional ass-kicking about as much as Nantucket needed more sand. The conversation deteriorated into stony silence on his part after that, until Leland gave up and said goodbye.

Stalking back to the inn, Trent began cobbling together a new plan of attack. He could sell the inn and get out from under it, as soon as he got that woman out of here.

He paused to take in the rooflines of the old building. Attractive, really. The gables sloped deep and sheltering over the wide porch. The windows were in just the right places to let sunshine into the rooms at the perfect time of day. The salt breeze carried enough bite to remind him of spring's chill, but the lingering warmth promised that the high season would arrive soon.

He found the window that—he guessed—looked out from the kitchen, but he couldn't see Morgan within.

Just as well. He shoved his hands into his pockets and went back inside.

On his way upstairs, he nearly ran into Agnes.

"Sorry," he muttered.

"That's all right, dear. You look preoccupied. Is something the matter?"

The concern in her voice drew him out of his black-cloud thoughts. "What? No, I'm fine."

"If you're not busy," she said, "I've just sent Morgan on a few errands in town. I thought you might like to go with her."

Wheels started turning in his head. Town. Town would have restaurants. Restaurants that might need an interfering busybody of a chef. "Sure, why not?" he said. "I could use a break from work."

Agnes gave him a pointed look, but all she said was, "Have a good time," and then she went downstairs.

Trent thought they would be driving to town, but Morgan walked right by his luxury sedan and led him to the carriage house. All he saw inside was a pair of ancient bicycles with wire baskets attached to the front. When he hesitated, she said, "We don't all drive a Lexus. Take one."

He grasped the handlebars of the first bike, an ancient, faded red thing that could have used a one-way trip to the salvage yard. He wondered how long it would take to disintegrate...and if he'd still be on it when that happened.

"Its tires and gears are fine," she said. She withdrew the blue bicycle leaning beside a trashcan, then rolled it out into the driveway. She passed him a skeptical frown. "Don't you know how to ride a bike?"

"Maybe when I was ten," he said.

She stared at him, and unaccountably, he felt like a complete idiot. "Are you serious?" she asked.

"When would I have time for a nice little bike ride?" he shot back.

"I'm sure corporate takeovers are very time-consuming."

He bit his tongue and counted to twenty. In German. Then in Spanish. And then Japanese, just for good measure.

"Come on, pokey!" she called, pedaling out of the driveway. She circled her bike in the street. "They say you never forget!"

With a sigh of resignation, he hopped on the bike. His feet dragged on the ground. Trent pedaled after her, wobbling a bit before he regained his balance. He doubted he'd forget the Seaglass Inn long after he'd washed his hands of it.

They rode into town. The sea breeze was mild and fresh, and the strengthening sun warmed their backs. They hadn't brought jackets, and he found himself glad of it. He would have died before admitting it, but getting out had done him some good after all. The fresh salt air helped ease the knots that his talk with his father had created.

Morgan seemed to enjoy herself, too. Every so often, she'd close her eyes and take a deep breath. He wondered how she did that without running into anything, but she always opened her eyes again and resumed her ride without incident. How did a woman from out west look so at home living on the East Coast? Didn't she miss her...whatever?

They swerved around a pack of running children. "That's Mrs. Mayweather's home," she said, pointing to a tidy little Cape Cod house tucked between a grocer and an antique shop. "She's such a sweet lady. Eighty-two years old, and she still gets out in her garden every single morning." Morgan then gestured to a café, pedaling ahead of him. "That's the Lightkeeper. Great blueberry pies."

Trent studied the bistro with its striped awning and tiny tables out front. He didn't see any Chef Wanted signs in the window, but it wouldn't hurt to check. "Want to get lunch there?"

She turned and shot an open-mouthed look at

him, and her bicycle veered toward a mailbox.

"Watch it!" Trent called. Catching up to her, he steered his own bike alongside her and caught her by the shoulder before she could crash.

They broke apart the moment they touched. Not knowing what to do with his hands after that, Trent busied himself pulling his bike away from hers. He closed his hand over the latent sensation of heat from her sun-warmed shoulder—to block it or keep it, he couldn't tell.

"Thanks," she said.

"Sure," he answered, not looking at her. But the image of her wide blue eyes as he touched her had imprinted itself on his retinas, and he couldn't shake it. Incredible eyes. What a shame they belonged to a woman he couldn't stand. "Lunch?" he prompted. "I don't know about you, but all this riding around makes a person hungry."

He risked a glance at her then, and found her smiling. Ah, yes. A desire for food must be music to a chef's ears. He avoided looking too closely at her smile the same as he avoided those piercing eyes.

They sat in a little booth toward the back of the restaurant. The waitress recognized her, and a few minutes after they put in their order, the chef came out. He gave Morgan a broad smile that reminded Trent vaguely of a hungry lion. "Testing out the competition?" the chef asked.

"I am," she said, spreading her napkin in her lap. "Are you worried I might steal your secrets?"

The chef's expression soured. "My dear, I never worry about that."

That about covered this place not needing a new chef. When the man left, Trent gave Morgan a mystified look and jerked his head in the direction the chef had gone.

"What, him? Never mind," she said with a touch of irritation that only increased Trent's curiosity.

She must have noticed him staring at her, because after a few seconds had passed without her making eye contact she added, "You'll be disappointed to find that they don't serve their coffee in beer steins here."

"What abominable service," he said.

The corner of her mouth twitched, and he decided then and there that he would make her laugh by the end of lunch. A woman with a mouth like that ought to laugh and smile.

Where had that come from?

Trent dug into the loaf of sourdough bread the waitress had brought and buttered a slice, taking his time.

He felt Morgan's gaze on him across the table. A few moments passed, and then she said, "Why did you buy the Seaglass Inn, Mister Williams?"

"I'm a businessman," he said automatically. "I find an opportunity, and I make the most of it."

She made a noise that could have meant anything. Trent focused on his slice of bread, sweeping the broad butter knife across it until the whipped garlic-and-parsley butter covered its surface. And still he felt her stare.

"Why did you *really* buy the Seaglass Inn?" she asked.

He looked up, but not at her. Instead he gazed out the restaurant's front windows. He couldn't see the ocean from here, but he imagined the waves breaking on the sand and the cries of seabirds in the salt-scented air. Had his parents ever been happy here?

Sometimes Trent thought Leland had sprung into existence fully formed, like Pegasus from Medusa's blood. Even the old black-and-white photos in Leland's office, though Trent knew they were of his father as a boy, seemed like forgeries.

He stifled a sigh and put his game face back on. "It's just business," he said, then bit into his slice of

Nicki Greenwood

Morgan looked as unconvinced as ever. The place settings included teacups turned upside-down on their saucers. She turned hers right side up, then watched him for several eternity-long minutes of uncomfortable silence. "Have you ever been to Nantucket?"

"No."

"Then I can safely assume you won't have been to the Nantucket Wine Festival."

"Can't say I have."

"Well, you're going to be here for it, so why don't you attend? The Seaglass isn't in it this year, but we have been part of it in the past." She fidgeted with the teacup. "I know the festival president, and I always get tickets. The wine's amazing, the food's even better—"

"I'm not here for social gatherings."

"You're planning to establish a business presence here, aren't you? You might think about getting involved with the community."

"Since when are you even willing to give me social advice?" he demanded. "This morning, you did all you could to kick me out of your kitchen."

Morgan sighed. The server arrived to fill her teacup. Plainly, she thought it as much a mistake as Trent did for them to have lunch together. Her gaze shifted to the front windows. She lifted the cup to her lips, and Trent found himself staring while she sipped. From there, his gaze wandered to her long, chocolate-brown hair. And from there, to her arresting blue eyes and fine features. What was this woman doing sweating her days away in a tiny, hot kitchen instead of modeling in New York City or Los Angeles? He rested his elbows on the table and made sure she saw him studying her.

She bore his stare for a few moments, then set her cup gently down in the saucer. "Yes?"

"Colorado."

"I don't think so."

"Why won't you tell me where you live?"

"Why do you care so much?"

He grinned. "Are you not proud of where you came from?"

"I am. Are *you*?" she shot back.

The waitress saved him by bringing the appetizer, a seafood sampler including marinated grilled shrimp and melt-in-your-mouth scallops. For a few stress-free moments, they busied themselves with eating.

"The food's really good here," he said, remembering the frostiness between Morgan and the chef. "What's Mister Never-Worries got against you, anyway?"

Morgan shook her head as if realizing she wouldn't get out of this lunch without an answer about either her home or the chef. "Sour grapes, maybe," she said at last. She selected a scallop from the appetizer plate, and dipped it into one of the cups of melted butter supplied with the food.

Some sort of devil drove him to ask, "How sour?"

"Sour enough."

"You know, it'd be a lot easier finding you some form of acceptable re-employment if I knew something about you."

"I hardly think my relationship history has any bearing on my work."

"Aha!" Trent sat back and gave her a smug smile. "So you did date the snob."

Her mouth twitched. "I wouldn't qualify it as a date. We went to the same trade show and had dinner there together. A process I'm not willing to repeat within this millennium."

"What'd he do? Drink his coffee from a beer stein?"

Success. Her laughter floated across the table,

and Trent returned it with a broad grin. Hard to recall why he disliked her when she laughed like that.

Keep your head in the game, kid, he ordered himself. But no matter how he tried, the mental scoreboard in his head dimmed in the brightness of the smile lingering on her lips.

They passed the rest of lunch in reasonable civility, but when Trent asked her about her family, her goodwill came to an abrupt halt. She seemed as reluctant as he to divulge family history. More so, if such a thing were possible. Were her parents as difficult as his had been? He adopted the easygoing façade he used when trying to ferret information out of a competitor. "Your brothers and sister must miss you, all the way out here."

She angled her head and gave him a look that should have warned him to shut up. "They manage fine without me."

"I don't know about that. Agnes seemed to think their meals will never be the same again—second-rate cooking in your absence, and all."

"How would you know? You've had all of one meal that I prepared."

"And it was every bit as wonderful as I'd been led to believe."

She scoffed and took a sip of tea. He enjoyed the view for a while, and then the server arrived with the main course. Trent didn't usually have time for lunch, yesterday's sandwich and today's hunger notwithstanding. He'd opted for a light crab salad, while Morgan had ordered what looked like a lobster dish. "What, no surf and turf?" he joked.

"When you've had home-raised beef, you don't go back," she said.

"A farm, eh?" Trent beamed.

With a tone of exasperation, she said, "Yes. A farm. Somewhere out west, Sherlock. Good for you."

Before he could prod her further, the chef returned. "How is everything?" he asked, but he spoke in Morgan's direction.

"Perfectly nice, thanks," she answered.

"I thought the crab a little on the bland side, actually," Trent said, though it wasn't. What on earth had made him say that?

Morgan's gaze came up from her plate. Her eyes held an intriguing little gleam of amusement.

The chef swiveled his attention onto Trent. He wore an expression that Trent could have bet lacked any sort of the sincerity it was supposed to convey. "I'm sorry to hear that, sir. I do hope you'll come back and try it again to see if I've improved."

Trent folded his hands and propped his elbows on the table, giving the chef an extra-stuffy A-list frown. "Well, I'm not in the area much, and things being what they are, I don't believe I'll have time to come back. But thanks for the effort."

"Of course." The chef fake-smiled his way out of the room and back to the kitchen.

Trent returned his gaze to Morgan to find her grinning. "You just earned yourself some points," she said.

"I'll try not to let it go to my head." He spoke with his businessman charm, but as he watched her turn back to her meal, he wondered whether something about her might not be going to his head after all.

What was the score again?

Chapter Three

After lunch, Morgan led Trent into town, pointing out local sights and punctuating her tour with anecdotes. She hadn't intended to have such—well, fun—but after the way he gave Spencer such a hard time on her behalf, she decided Trent had some redeeming qualities after all. The chef had been a fly in her soup since her arrival in Nantucket, and frankly, she'd have welcomed a round of tormenting him from her worst enemy. Even if Spencer's food was good, his everything else left a lot of room for improvement.

She and Trent stopped to mail the letters for Agnes, and got whitewash last thing. By then, Morgan was startled to realize the sun had begun to set. "Would you like to ride back by way of the beach?"

"Sure. 'Cause there's no beach back at the inn, and all."

Ugh, just when she was starting to think well of him, he spoiled it by opening his mouth. "A simple 'no' would have been sufficient." Exasperated, she pedaled off.

Trent muscled his bike alongside hers. "I'd have said no if I didn't want to do it. Don't they have jokes where you're from?"

"Don't they have enjoyment where *you're* from?"

"I've got to say, I'm impressed with your touchiness."

"Let's revisit how you're buying out my livelihood, and trying to pawn me off like someone's old tea set."

He laughed. "I can think of a number of things to compare you with, Miss Clifton. 'Tea set' doesn't make the list."

With a growl, she sped down the sidewalk.

He caught up again, pedaling in and out of a trickle of pedestrians. "I guess that means my earlier points have been deducted back off your tally."

She didn't answer, merely sped up until her bike surged ahead of his once more. She dodged a pair of hand-in-hand Rollerbladers.

"All right, all right," he called. "Let's go back along the beach."

She shot him a scathing look. "Don't make it sound so much like I'm twisting your arm." She turned her bike at an intersection, and they veered off toward the omnipresent sound of ocean waves.

Their path took them along the shore. Morgan detoured at the Nantucket Town Pier. She leaned her bicycle against a convenient piling, then walked to the edge of the beach to remove her shoes. Gritty sand oozed between her toes. She needed the soothing feel of water against her skin right now. Trent had a maddening knack for testing her patience. And she was supposed to be the patient one in her family. Ha.

After an awkward moment where he merely stared at her, Trent got off his bike and followed her. "What are you doing?"

"Sitting. Is that particularly shocking?"

"What's with the bare feet?"

"Absolutely nothing." She pushed her feet into the chilly shallows, then closed her eyes. With her hands tucked under her hips, she let the feel of the ocean soak into her. The soothing touch of the water rushed through her, and she shivered with pleasure. Much better.

She heard Trent walk to the edge of the dock,

then he reached the beach and sat beside her. Shocked that he would risk getting wet sand on his clothes, she almost didn't hear him when he said, "Keep that up, and you're going to lose your feet."

"It's nicer than you think," she said, her eyes still closed. "You should try it." How she longed to let her power loose and connect fully with the ocean currents, to moderate that chill she didn't want to admit to—but not with *him* sitting right next to her.

"I'll pass," he said.

"Suit yourself." She opened her eyes to stare westward, where the sun had begun setting in a brilliant late-spring blaze that washed the fluffy clouds in watercolor pinks and reds. She drew a soul-deep sigh that sank into every extremity, and listened to the swish of the ocean and the lonely wail of birds. The island felt almost deserted this time of year. The number of boats speckling the ocean's surface were a fraction of their mid-summer mob.

Trent stared not at the incredible sunset, but at her. His predatory gaze burned—or was that a blush she felt in her cheeks?

Dear God.

"What?" she snarled without moving her gaze from the setting sun.

"Don't you get bored watching this stuff?" he blurted. "I mean, you live here."

She looked at him then. "Don't you get bored with buying out the little guy?"

The line of his mouth thinned. Something flickered through his eyes, but he snapped, "Do you ever not answer a question with a question?"

"No, I do not get tired of watching the sunset." She held his gaze, expecting him to look away, but he didn't. Their mutual stare lengthened until she wanted to squirm. Her hands began tingling—her gift, reacting to the discomfort. *Pledge of Allegiance. Okay, not working.* She flexed her hands, but kept them tucked under her legs. Sand grit sifted through her fingers. Seconds drew out into centuries, and still she couldn't look away.

He kept right on staring. His eyes darkened from the color of fresh honey to a cinnamon-bun golden brown. *Ten, nine, eight, seven—oh, God, I've got to get out of here.*

Too late. The pins-and-needles sensation of her power flowed up her arms and over the top of her head, then down through her body to her toes where they sloshed in the cool water. Horrified, she froze where she sat. Next thing, her skin would be glowing. She held her breath, wishing he'd look away. Wishing he'd *go* away. *Please, please, don't let it get that far out of my grip.*

"What is it about you?" he asked at last. He leaned forward, studying her face. "I can't figure you out."

Too close. Way too close. She ripped her gaze away and leaped to her feet. "We'd better go. If we get guests tonight, I'll need to be there—"

"Who's going to come now? It's after seven o'clock." She heard Trent stand up behind her. "Besides, you just sat down."

"I didn't know what time it was. Let's go," she said, pulling on her shoes and avoiding his gaze as if it could turn her to stone.

"You're twitchy. Is that a chef thing, or just a you thing?"

"It's an I-don't-like-you thing," she snapped. She could almost see Agnes frowning at her in disapproval. Her skin itched. She wished she could just jump into the water, and let her power loose to do as it would. A little dip of the feet this time of year wasn't so outlandish, but barreling in fully clothed might convince Trent she was off her rocker.

She jerked her bicycle upright and plopped onto the seat. Jamming her feet onto the pedals, she cranked the bike along. "Better hurry."

"Montana."

In spite of her every intention otherwise, she screeched to a halt. Cookie-jar guilt wormed under her skin to mingle with the itchy echo of her power.

Busted.

This must be how Ethan felt whenever I yelled at him for burning his junk mail in the kitchen sink. How many times had she yelled that smartass grin off her younger brother's face when she found him using his gift to make a mess in her kitchen?

For once, she empathized with him.

Shaking it off, she began pedaling again.

Deep-chested laughter floated through the air. "I'm right, aren't I?" Trent called.

"What if you are?"

"You continue to avoid telling me anything about yourself—"

"I've known you a day and a half."

"—so I've got to guess."

"Congratulations."

Still chuckling, he pedaled alongside her.

Instead of the outrage she expected to feel, Morgan shivered at that sizzle-inducing laugh. Her belly, normally perfectly well-behaved around men, and men like him in particular, gave a shocking little jump. *Oh, no. No, no, no, no, no.* She rode faster.

"You trying out for the Ironman?" he asked.

She glanced back to find him grinning like he had the world by the tail. Her power bubbled in her fingertips. Panic shot through her, and she pedaled away as fast as possible.

Still smiling, he cycled past her and wove between the pedestrians as they rode back to town. Damn him. He lifted smugness to a whole new level. What she wouldn't have given to knock him down a rung. A few rungs. A whole stinking ladder company worth of rungs.

As infuriated as she was, she couldn't help noticing as they rode along that Trent drew an alarming multitude of stares from women. The first one gave him a subtle, lingering look. A pair of walkers giggled as he coasted by. When he passed a chattery group of jogging women who gave muffled gasps and craned their necks to watch him, Morgan finally lost her hold on her power. Swearing, she tried to grasp it, but it slipped from her reach with a mind of its own. She muttered a desperate prayer. Oh, why hadn't she worn a long-sleeved shirt? Or a sweater? Or a down parka?

The sunset clouded over. Within seconds, it was drizzling. A minute more, and it was pouring. People held papers and jackets over their heads, and rushed for the nearest store with squeals and exclamations.

Trent's pale-blue oxford shirt went transparent with the rain. He slowed down, slicking his dripping blond hair out of his eyes. He gave a shuddering grimace, clearly feeling the cold she never experienced. Water temperature was never a problem for her. "Where did all this come from?" he demanded.

Where, indeed. She clenched the handlebars of the bike until the ridges of the grips bit into her palms—which were probably glowing at this very moment. She avoided looking at them, afraid to draw his attention.

He definitely drew hers. The wet shirt clung to his upper body. Her dry tongue stuck to the roof of her mouth as she stared. He must have spent as much time in the gym as he did in boardrooms playing king of the world. The sleeves hugged his prominent biceps and sculpted forearms. *Of course,* she thought—a man that arrogant would be as attentive to his appearance as he was to ruining people's lives. She wondered if he owned a gym, among his other real estate conquests. Maybe a string of them.

Even drenched, he managed to look more sinful than her triple-chocolate layer cake. She deliberately turned her attention away, and kept it fused to the sidewalk ahead of her bike for the rest of the ride.

No matter how much she wanted otherwise.

Trent said nothing further, probably lost in some imaginary corporate coup. They pulled into the driveway of the inn, then she stood her bicycle in the garage. Without looking at him, she hauled the bucket of whitewash out of the basket on her bike and rounded toward the inn's service door.

He grabbed her arm.

They froze. With his other hand, and without breaking eye contact, Trent leaned his bike alongside hers. In his eyes, she saw the same surprise that must have been on her face.

He let go like she'd stabbed him. "Sorry," he muttered. He hitched his broad shoulders and looked away. "Thanks." He slicked his hair back again, hesitated, and then tugged the whitewash from her hand.

"What for?" she asked, but he'd already started away toward the door, carrying the heavy bucket.

****

"No," Trent growled into his phone for the third time. "I said sell the stock in the cardio device, and put the money into this auto manufacturer. I mean it, Sam."

His stockbroker made a noise of anguish. "You do realize this is financial suicide, right?"

"What am I paying you for?" Trent demanded. "My hunches are right more often than yours."

"All right, all right. I bow to your clairvoyance," his broker said. "Don't forget my cut when your hunch pans out, bro."

"Yeah, yeah." Standing at his bedroom balcony,

Trent hung up the phone.

The floodlights on the back of the inn weren't enough to illuminate the beach below, but the extra lighting would have been unnecessary. The shore stretched out below him in all its moonlit glory. The salty breeze toyed with the curtains on the open balcony doors. Weird how warm it was for this time of year.

Agnes had given him the best room available without even asking. While he was accustomed enough to such treatment not to question it before, he took in the view of the beach now with an uncomfortable sensation of obligation.

He didn't want obligations. He wanted to break this place down and piece it off as fast as possible, then get out of here and back to his life in Boston. Back to full days at the office, unfussy games with his poker buddies, and the peace of his condo and a chilled glass of pinot.

There were too many distractions here.

Turning away from the breathtaking view, he focused on the hardwood floors and detailed architecture of his room. No one built places like this anymore. They were worth more in pieces than as a whole building. Goldmines waiting to be plundered.

He stared at his cell phone. He had a lot of catching up to do. He'd wasted a whole afternoon fooling around in town with that—that woman.

A flash of her grinning face thrust itself into his memory. Christ, she had the sexiest laugh he'd ever heard. And her voice—when she wasn't flinging insults at him—could have talked the devil into reformation. To say nothing of that body, curvier and more hazardous than an icy mountain road.

Lust slashed through him. He shoved it back into its box with a quiet groan of frustration. He needed to get out of this doily-filled tourist trap.

He dropped into his desk chair, then flipped

through his day planner for the number to his latest client, the temperamental owner of an insurance agency looking to expand. He didn't care about the late hour, and he suspected she wouldn't either, if it meant getting her way when they closed a deal. He hated talking to her, but at least the old grouch would take his mind off the *other* annoying female in his life.

The moment he dialed the number, female laughter floated into his room through the open balcony doors. The sound chiseled at his concentration, and while his cell rang, he drifted back to the balcony to investigate.

He'd left the doors open hoping the fresh air would sharpen his thoughts. Now he wished he'd shut them.

Morgan strolled along the beach beside a large, lanky dog. The animal's shoulders reached above her hip. Every yard or two, the canine horse turned to her and leaped up. It slapped its paws against her snug T-shirt and wraparound skirt, an outfit which outlined in vivid detail the curves Trent had been thinking about only moments ago. Morgan seemed not to mind the dog getting her dirty.

She laughed again. The sound shot through Trent from the top of his head down to his feet, then set up shop low in his belly. He let his gaze rest on the long, long legs visible when her skirt fluttered in the breeze. The dog raced away down the beach, presumably returning to its owner.

Then Morgan shucked out of her clothing, revealing a modest one-piece bathing suit that made him suck in until he choked. Any intention of calling his obnoxious client flew out of Trent's head. He lunged away from the open doors, hoping she hadn't seen him watching.

Holy hell.

"Yes?" grumbled a sleepy voice over his cell.

Trent disconnected the call without a word and squeezed his eyes shut on the vision of Morgan in that skin-hugging slip of fabric. If any other woman had worn that bathing suit, he might not have thought twice. On *her*...the image hovered in his mind like an aftereffect of staring at the sun, somehow a million times more sensual than a tiny bikini that left nothing to the imagination.

The businessman in him wanted nothing to do with her—wanted only to speed back to Boston to avoid looking out that door again.

But the businessman wasn't doing the thinking right now.

Trent turned the phone off. What the hell did she want to do out there, freeze? The water had to be under sixty degrees. He strolled back to the balcony with a put-on ease she wouldn't have seen anyway, then braced his hands on the painted white balustrade.

He saw no sign of her on the beach. Scanning the water, he wondered with a pinch of discomfort whether anyone besides himself knew she'd gone swimming. It must be past eleven o'clock. Did she do this a lot? What if she were swept out by an undertow?

He'd almost made up his mind to go down there—hell, he didn't like her, but he didn't want her to drown—when he spotted a pale shimmer in the water about twenty yards out.

Moonlight? No—the moon shone in a watery white streak on the ocean surface, well away from the whatever-it-was that had caught his eye.

Not rocks. He remembered from daylight observation that the water spread out smooth and uninterrupted from this part of the beach.

He thought about the dog, and the way the moonlight shone on its fur as it ran beside her.

An animal.

43

Did Nantucket have shark problems?

Trent didn't know. But in the next moment, without conscious thought, he was downstairs and out the door. He rushed toward the water, stripping off his polo shirt and shoes as he went. "Morgan!"

The shimmer flickered and disappeared. Seconds later, as he was plowing into the frigid shallows in his dress pants, she surfaced and brushed her hair back. *"What?"*

He stopped dead, feeling like the biggest idiot this side of the Mississippi. Swearing under his breath, he backed toward the shore a step. "Nothing. I thought I saw..."

Her lips parted and her eyes went wide. Trent couldn't believe it. Late at night, alone in maybe shark-infested water, and she'd had no reservations. Now that he was there to—God, *rescue* her—*now* she looked scared. What the hell was it with her?

"What did you see?" she asked. Her unsteady voice reached him across the moonlit water's surface, just audible above the quiet waves.

"Never mind," he said, turning back to the beach. Every step shot an arc of seaweed-scented ocean froth up the legs of his four-hundred-dollar pants.

Water sloshed behind him. "Wait. Did you—did you come out here to *save* me?" Amusement and disbelief filled every syllable. She laughed, actually laughed.

He gritted his teeth. *Do. Not. Talk.* Jamming his fists in his pockets, he splashed onto the beach.

"Trent, please wait."

He jerked to a halt, unwilling, but unable to resist the sound of her voice saying his name. Soft. Impatient. Too damn inviting. A lot like her. A warning voice in his head began screeching *get-out-get-out-get-out*, but he couldn't obey that any more than he could obey the twitch of leg muscles primed to run. A Williams never ran from anything.

Her hand settled on his bare shoulder, cool and damp. Burning anyway. Trent had never lacked for women to decorate his arm—or his bed—but none of them had ever done to him what that touch was doing right now. He strove to ignore the alarming way his body reacted. Heat spread through his veins as though he'd chugged a glass of single malt whiskey. Infuriating woman. Obnoxious. Presumptuous. God, he couldn't stand her.

He spun around and kissed her hard.

Chapter Four

Morgan yelped into Trent's mouth and tried to step back, but he snaked his hands around her waist and tugged her to him with potent male ferocity. He kissed with a hunger that unwound her misgivings one by one and retied her into a hopeless tangle. She whirled like a drowning shipwreck victim. Clutching at his shoulders, she clung to him, the only solid thing her senses understood.

Sizzle. Her power flung itself along her nerve endings and rebounded into her fingertips.

She reeled backward. Terrified he'd seen the evidence of her power, she crossed her arms over her chest and jammed her fists underneath her elbows. Her gift throbbed in her palms. She sensed every droplet of water on her body.

And the ones she'd left on his shoulder, too.

Had he seen her using her gift underwater, soaking in the desperately needed comfort of ocean currents?

Seawater dripped down his arm. Riveted, she followed the trickle of water down his powerful shoulder, over his bicep, and along the sinewy forearm. Realizing she'd begun to stare at skin instead of water, she dragged her gaze back to his eyes.

His expression ran the gambit from surprise, to confusion, to anger. "Sorry I bothered you," he said.

Before she could stop herself, she'd reached out toward his arm. "No! I mean...thank you."

At the softening expression in his eyes, she lowered her hand. She went to cross her arms again, hesitated, then did it anyway. Awkwardness hovered between them like a stifling vapor.

The split-second vulnerability in his eyes swept away, and he returned to his stone-faced cool. "You're welcome. Aren't you cold?"

"No." Not with her gift moderating the water temperatures around her skin. Certainly not while feeling the residual crush of his kiss on her mouth. Quickly, she pressed her lips together.

His brows twitched up, then he frowned as if he was trying to convince himself she wasn't his problem. "Enjoy your swim." He stalked back toward the inn.

Chilly air slid into the spot he'd vacated. Morgan rubbed her damp arms and stared after his broad back. At the top of the beach, he bent to scoop up his shirt and shoes. Her gaze went right to his ass, clad in a pair of wet slacks that clung to his body and displayed him as plainly as if he were stark naked. A little moan stuck in the back of her throat—part admiration, and part frustration that he was the one responsible for it. But that body...

Oh, don't go there, girlie, she told herself. But her mouth jumped ahead of her brain. "Trent," she called, splashing after him.

He turned halfway around, sneering as he scrubbed sandy water off his pants with the wadded-up shirt.

Dear God, was she really about to invite him to stay on the beach? She tried to stop herself, but one glance at the way the moonlight traced the planes of his broad chest loosened her tongue. "Did you want to—"

"I'm going to make some calls tomorrow," he interrupted. "Get me a copy of your résumé first thing in the morning, and I'll have you a list of potential employers by dinner."

The rest of her words died in her throat. The

memory of his lips pressed roughly against hers pelted through her body. Torn between that and the insult burning in her chest, she clenched her fists at her sides. "Fine. Next time you think I need saving, keep your mouth off me."

He held her stare, his handsome features full of disgust. "No problem." He whipped around and stalked away, leaving her fuming.

What a— How dare he— Insufferable! The sooner she got him out of the inn and back to Boston, the better. He had no right to kiss her. No right.

But what a kiss. The mere thought of it slipped in along her nerves, touching off little pings of frustrated fascination. Her power flitted after it, *zip-zip-zip*, until she found it impossible to stand still.

She jogged along the beach, heedless of the cool air on her still-wet skin, trying to force the slight chill to drive off the way her body echoed with the blast of his kiss. No luck there.

She didn't even *like* him. He'd made it clear he didn't like her, either. He wanted to wreck her home. He had no tact, and no consideration.

But tons of charisma, when he wanted to.

Bad ideas began bubbling to the surface of her thoughts. He couldn't very well send her packing if he didn't *want* her to leave. She could tempt him into letting her stay on.

No. No, no, no. She wouldn't sell herself to him, not even to remain at the Seaglass Inn. He might be able to write his own ticket where most women were concerned, but it would be a cold day in hell before she made herself one of them.

She swept up her clothing, then marched back to the inn, painfully aware that every step brought her nearer to him.

When she crept inside, he was gone—upstairs, she hoped, well out of her way. Instead of going up to her room and risking a run-in with him, she slipped back into her skirt and T-shirt and went to the kitchen. She doubted she'd be able to sleep anyway. Since his arrival, she'd gotten poor sleep, or no sleep.

Baking a batch of her signature muffins ought to get him off her mind. A quick search through the kitchen yielded flour, cinnamon, blueberries, and lemons.

She turned from the refrigerator, milk pitcher in hand, and rammed into Trent. She squeaked and let go of the pitcher.

He caught it by the base. Milk sloshed out of the spout and dribbled over his arm. His brows quirked. Broody hazel eyes locked on her face. "Taken to throwing things at me now?"

She grabbed the pitcher out of his hand. "What do you want?"

"Coffee. What else would I be doing in the kitchen past midnight?" He angled his head and laid that sexy look on her.

How did he *do* that? While she was still spinning over that kiss, he switched moods as easily as flicking a power button. She backed away as if he were a rabid rottweiler. "I'm not starting the percolator. You'll have to make do with instant."

"You're killing me." He edged around her to the cupboard.

He'd changed into another shirt and a pair of khaki shorts that exposed powerful legs. She wrenched her gaze away, but it snapped back to him like a rubber band.

He didn't even notice. Whistling, he found the coffee and that infuriating beer stein, then moved to the stove to start the teakettle.

Realizing he wasn't going to leave after all, she grumped, "Why do you even want to be awake at this hour?"

He pivoted on his heel, and his gaze went laser-hot. He slid the short distance across the floor and leaned, smiling, close enough that she smelled peppermint on his breath. "I do my best work in the middle of the night, Montana. What are *you* doing up?"

She stood her ground, and gave him the look she used to give Ethan when he got out of line. "I was trying to avoid you, until you barged in here."

"Sorry to be so distracting." He looked anything but sorry.

"Just get your coffee, and get out of my way."

He dropped onto a barstool. "Can't do that until the water heats up. Notoriously slow, teakettles. Watched pot, and all."

"Microwave it, then."

"Have you ever microwaved your water for coffee? Nasty stuff."

Muttering an unfriendly word under her breath, she stalked to the stove and turned her back to him. Certain she wouldn't be seen, she touched the teakettle's lid.

He'd been sloppy about filling it. Water droplets clung to the lip around its lid. A tiny rivulet ran from there to the inside of the kettle, and down to the rest of the water in its bottom. Loosening the reins on her power, she gave the molecules a boost of energy. Seconds later, she felt them smacking into each other and creating friction—heat. Only a tiny shimmer on the skin of her fingertips gave away the evidence of her gift in action. A little risk was worth it, if it got him out of her kitchen faster.

Normally when she cooked for the inn's guests, she drew on her power's sensitivity to filter impurities out of the water—anything that wasn't straight water—before cooking with it. She didn't bother this time. Served him right if his coffee came off with a little extra sediment flavoring. Heck, it might even drive him out of her kitchen in search of something else to fill that stupid beer stein.

With its own aquifer, Nantucket had better water than most places—better than Sagerton, Montana's had been—but Morgan had always sensed a difference when she distilled it with her gift.

Maybe he wouldn't know the difference. Maybe she ought to be *adding* something unpleasant to the water.

Yeah, she thought with a smirk. *A little hemlock might do him some good.*

She let the water get to a simmer, then began gathering bowls and graters for her muffins. All the while, Trent watched her, a nagging presence at the corners of her vision. By the time the kettle began to hiss its precursor to boiling, she couldn't take it anymore. She watched him spoon the usual pound of sugar into the stein. "I'm going to start charging you for that."

"Put it on my tab," he said.

"Don't you have someone to annoy somewhere?"

"Just you, honey."

"I'm flattered. Go away."

He pinned her in place with those liquid hazel eyes, a leisurely stare that wandered from her face to her damp T-shirt. She wished she'd tied her apron in place over it. Heat rushed through her all the way up to her cheeks, where it flamed like a bad sunburn. "You first," he drawled.

She beat back a growl and turned to mixing batter for her muffins. Sugar. Baking powder. Eggs. Oil. Milk, where had she put the milk?

She snatched it and poured it in without needing to measure it. What next? Lemon zest. Scrape, scrape, scrape. For one instant, she let herself imagine how it might feel if she swiped at his nose with the grater. Scrape, scrape, scrape— harder.

No. She would not, would *not*, give him the

satisfaction of getting her temper up.

Well, at least she wouldn't show it.

The Kit-Kat clock on the wall ticked away, wagging its pendulum tail with a lot more nonchalance than Morgan could muster. Still fuming, she thought of all sorts of ideas to get Trent out of the inn, none of them fruitful.

Finally, he asked, "Are you always this...interactive...with your cooking?"

"What are you talking about?"

"Your lemon's going on the counter."

She shifted her glare from the gleaming grater to the bright-yellow curls of lemon rind on the countertop. She'd missed the bowl by four inches. She scraped up the peels and deposited them where they belonged. "Are you just here to irritate me, or do you have something useful to say?"

"Well, you'll notice I'm not the one messing up your counter this time. That's useful."

She looked up to find him laughing quietly. Memories of their bike ride and the stop at the pier rushed back. Memories of that alarming way he leaned toward her. Looked at her. The way he looked at her now. The way he'd kissed her on the beach, with devastating passion.

She jerked back so fast, she ought to have left skid marks on the linoleum. "Whatever you're thinking," she said, "you'd better un-think it."

He never let up that unhurried, smoldering stare. Seconds passed. With distant shock, she felt his steady gaze loosen the knots all the way up her spine. How could he be so hypnotic, when not half an hour ago, he'd been as unapproachable as a pit of razor blades? The inn hadn't received any guests tonight after all, and she'd never wished more for a house packed to bursting with diversions.

The kettle whistled in time to save her from doing something stupid—lean toward him, or throw something at him, she didn't know what. She poured hot water into the stein, and then pushed the canister of instant coffee toward him without looking at him again. "Have a nice morning," she said, hoping he heard the frost in her tone. She kept her focus on mixing the muffin batter.

His low laughter chased along the loosening knots in her body. "See you around, Montana."

He left the kitchen, but she found no relief once he was gone.

****

The instant Trent reached the stairs, he dropped his golden-boy routine. By the time he got to his bedroom door, he'd traded the grin for a fire-and-brimstone mood that would have done his parents proud.

In his room, he set his coffee on the secretary desk, then stripped out of his polo shirt. *All right,* he admitted to himself. *She's smoking hot. Get it off your chest, and move on.* He allowed himself to revisit the image of her in that bathing suit, and then the feel of her against him as he kissed her.

He ought to call up some of the women whose numbers filled the directory in his cell phone. A little distraction could be just the thing he needed.

Not at this hour, though. Even his sometimes-date Laura would chew him out for calling this late.

Moody, he flipped open his laptop and skimmed the contract for his latest real estate purchase without any particular attention or interest. Every time he read something about power supplies or water lines, his mind drifted back to the woman in the kitchen downstairs. And then lingered there. Way too much.

With a sigh, he opened a Website for want ads. Someone on the New England seaboard had to need a chef. And if he couldn't find someone who wanted her on this coast, he would damn well try the other one.

Within an hour, he'd ferreted out three potential jobs for her, two of them about an hour inland. One was a private chef for some corporate big shot, and the other two were in chain restaurants. He hoped like hell she got him that résumé first thing, because the thought of lingering here with her any longer than necessary did things to his body that he wished he could get the rest of him to ignore.

He shouldn't have kissed her. What—besides the obvious—had he been thinking?

He stared at the screen of his laptop, resenting that he even had to waste time on hunting up a new job for her. One of his underlings at the office could have done it...tomorrow. He didn't have the patience to wait.

Parts of him didn't, anyway.

He sprang up from his desk chair to stalk the room. He couldn't even start tearing down the building until he'd waved Morgan off to her new job. He stripped off his shorts, then shut the balcony doors. It was mild enough that he could have left them open a bit longer, but he didn't want to be reminded of who'd he'd been watching on the beach tonight. He much preferred to deal with a stuffy room than with reminders of her.

Damn woman.

He stretched out facedown on the bed, and groaned into the pillow. He found it almost impossible to sleep for the rest of the night.

Late the next morning, he woke to the mesmerizing smell of cinnamon and sugar. He hurried through a shower, then slipped on one of the few pairs of blue jeans he'd brought.

His mother thought them vulgar. He hadn't owned a pair until age fifteen, when he scraped up the pocket money for them. She promptly threw them out with the trash, and told him never to let her catch him in them again.

He wondered how he didn't own a whole closet full now.

As he went downstairs, he heard the chatter of unfamiliar voices. Strange. Anyone that would have stayed at the inn should have checked in last night.

Agnes's voice punctuated the talk, and then the unmistakable sound of Morgan's laughter rose above the din. A mental snapshot of her smile skewed his concentration.

He ventured into the dining room, where he found a table full of people. The smell of coffee—good coffee, the kind you found in a bistro, paired with biscotti and indie music—rolled across the room. He sucked it greedily into his lungs.

Then he noticed everyone had stopped talking.

A young blonde woman had paused with a cinnamon bun halfway to her mouth to stare at him. Her gaze flicked toward Morgan and back, then carefully down to her plate, strewn with the remains of scrambled eggs.

The rest of the strangers continued to stare openly, a rough-around-the-edges assortment that Trent couldn't imagine would choose to stay at a Nantucket bed-and-breakfast. Seconds dragged past. He fumbled for his golden-boy camouflage. "Good morning."

Agnes found a serene smile for him—*Not going to do the guilt thing again, damn it, I'm not,* he ordered himself—and then Morgan stood up. "Everyone, this is Trent Williams, the...buyer...of the inn. Trent." Morgan ticked off the heads around the table. "This is Rory Grant, Seth Loughlin, Nina Parnow, Brian Wozinsky"—she reached the young blonde—"and my sister, Elsa Pemberley."

The different last name brought Trent's attention automatically to the young woman's left hand in search of a wedding ring, but he found none.

Unwilling to admit curiosity toward any part of Morgan's life, he slid into the only remaining empty chair. A cup sat at the untouched plate, turned mouth-down on its saucer. He upended it, lamenting its small size, and cast a look toward the carafe standing beside a tiered server of baked goods.

Elsa pushed it toward him with a warm smile. "We barged in first thing this morning. Cream and sugar?"

Well, she was friendlier than Morgan. He doubted Morgan had told Elsa the full story behind his purchase of the inn, since Elsa didn't seem to want to shoot him on sight. Yet.

"What brings you all to Massachusetts?" Agnes asked the newcomers, while Trent helped himself to two plump blueberry muffins. "You know I never mind you kids dropping in, but it is a surprise."

"We heard there'd be some big boomers coming through this summer," said Brian. "Just wanted to put the warning out there."

Morgan sat down again. "Thunderstorms," she said when Trent caught her eye.

"I gathered that, thanks," he said. He scooped a dollop of honey butter out of its dish.

"We work in the Midwest, chasing storms," Elsa told him. "We...observe and record."

"Bit of a hobby, really. Not much of a money maker," Brian added.

"Sometimes we're able to help people by warning them of emergency conditions," explained Elsa.

Morgan fidgeted. A strange, indecipherable look passed between the sisters, but before Trent could question it, Morgan said brightly, "But they really came out here to eat and pester Agnes."

"Sure," said Brian. "A little free food and a warm bed never hurt anyone."

"We're paying for the rooms," Elsa said. She and Morgan exchanged another look, this time clearly one of admonition. "Morgan, don't argue. You know Agnes can use the—"

"That's fine," said Morgan. "Why don't we take advantage of all this food, and then you can tell me more about these storms?"

Trent's cell rang. He fished it out of his pocket and tucked it into his shoulder while he finished buttering his breakfast. "Hello?"

The caller turned out to be his cranky insurance-agency client. At once, he regretted not looking at the caller ID before picking it up. He murmured a few apologies, and she said something about late calls and hang-ups and common courtesies...but more interesting was the frown on Morgan's face. She obviously didn't appreciate his taking a phone call in the middle of their breakfast. He returned her frown with a *What am I supposed to do, ignore my clients?* sort of look. Insurance Hellion chewed him out for a few more minutes, and they hung up with the understanding that when he was back in Boston, he'd show her the office building he was renovating.

He pocketed his phone and returned to the conversation. "What's a few thunderstorms? The East Coast is riddled with them every summer."

"Big ones," Brian said. He made a large circle with his hands. His eyes gleamed the way Morgan's did when she puttered in the kitchen. "Radar's all green, buddy. Or it will be."

"Woz," Elsa cut in, "how about you get some more orange juice for the table?"

Brian pushed up from his seat, grinning at Morgan, then trotted off toward the kitchen.

Trent regarded the exchange over the rim of his raised coffee cup. What had he just missed? He glanced at Morgan, but she looked away as soon as their gazes met. "So," he said, keeping his attention on her, "chasing storms must be...time-intensive."

"Oh, it is," Elsa said. Enthusiasm rang in her voice. "Not as exciting as you might think. Lots of staying at motels and hotels, lots of time sitting in the car with your cell phone. But we have had the occasional nail-biter. My truck skidded into a ditch once during a bad rainstorm. Flooded out the whole works, and I had to wait for a taxi to bring me forty miles back to the nearest hotel. All this in driving sheets of rain, of course."

"And don't let us catch you doing that again," Nina said, wagging her finger at Elsa. The woman couldn't have been more than ten years older than Morgan's sister, but Trent spied a stern, motherly look in Nina's eye.

Morgan, he noticed, wore the look tenfold. She curled a hand around the half-empty top tier of the baked goods server. "I'll just go refill this, and see what's keeping Brian."

When she left the room, Trent zeroed in on Elsa, unable to smother his curiosity any longer. "What's her deal?" he asked as casually as possible.

Elsa drew a long sigh, then refilled her coffee. "Her deal is that she still seems to think I'm a helpless three-year-old. Morgan hasn't quite gotten used to the fact that we've all grown up. The only one she never questions is Cade. Me, I'm on the other end of the scale."

"Who's Cade?" Trent wrestled a little with the urge to pry, but managed to kick it into some dark corner. Mostly.

"The oldest. He still lives in Montana."

Ah, the brother. He grinned at the mention of Morgan's home state, a flash of inexplicable cheer, but it washed away a few seconds later. Remembering his phone conversation with his father yesterday, Trent gave the scalloped edge of his breakfast plate a thoughtful rub. He wondered what communication in a normal house was like. Normal, as in not at ear-splitting decibel levels. "I wouldn't be too hard on her," he said. "You could do worse than having someone worry over you."

Elsa's gaze shot to his, wide-eyed. He gave a dismissive shrug and added, "Don't tell her I said that. Wouldn't want her to think she's right about something."

The young blonde grinned broadly. "She's got you all wrong." When Trent asked what she meant by that, Elsa merely turned back to her cinnamon bun and coffee with that Mona Lisa smile.

His inner warning button began flashing DayGlo red, and he itched to get away from that look and whatever it portended. He forced the need for Morgan's résumé to crowd out the persistent, remembered feel of her mouth and her curvy, damp body pressed to his. Pushing to his feet, he said, "I've got work to do. Nice meeting you all." Without waiting for a response, he stalked to the kitchen.

He passed Brian on his way. The man saluted with the carafe of juice, and Trent entered the kitchen.

Morgan didn't spare him more than a perfunctory glance. "Yes?"

The sharp note in her tone lit the fuse on his temper. "Want to tell me why I'm still wasting my time here?"

"Don't ask me," she said. "I've been trying to get you to go back to Boston since—"

"Since I barged into my own room to find you with your hands all over my stuff?" he suggested.

Her cheeks pinkened. She kept her gaze on the serving platter she was refilling from a container of fresh baked goods.

He rounded the butcher block, then leaned against it—much closer, he was sure, than could be comfortable for her. Her posture sure said so. She leaned away from him as if he were a hot stove. "I seem to remember asking for your résumé last night," he said in a suggestive tone that had nothing to do with job histories. When she didn't answer, he stepped even nearer. "Where is it, Miss Clifton?"

"You'll get it when I've had five minutes to print it out," she said. She snapped the lid back on the container of baked goods, then set it aside.

The motion swept a whiff of something cool and fresh toward him—a startling reminder of the rare, naïvely happy childhood days when his parents had taken him sailing. Morgan wore a low-cut white blouse that offered a tempting peek of lace underneath, and one of the airy skirts he had already come to expect from her. The top of the skirt hugged her body, then it cascaded out in a flowy, frilly expanse of cloth that swished around her ankles whenever she moved.

How had she gotten up early enough to get breakfast ready for a table full of hungry guests after their late night, and still managed to look like she'd gotten more than her fair share of beauty sleep?

His gaze fastened on the curve of her neck, where a few wisps of her upswept hair had escaped from the soft bundle caught in her clip. When his attention migrated to her lips, he began to regret his nearness to her.

He couldn't back away without losing some unspoken battle, so he did the only thing left to him. He stepped close enough to brush his shoulder and hip against her. "Am I to take it that you're in this tiny kitchen, refilling a platter for people you've already stuffed, simply to avoid me, Montana?"

"Whatever works in a pinch," she said.

"What is it that bothers you so much?" he asked. "I can find you loads of better jobs than this one. Better-*paying* jobs, I'll bet."

"*You* have obviously never been enamored

enough of a place to call it a home," she said, "and I'd have words with anyone who's willing to take advantage of an elderly woman in an awkward financial spot."

"What?" he sputtered.

"You want to back-charge Agnes for her own room while you're closing this deal. I heard about the adjustments you were planning to make to your contract. Aren't you already soaking her for enough money?" Morgan snatched up the serving dish with fine lines between her brows. "You and your snake of a lawyer must be laughing it up..."

His mind raced. He hadn't made any such adjustment. "Were you snooping in my room again?"

"John Lattimer called Agnes this morning." Morgan's voice trembled—with anger or upset, he couldn't tell, but probably both. "She can't afford what you want her to shell out every month to continue living in her own home. She needs all the money she has, and—"

"Whoa, whoa," Trent said. He took a step backward. "I haven't even spoken to John since I got here. I never told him to do that." Even as he said it, even as he wanted to swear at his lawyer for going over his head and trying to make a provision without his knowledge, Trent had to admit it was a good escape route from the potentially endless waiting on Morgan's job acceptance. A little pressure on the old lady might convince both women to hurry up and leave.

But when Morgan finally looked up, the distress in her eyes speared a hole right through his conscience. She set the dish down again and added, "Agnes doesn't have that kind of money even for a month, and I can't cover it either. Just get me a new job." She looked away as soon as she finished speaking, rearranging pastries that didn't need rearranging. Her fingers shook as she replaced a raisin bagel precisely where it had been.

"Hold your...bagels," he said. "No one's made any changes to anything...recently." She reached for a bowl of sugar glaze, and he clapped her hand down on the butcher block. He met her affronted stare with a look he hoped showed none of the guilt roiling through him. "Did you mean what you said? You'll take the first thing I offer?"

She lifted her chin. "If the alternative is you driving Agnes into bankruptcy before she has a chance to buy a new home down south...yes."

Everything he wanted out of this deal was right in front of him...and he couldn't bring himself to take it. Not with that look of pained pride on Morgan's face, a look he hated to admit he'd worn many times. He pulled his hand from hers, and examined the raisin-studded bagel. Frustrated, knowing it was a bad decision, he said, "Look, there's no reason I can't find you something other than a fast-food restaurant. I have a few contacts to mine. Give me a day or two, and—"

Christ, what was he doing? Her mouth had frozen open as though she suspected him of foul play. Her hand hovered motionless over the bowl of sugar glaze.

He sighed and stalked to the sink for a glass of water. When he turned the tap, nothing happened but an ominous banging that seemed to echo from inside the wall. "Have you been having water trouble today?"

"No." Her tone had shifted to one of businesslike concern. She tested the faucet herself, with the same result.

"Wait here." Trent left the kitchen for the first-floor bathroom, where he tried the fixtures again. Still no water. He returned to the kitchen, where Morgan was drizzling the glaze over some of the pastries on her serving dish. "Nothing coming in anywhere down here," he told her. "Might be a valve thing. Has the water been acting up?"

She blushed a little, but before he could figure out why, she shook her head. "Pressure's a little slow-flow at times, but this house is over a hundred and fifty years old."

"For chrissakes, the pipes are probably original," he muttered. Louder, he said, "This needs to get looked at, and probably repaired. Where's your water access, and where are your tools?"

Her mouth dropped open again. "You're going to do it yourself?"

She sounded as if she didn't believe him capable of a home repair, and that rankled him. "You just got through saying Agnes has no money," he snapped. "This place has to operate until the deal's closed, doesn't it? Where are your tools?"

"D-Downstairs," she stuttered. "The cellar." She pointed into the hall leading out of the kitchen and to the left. "The white paneled door."

Trent stomped out of the kitchen, almost as surprised at his actions as she must have been. Every time he tried to stop and head the other way, he thought of that look on her face, the one of dismay at having some high hope shot down before her eyes. Then he thought of the little blond boy buried in his past, struggling though the same reaction when his parents disapproved of him.

All those childhood hopes. All those dogged, wasted efforts...never enough. Never enough to make them happy.

If all it took was a minor repair, he'd get that look off Morgan's face. He hated seeing it.

Even on her.

Chapter Five

As soon as Trent left the kitchen, Morgan rushed to the tap and stuck her finger on the nozzle. For one breath-holding moment, she'd thought he had rattled her so much that she'd somehow short-circuited the inn's water supply—but no, the water refused to come even when she coaxed it from the faucet with her gift. It really was a mechanical problem, then.

Which begged the question, what did Trent plan to do about it? *Why* did he plan to do something? The further into dire straits the inn sank, the more the sale favored him. Vacationers wouldn't stay at an inn with water problems. No vacationers, no income. No income, no inn.

And yet, he was helping them.

Morgan couldn't concentrate for the rest of the morning. Elsa and her crew finished breakfast, then left the inn to do some sightseeing. Morgan tried to turn her attention to the lunch menu. When that didn't pan out, she focused instead on helping Agnes strip the beds down, and furnishing them all with fresh sheets in anticipation of their guests' overnight stays.

As she shook the last quilt out over the last bed, Morgan looked around the bedroom with a little thrill of pride and affection. In the two years since she'd arrived here, the Seaglass Inn had become an extension of herself. This very room had been her first one here, her first real home since Hope Creek. She knew every crevice. She'd painted it herself— sky blue with white beadboard, and Shaker pegs on the walls for hats and coats to ward off late-night coastal chills. Her power was proof enough against cold water, but it couldn't circumvent everything Nantucket dished out.

A chill of another kind ran through her as she recalled Trent kissing her last night—all the more disturbing because it wasn't an unpleasant memory. Pausing with an embroidered pillow under her arm, she touched her lips.

"Daydreaming, sweetheart?" called Agnes.

Morgan started and dropped the pillow on the bed. Agnes stood in the doorway with her usual kindly, too-observant smile. "Whitewash," Morgan blurted.

"What's that you said?"

"The fence, I was thinking of the fence. I'm going to whitewash it this afternoon. I'm sure I can convince Elsa to help." Even as she said it, Morgan clung to the idea of a project to lure her attention away from Trent's mouth.

"All right, dear."

"I've already got something in mind for lunch. We're having a roast for dinner, so I thought I should prepare a light meal for midday. It'll take no time at all, and when I get done—"

Chuckling, Agnes came into the room and straightened the pillow on the bed. "I've already said it's all right." She gave Morgan another discomfiting smile. "You seem a bit...preoccupied this morning. Anything you want to talk about?"

Oh, everything. Nothing. Morgan's nerves strummed like plucked guitar strings. She bent and smoothed out invisible wrinkles in the quilt. "I'm just—I'm just surprised that he even *wants* to make repairs. He's not like that. I mean, if he wants the inn so badly, what would stop him from letting it fall down around our ears? He's probably never—"

Agnes laid a quelling hand on Morgan's

shoulder, and Morgan jerked upright. The older woman gave Morgan's shoulder a gentle rub. "I know how you love this place. I'm sorry to have to leave you."

Morgan looked away. "You need to."

Agnes stroked her hair. "And you need to make some new ties, honey."

Not to him, Morgan thought automatically. Then she wondered why that was even a question. She shook off the thought and gave Agnes a brave smile. "I'll make do. Please don't worry about me."

Elsa and her team returned a few hours later, and Morgan had lunch ready. Trent didn't emerge from the basement. When she called down from the landing, he answered with a muffled "Busy," and a disturbing amount of clanging and squeaking.

Would he try to sabotage the inn, she wondered, or was he really fixing the water supply lines? Uncertain, unwilling to give in to curiosity and see for herself what he was up to, she left his lunch tray on a cardboard box, then returned upstairs.

That afternoon, she dressed in an old pair of jeans and a worn sweatshirt, and she and Elsa started whitewashing the picket fence surrounding the property. Salt and inclement weather had worn the old fencing to a silvery gray.

Elsa, used to chores of this sort, normally worked fast, but today she took her time with the paintbrush. Whenever Morgan looked, her sister seemed on the point of saying something, but didn't. Morgan gave up expecting any conversation, and threw herself into the project. An hour passed in pleasant silence, with the rhythm of the waves as punctuation.

"He's cute," Elsa said finally.

Offended, Morgan glared at her.

Elsa shrugged. "Don't get me wrong, I can see why you're upset. But I haven't seen a smile like that since...ever."

"Yeah, crocodiles do have lots of shiny teeth, don't they?"

Laughing, her sister started a new section of the fence. "He has you in knots I never knew you could get into. I kind of like him."

"Take that back, or you're getting a face full of whitewash!"

With a lofty swipe of her paintbrush, Elsa covered the next picket. Her chin inched upward. "I cannot tell a lie, sister." She swished a paint stick in the whitewash bucket, then shot a sidelong look at Morgan. A smile curled along her lips. "This stuff is starting to settle out. Care to fix it?"

"Don't change the subject. There is no possible way to like, admire, or otherwise think kindly of a man who goes around...*demolishing* people's happiness."

"I did say I saw your point," Elsa shot back. "Don't tell me you've been able to ignore that a man who looks the way he does is staying under your roof."

"*His* roof, once he gets his way."

"Is he single?"

"Oh, Elsa, give it a rest."

"Give me an answer, and I'll give it a—"

"Yes! Yes, he's very attractive. He's also a..." She couldn't complete the thought. Standing there, paintbrush in hand, dripping whitewash in the grass, Morgan tried to form the picture of the arrogant, callous businessman she knew. But at this moment, that arrogant, callous businessman was sweating away in a stuffy cellar, fixing something for her, and he didn't have to.

She didn't want to like him for anything, for any reason. He could have called a plumber and avoided dirtying his expensive clothes. He *should* have, damn it, and saved her the trouble of having to thank him, when he was only planning to repair the inn long enough to snatch it from her.

Flustered and angry, uncaring that Elsa could have done it herself with the paint stick, Morgan stuck her free fingers in the bucket of whitewash and forced the water to re-disperse evenly throughout the pigment. With her hand still glimmering, she stood upright and glared at her foster sister.

Elsa wasn't looking at her. She stared, open-mouthed, over Morgan's shoulder.

Morgan lunged around. The drippy whitewash clinging to her paintbrush flung outward and splattered all over Trent's face.

Elsa dropped her brush and clapped her hands over her mouth. Morgan whipped her still-glowing hand behind her back. "I'm so sorry," she blurted.

He swiped a hand across his face, then flicked droplets of whitewash into the grass. "Me, too. What are you hiding?"

"Nothing." She held up the paintbrush.

"And in your other hand...?"

Mortified, she struggled to stuff her power back into its mental container. Unused to being chained, it pressed back against her plea.

She struggled to hone in on the sensation, tried to sense the moment when she knew the evidence of her gift would be gone from her skin. But she found herself staring at Trent instead. His shirt and jeans were streaked with grease. His usually neat hair stood in damp spikes. A bead of sweat trickled down his whitewash-smeared cheek. Holding her breath, she began to pull her hand from behind her back.

"Morgan," Elsa said, snatching her wrists.

Morgan whirled around. Her back to Trent, she stared in horror at her hands. Both were glowing with a mother-of-pearl shimmer. The smears of whitewash did nothing to hide it.

Elsa gave Morgan's wrist a shake. The paintbrush dropped out of her hand and into the whitewash bucket. "Whoops," Elsa said. "You'd better get that." She gave Morgan a meaningful, urgent look.

Morgan crouched and plunged both hands into the whitewash, making an exaggerated show of swishing around for the brush. She gave Elsa a grateful look, and her sister smiled.

Trent's shadow loomed over her. The scent of clean sweat and copper tickled her nose, mixed with a musky undertone she recognized as Trent's cologne, and something purely male—purely *him*—that made her wonder if her legs would support her when she stood again. Heated shivers began at the top of her head, traveled through her body, then spread straight down to her tennis-shoe-clad toes.

"I finished with the basement," he said. "Your water's back on." He rubbed his scalp, getting whitewash in his golden-blond hair. "You've got some dry rot in one of your floor joists."

Agitated by the near-blunder of revealing her power—more so by the way he stared at her, too attentive—Morgan snapped, "Fishing for a way to reduce the sale price?"

"The creaky floors you love so much will be dropping out from under you before I get the chance to buy," he shot back. "I'll have it resectioned, but it'll take a couple of days—"

"What do you care?" she burst out. Torn in three directions—loyalty to Agnes, steaming attraction to Trent, and hatred of his lack of principles, she thrust an arm into the whitewash, never mind her sweatshirt sleeve. She came out with the saturated brush. Anything to get the man away from her, anything to drive him off before he saw how his nearness frazzled her. Before he saw how she wanted to kiss those sardonically twisted lips again, in spite of every reason not to. "You're a buyer, not a builder."

His mouth twisted further. Sparks of flame leapt up in his hazel eyes. "Right. I'm buying those floors. I don't want to buy them warped and damaged."

"How dare you? If there's anything at this inn that's warped, it's *you*." She made a fist, intent on slugging that smarmy look off his face.

Elsa tugged at her arm. "Morgan, why don't we just finish up here? The boys will be back soon." She tugged again, more insistent.

"I'll do it," Trent said.

Elsa's hand froze on Morgan's arm. Morgan herself went motionless as shore breakers. She fumbled for her tongue. "I don't need your help."

"I'm already dirty. A little whitewash isn't going to make matters any worse." He turned his gaze on Elsa. "Brian's already back. He asked for your help with some sort of weather program on his computer."

Elsa hesitated, clearly unwilling to leave them to what would be a world-class boxing match. When Trent stuffed his hands in his pockets and grinned, however, she melted like an ice-cream cone in high summer. She laid her paintbrush on a pile of old rags beside the fence. "Thanks." As she jogged toward the house, Morgan spied a blush pinkening her sister's cheeks.

"At least one of you can say it."

"Say what?" Morgan snapped, while searching her whitewash-smeared hands to be certain any evidence of her power was concealed.

"'Thank you,'" he responded, his voice oozing haughtiness.

"Is that what you came out here for? Acknowledgment that you did something nice?" She'd been planning to say it anyway, reservations aside—but now that he expected it, she clamped her lips shut with a silent will that would have shamed the Queen's Guard at Buckingham Palace.

She resumed painting without looking at him. Instead of having out with the expected snide comeback, he picked up Elsa's paintbrush and joined her. The swish of waves and the plaintive cry of shore birds filled the air for several minutes, serving only to magnify the way they weren't speaking. His maddening calm raked her raw nerves like a cheese grater. Her power pulsed insistently under her skin.

At last, her tolerance at its limit, she glared at him. "What's in all this for you? Why do you want to fix a place when you don't even own it? Yet."

He angled his head and studied her. His gaze traveled, unhurried, from the top of her head to her feet. Something in his perusal left her strangely adrift, as though she were a rowboat unmoored in a current that knew not where it wanted to go.

Unsettled, she dug the toes of her old tennis shoes into the turf as if that alone could keep her in place. "For a man intent on helping me, you're doing a lot of not."

Whatever had caused that focus in his eyes swept away, and he applied himself to whitewashing the fence with a will. Again, wind and water filled the silence.

Left to herself, she had no choice but to follow suit and resume whitewashing. Guilt began gnawing at her—first in tiny nibbles she could ignore, and then gradually more insistent until she felt like a well-chewed bone. She envisioned Agnes, calling Morgan "uncharitable" and pairing it with that disappointed look. Would she ever be as decent a person as Agnes, willing to see a good side to everyone? Her heart sank. "Thank-you-for-fixing-the-water," she spat out.

He angled a lazy grin at her. "Bet that was a real sonofabitch to say."

"You'll never know."

To her amazement, he laughed. He swept his brush along a fence picket—fast, efficient, a few swipes and he was on to the next. A few seconds passed before she realized he was the only one working. "Used to this sort of thing?" she asked, trying to shove her discomfort under a mental rug.

His brows drew together. He took a moment to speak. "I spent some summers doing fix-it work when I was a kid."

"What did you do with the money?"

"Had some invested. Had the rest put away to pay for college."

"Where did you go to college?"

"Harvard, where else? Business."

A swirl of wistfulness eddied through her. She had never been to college, not even distance learning. She thought of all the things she'd missed—parties, rallies, and the unspoken energy of hundreds of people gathered in one place, aiming themselves at an education and a better life. Until Allyson arrived at Hope Creek, Morgan's sphere had been that ranch and the people who lived on it. She did what she had to, and focused her energies on her foster siblings. If Kincade had kept them together, she had kept their home. It was for the best that she, Elsa, and Ethan had left, but still...

She would never tell Kincade so, but she missed being needed.

When she discovered Trent watching her, she threw herself back into whitewashing. "Did you like it there? Harvard?"

His hand twitched. He frowned and carefully finished another picket. "I got through it."

Intrigued, she followed his motions with the paintbrush. Had he ever been happy? The urge to ask pricked at her, but somehow she knew the answer wouldn't be yes...if he even responded. Did he know how it felt to want so badly to belong somewhere?

She forced a lighthearted tone and said, "I have a few loose cupboard doors in the kitchen. If you're still in the mood for fix-it work when we finish up here, the hinges and latches could probably use some tightening."

A smile crossed his face again. She found herself relieved until it disappeared as quickly as it had emerged. "Sure," he said.

And suddenly, though she would have endured torture before admitting it, the smile wasn't enough.

****

Trent finished the kitchen cupboards with discomfiting awareness that Morgan stood behind him, working on dinner for the inn's guests. The aromas of spices, sherry, and roasting beef filled the kitchen. His mouth had been watering for twenty minutes straight. He stepped down from his borrowed footstool, then stowed his screwdriver in the toolbox he'd extracted from the cellar. "I'm finished here," he said.

He turned around to find her fussing over something on the butcher block island. A lock of her hair had escaped its ponytail and fallen forward over her shoulder. A shoulder left maddeningly bare by her sleeveless sundress and that ridiculous apron.

An hour ago, she'd been covered with whitewash. Now, she looked country-club perfect. He tried to turn away. His gaze went instead to her curvy silhouette, and a perfect ass that the apron and sundress couldn't hide. Desperate to escape that view, he zeroed in again on that lock of her hair. He moved across the floor, not realizing he'd done so until his hands were already on her.

She stiffened. His senses returned with sucker-punch force. Her hair slipped like silk through his fingers. His head swam with the heady, fresh-water scent of whatever perfume she must have been wearing. And her shoulder, when his fingers brushed it, burned a trail of lust straight up his arm into his brain.

"What. Are you. Doing?" she asked in a voice stripped of inflection.

He slipped the ponytail band from her hair and re-tied it fast, trying like hell to make the motion as clinical as possible and failing utterly. "Unless you want hair in your food?"

She arched around, wary-eyed. The back of his hand brushed the nape of her neck. She had skin so fine he sensed the ridges of her vertebrae underneath. So damn delicate to the touch.

When she faced him, his hand slid over her shoulder, still trailing her ponytail. He let go and his fingers brushed her collarbone. Her gaze flicked to his hand, and then back to his face. A blush bloomed on her cheeks. She opened that sinful, sexy mouth. "Trent—"

A tiny shudder ran through him at the way she said his name—softly, on a suspended breath. The last of his self-control blasted apart. Uncaring about her reaction, he pinned her against the counter and slammed his mouth over hers.

Crash. Metal went clanging to the floor. Something cold splattered against his jeans. Morgan yelped into his mouth, but he corralled her with his arms braced against the counter and went right on kissing her.

She jerked backward, furious-eyed, her chin in the air and her lips wine-red from kissing. "Damn it, that was my—"

He slipped his hand under her hair and turned her head back toward him, massaging the tender skin at the base of her neck with his fingers until she let him direct her mouth to his again. "Shut up, Montana." When he slanted his lips over hers once

74

more, she didn't resist. He gave an inward rumble of satisfaction. God, she was everything he'd been obsessing about since that kiss on the beach. He arched his hips against her. She gave a muffled little sigh and blew his concentration when her tongue slipped into his mouth.

"What happened in here?" called a voice.

Morgan shot out from under his arm and raced around the kitchen island. Still drugged with her, he searched for the source of their badly-timed distraction.

Agnes stood in the kitchen doorway with her cloud-white eyebrows arched over pale blue eyes.

"Just an—an accident," Morgan stammered, already wiping up some sort of custard from the floor with one hand, and sliding an aluminum bowl and mixing spoon onto the counter with the other.

"So I see," said Agnes, in a tone of amusement that tugged at the corners of Trent's mouth. Then she looked at him with such approval that he quickly wiped any expression from his face.

Agnes entered the kitchen and slipped easily around the counter to the sink. She pulled a dishtowel from one of the drawers and wetted it under the tap. She twisted most of the water out of it, then handed it down to Morgan.

"Well, there goes the pie," Morgan growled. On hands and knees, she scrubbed the linoleum floor hard enough to gloss the finish, and didn't look at him once. Trent guessed she was angrier about being caught kissing him than about her ruined dessert.

"I have an idea," Agnes said. "Why don't we all go out for ice-cream after dinner? There's a nice little shop, walking distance down the beach."

He suspected from Morgan's hesitation that she didn't want to go any more than he did. The longer he stayed here, the more he seemed to do anything but attack the pile of work on that little desk

75

upstairs. A couple more days of this, and he'd be lounging on the sand with Baha shorts and a scruffy beard.

So it was with complete surprise that he heard his own voice say, "That sounds good, Agnes."

Morgan's gaze shot up. Her eyes held such a satisfying look of shock that it was almost worth the annoyance of having obligated himself.

Smug with the success of setting her off-balance, he wetted another towel to help her finish cleaning up the mess. He'd helped make it, after all. But his generous mood clouded over with a storm of remembering just how he had helped make it. For crying out loud, he could barely crouch beside her cleaning a kitchen floor without wanting to be kissing her instead. He'd never felt more like the rope in a tug-of-war in his life.

He'd left his towel a bit too soggy. Water splattered across the floor, onto the legs of the kitchen island, and over Morgan. He caught a flash of light from the corner of his eye, and looked up from his scrubbing.

Morgan had wrapped her dishtowel around her hand. She held it close to her belly with a look of alarm as if she had injured herself. "Are you okay?" he asked with more concern than he'd meant to show.

"Fine," she snapped. "Agnes, can you finish up here? I—I have to...I'll be back." She sprang to her feet and pounded out of the kitchen hard enough to shake the china in the cupboards.

Trent stared at the empty doorway. He scanned the floor, but saw no blood, no broken glass, nothing with which Morgan might have cut herself. The half-seen flash of light nagged at his memory. "What in hell just happened?"

Agnes gave a little wave toward the door. "Oh, it's nothing, dear. She's all right."

Then he recalled that same flash of light from the night before—just offshore while Morgan had been swimming in the ocean. He opened his mouth to say something about it, but Agnes interrupted.

"I forgot to tell you, dear," she said. "Your parents called. They tried your cell phone, but you had turned it off."

Likely after the last failed attempt to make them happy, Trent thought sourly. "Yeah? What did they want?" he asked, not really caring.

"They're on their way back to Boston now. They decided to stop here and visit. They ought to be here in an hour."

A knee-jerk awareness of how he looked hit him broadside. Paint-smeared jeans. Greasy shirt. Unshaven face. Sneakers. God, his mother would have a stroke. He rubbed a hand through his sweat-damp hair. "Aw, shit."

Chapter Six

Morgan slammed the bathroom door. "Oh, God, what an idiot I am," she whispered. She pulled the dishtowel away from her hand.

Her skin glowed, opal-white. The glow was even now spreading up her arm. Why in heaven had she let him kiss her? Why had she kissed him back? "Stupid, brainless fool," she muttered, twisting the tap on the bathroom sink. She splashed water on her face, but the sensation only intensified her power. She dried her face at once. No good. Shudders of power raced under the surface of her skin, uncontrollable, refusing to submit to her usual methods of harnessing it.

Staring at her wide-eyed, flushed face in the mirror, she brushed her fingers against her lips. The shimmer on her skin mocked her, threatened her, dared her not to flee the inn that had been her home for two years before Trent could learn her secret. Had he seen it? Why did she have such trouble hiding it from him, a man who didn't even like her— a man *she* didn't like—when she could hide it so easily from anyone else?

What was it about this man?

The squeal of a smoke detector tore through her thoughts. Hoots of surprise rang through the inn, and Morgan smelled charred meat.

Oh, for Heaven's sake. Dinner.

The alarm stopped, and she heard Brian's voice above the others, announcing it was a good time to order out.

Morgan flew out of the bathroom and down the

hall to her bedroom. A frenzied scuffle through her closet yielded a long-sleeved blouse and a pair of denim overalls she hadn't worn since leaving Montana. The only clean garments she had that guaranteed enough coverage. The more cloth concealing her skin, the better, but she disliked the option. While Agnes wouldn't care what she wore, Morgan hated to look anything less than professional—especially now that her employment here had become such a point of contention.

Elsa and her crew knew of their family's abilities. Agnes knew. The only one Morgan needed to hide it from was the same one she couldn't.

Damn Trent Williams and his nosy, sexy...everything.

Who was she kidding?

She pulled on the change of clothes and, forcing a serene smile onto her face, returned to the kitchen. An unpleasant, smoky haze lay thick on the air, in spite of the open window over the sink.

Trent was still there, facing the sink with his omnipresent cell phone clapped against his ear. He spoke in a low voice, but even without hearing the words, she knew it wasn't a pleasant conversation. He turned around, and their gazes met. He looked elsewhere at once—to her sister, who stood in the corner of the kitchen.

Elsa watched as Morgan reached toward the counter for the custard bowl. Her sister's mouth fell open, and she shook her head frantically.

Morgan looked down. The skin of her hands glowed white. With a stifled cry, she shoved them in her pockets.

Trent's stare came back around to her. His brow furrowed, and for several suspended seconds, she froze on the spot. Then his gaze snapped away, and he barked something into the phone. The caller's response plainly wasn't what he wanted to hear, because he jabbed a button and shoved the phone into his pocket. "I'm going upstairs," he muttered.

He offered no further explanation. When he swept out of the kitchen, Morgan let out her breath. "Do you think he saw?"

"I sure did," Elsa said. Worry lines formed across her brow. "What is it about him, Morgan? Why can't you control yourself—"

"Don't you think I've been trying? Good Lord, El, it's not like I want to go around gleaming like a demented lightbulb when he's in the room. I..."

Kissed him. Twice. Eagerly, the second time. A guilty shiver of pleasure ran through her body. Anxious to change the subject, she added, "What was the matter with him? Other than the usual?"

Hands on hips, Elsa scrutinized her with a look reminiscent of Agnes. "His parents are coming," Elsa said.

Curiosity almost washed away Morgan's discomfort about her power. "When?"

"Any minute now, from what I overheard."

So that was why he'd flown out of here. Was he coming back, or did he intend to hide in his bedroom until Mr. and Mrs. Williams tired of their visit to the inn?

With that same studious look, Elsa said, "Looks like the dessert foray has turned into an entire dinner run. We're all going to the Lightkeeper once his parents get here."

Morgan made a fast mental head count. "On whose tab? You barely have enough money to buy peanut butter and jelly. I'm not letting you—"

"I didn't say I was paying." Elsa gave her a cryptic smile, then sauntered out of the kitchen.

Morgan pursued her. "Spencer doesn't cook for a ten-person party without notice. Certainly not without a hefty surcharge."

Elsa waved her hand in a shushing motion. "It's

covered. Stop fussing."

The sound of a car door banging shut outside prevented her from arguing further. A moment later, footsteps thumped on the driveway porch, and the inn's doorbell chimed.

Agnes bustled into the room from the direction of the dining area. She opened the door with a broad smile. "Mister and Mrs. Williams? How nice to meet you. Come in, come in. I've had a room made up for you—"

"We won't be staying," answered a cultured female voice. The comment was smooth and open-ended, and Morgan sensed the implied *Not here, anyway* that the woman hadn't voiced.

Into the room stepped a middle-aged man and woman as graceful and somber as a pair of black swans, but without the obvious mutual devotion of those birds. They moved away from one another as soon as space allowed. Mr. Williams swept the room with a look like a man appraising goods before the auction started. His wife gave the people present a perfunctory look that carried less concern than her perusal of the well-loved furniture.

Poor Trent, Morgan thought.

Studying his father, she noted certain resemblances. The shape of the man's ear. The serious, flat line of his mouth. The focused-on-something-else air he exuded even when introducing himself to Elsa and her team.

Trent's mother was even frostier. After her initial steps away from Trent's father, she remained still, looking like she feared she might step in something unpleasant if she moved.

Morgan made herself walk across the room to extend a hand. "Hello. I'm Morgan Clifton, the Seaglass Inn's chef."

The woman's nostrils flared, and Morgan realized the faint odor of her charred roast lingered

81

in the air. "I see. How charming." She extended ruby-tipped, diamond-lavished fingers. They shook hands. Morgan strained not to wipe her palm on her overalls. The woman had a grip like a dead mackerel. "We were about to go out to dinner, actually. My sister and her team don't visit us very often—"

"We'll be looking at Trent's purchase, and then we're going back to Boston," said Mrs. Williams.

"Mom, give it a break," interrupted Trent. He stalked into the room, adjusting a tie over his dress shirt, which was tucked into a pair of slacks with razor-sharp creases. His hair was damp, and he'd shaved. How had he cleaned up so fast?

Mr. Williams treated his son to the same appraisal he'd given the inn's receiving room. "Trent."

"Sir."

The elder Williams waved his hand. "Well, show us around, time's wasting. And I want to talk to you."

Trent's gaze flicked toward Agnes, then he lingered on Morgan. She could have sworn she glimpsed an apology, but he looked away before she could be certain. "Excuse us," he muttered. He and his parents filed out of the room.

Brian exhaled on a loud *phew* and headed for the door. "That was almost as much fun as a rattlesnake bite."

"Woz," Elsa reprimanded.

The group collected lightweight jackets and poured outside. Morgan seethed. Trent's parents had no right to be so dismissive of Agnes in her own home. "I'm sorry, Agnes," she murmured when she found the older woman walking beside her to the front driveway.

Agnes studied the sky with a serene smile. "Sweetheart, the world is full of all kinds of people.

At my age, you learn which ones to take to heart, and which to take with a grain of salt."

Thinking of Trent and her own short experience with his parents, Morgan decided there probably wasn't enough salt in the entire Atlantic Ocean with which to take them. All at once, she missed Kincade, and even Ethan, as much as he exasperated her. Grateful for where she'd ended up in life, she drew alongside Elsa, who smiled and linked her arm through Morgan's.

Elsa leaned in close, laughing-eyed. "I missed you, too."

****

Trent stuffed his hands into his pockets, trying his damnedest to appear casual, instead of like the chastised five-year-old he felt. He leaned against the doorjamb of the inn's upstairs bathroom.

"One bath for all the residents?" Leland's censorious tone grated on Trent's ears. He didn't even bother telling his father the inn would be deconstructed and the property used for something else, maybe a summer home for their family. Looked like that bright idea was just going to be a pipe dream. Leland would grouse about the inn's flaws regardless of whether Trent tore the property down or not. Sometimes he thought Criticize was Leland's only setting.

His father spared the bathroom one more glance before continuing down the hall to duck into the doorway of each of the remaining rooms.

"It's an old house," Trent said. "They haven't had much money to remodel." He hated how defensive the words sounded.

"Probably why you got it so cheaply. How is the foundation?"

"Good, considering the house's age."

"Well, that bathroom situation will have to be fixed if you keep the property. Costly. What's the heat?"

"Boiler."

"Hmm," said Leland, a monotone syllable that could have meant anything from *Fine, then* to *This is a waste of your money.* Trent could never be sure.

His mother strolled out of the bedroom at the far end, pulling a pair of leather fashion gloves from her coat pocket. "Are you ready, Leland?"

His father drew a long sigh, strangely reminiscent of Trent's own irritation at his mother's constant impatience with standing still. He frowned at Trent. "I don't know what you intend to do with this place, with that woman hanging onto it. What were you thinking, boy? I taught you better than to accept a contract with—"

"I've got it covered, Dad," Trent lied, impatient to deflect the usual barrage of How He'd Done Wrong This Time. "Are you coming to dinner?"

"Leland, really," said his mother, sounding put out.

"We're stopping for dinner, Maureen," said Leland. "We can spare a couple of hours."

"Yeah, Mom," said Trent, barely able to contain a sudden rush of sarcasm. "I'm buying, and everything. You should take advantage."

His father shot him a warning look. Hitching his shoulders, Trent softened the edgy remark with a muttered, "See some of your old stomping grounds, anyway. You haven't been back since you were kids—"

"That's quite enough out of you, young man," his mother snapped.

Trent clamped his mouth shut and kept it that way through the remainder of his parents' tour. When they left the inn and started toward the driveway, he walked beside his father. "How long will you be in Nantucket?"

"The night. Your mother wants to get home."

To what? Trent wondered. When he was young, he'd imagined that if he stood at the top of the stairs at his parents' Boston home and whispered, the sound would carry in a lonely echo to the farthest corners of the old brick structure. Even when his mother and father were home. Once, he'd asked for a baby brother or sister. Only once.

Dinner was awkward, painful, and not short enough. His parents ordered the lobster and his mother loudly pronounced it terrible—the one thing that seemed to draw a genuine smile from Morgan the entire evening. Trent found himself fixed on that smile with all the attention of a border collie. She caught him looking, and instead of turning to his baked salmon, he grinned. Spencer ought to be wringing his hands in the restaurant kitchen at this very moment, lamenting another culinary failure.

Morgan blushed and looked down at her plate. He'd have bet that her ears, if they weren't covered by that glorious fall of dark-brown hair, would be an intriguing pink. As it was, he could hardly tear his gaze away from the rosy glow surfacing on her cheeks. He stared at her lips and wondered if she were thinking about that interrupted kiss back at the inn.

"Trent," his mother cut in over the genial chatter of Elsa's team, "your father wants you home for Mother's Day, so we'd like you to conclude your business here as soon as possible."

Not *I want you home.* The conversation at the table took an uncomfortable pause. With barely a glance at him, Elsa began again with a discussion of weather patterns. Her team dived in once more.

He had only a second to admire the young woman's social tact before Morgan sat up taller in her seat beside Trent's mother. "Trent has quite a gift with fixing things," she said brightly. She ducked around his mother to smile at his father.

"Did he learn that from you, Mister Williams?"

Trent got the shock of his life when Leland paused with his fork in midair. His father studied Morgan for a silent moment, then lowered the utensil. His expression softened, a shocking transformation Trent had never seen on his father's face before. Leland's gruff voice broke through Trent's stunned fog. "The boy comes by that through his grandfather. Man was always fixing things. Basement looked like a used-parts store."

Trent barely recalled his grandfather. He had the faintest memory of pipe tobacco, aftershave, and hazel eyes that resembled his own. Trent had never in all his life heard his father refer to the man in conversation, let alone been compared to him.

"I remember those messes," his mother said. She sipped her wine, then lifted her chin at Morgan. "Ridiculous. Stephen had a repair shop. There was no reason to clutter up his house with all that junk, too."

Leland's expression reformed into sternness, and Trent had the impression he'd just missed something important. "We need to leave, if we're going to get home," he said to Trent. "Be back in Boston in time for Mother's Day."

Trent glanced at his mother, who was already throwing down her napkin and rising from her seat. She didn't even turn to him. Trent looked back to his father. "Yes, sir," he muttered.

Leland paused then. Trent felt he ought to say something, but words escaped him. Leland tossed a fifty on the table. "For the tip," he said. He took his leave with a gruff nod to the table's other occupants, and he and Trent's mother departed.

Fuming silently, Trent stabbed the last forkful of his salmon and stuffed it into his mouth. Once again, his parents had managed to make him feel more like a hired hand than a member of the family.

Leland's business advisor was closer to him than Trent would ever be.

"Tell you what," said Nina. "Why don't we all head to that ice-cream shop Agnes keeps raving about? I feel a butter crunch requirement coming on."

"Wait until you've had their mint fudge ripple," Morgan said. "They make it all from scratch. And when they reopen for the season, they have a special ice-cream flavor that they make just for that year."

The talk turned to dessert, effectively derailing the questions the others must surely want to ask about the dynamic between Trent and his parents. He stole a look at Morgan then. She had turned toward the others, engaging their attention with an explanation of hand-churned ice-cream.

Not shutting him out. Deflecting.

A tiny spot of—something—thawed inside him.

The group returned to the beach and walked the short distance from the inn to the quaint shop. Still brooding over his parents' frosty departure, and his troubling gratitude toward Morgan's kindness at dinner, Trent said little. He ordered a vanilla sundae, but ate barely any of it. While Elsa and her team chattered about cloud patterns and prevailing winds, his attention strayed to Morgan. She stared at the ocean with a far-off look that made him wonder what—or who—was on her mind.

Recalling the way his mother had treated both Morgan and Agnes, he tossed his half-eaten sundae in a trashcan. Was that the way Morgan thought he treated her?

An unaccustomed discomfort slithered through him. He shied away from it and lagged behind the group, mystified by the way it even bothered him that it *did* bother him.

Elsa moved toward Morgan and said something inaudible. Morgan threw away the rest of her ice-cream cone, and then stuffed her hands in her pockets with a curiously guilty expression on her face. Her gaze flicked toward him, and then away to the water again.

What was she hiding? Was it that she thought him attractive and didn't want to admit it, or did she have a deeper secret? One that involved the contract for the inn, maybe?

A moment later, he realized he'd begun to stare, and turned his attention to the ocean with a moody shrug. The water spread out in an endless cobalt expanse under a sky stained sunset-red. Oddly warm, this year. He hadn't needed more than a lightweight jacket since his arrival. He sucked in a breath of fresh sea air and killed a few minutes watching the water.

The call of squabbling birds woke him out of his trance. One of Elsa's team—Seth, or Rory, whichever it was—had tossed the remainder of an ice-cream cone onto the sandy boardwalk, and a flock of gulls swarmed down to fight for the tidbit. Nina scolded them for egging the birds on.

I need to get out of here before this place sucks the ambition out of me. Trent considered the stack of work on the desk back at the inn, deciding which item to address as soon as they returned. He'd wasted too much time fiddling around with whitewash and plumbing and cupboards, and *not* finding a way out of this contract. No wonder his parents were pissed off at him. In a few days, he'd gone from focused businessman to complete slacker. *I taught you better. I taught you better. I taught you better.* Biting back a curse, he flexed his fingers.

"Trent?"

Morgan's voice scattered his thoughts. She had broken away from the group to join him at the shoreline. "Is this your master plan?" he snapped. "Every time I get my mind on work, you come by and throw a whitewashing or a broken cupboard or an ice-cream cone at me until I'm so broke I gotta break the contract first?"

Her eyes went wide, and a surprising pang of remorse assaulted him. Before he had a chance to act on it, she advanced on him, flush-faced. "I wish I were that much of a snake in the grass," she replied, "but I guess I'll leave that sort of behavior to you." She shot past him, banging his shoulder as she went, and stalked back toward the inn.

He refused to watch her go, refused to look toward Agnes or Elsa, who would surely be staring at him with that reproachful expression. But he couldn't refuse the nagging stab of regret that drowned out all those thoughts of the work on his desk.

Every damn thing he did just went wrong here.

****

"Jerk," Morgan snarled. "Self-righteous, inconsiderate, unfeeling, arrogant jerk." Gripping her baking pan with a vengeance, she scrubbed the burnt-on residue of the charred roast she'd had to dump in the trash. "What a waste of effort. I can't believe what a stupid—"

"Boy, that pan must have offended you pretty badly," came Elsa's voice.

Morgan spun around. Her sister stood hip-shot in the kitchen doorway with a know-it-all smile. Morgan turned back to the sink and scrubbed faster. "I'm imagining it's his face."

"Ah, so *he's* the waste of effort."

"What makes you think I would want to spend any effort on him? A man like that is a lost cause, Elsa, believe me. A soulless, unfeeling lost cause who speaks in dollar signs and nothing else."

Instead of replying, Elsa laughed.

The sound of her sister's mirth alone was enough to stomp on Morgan's last nerve. "That. Is.

It," she said, tossing down her scrubbing pad. "I'm moving south with Agnes."

Elsa approached the sink with a frown. "I thought you loved Nantucket. That the water here was perfect, and you never wanted to live anywhere else." When Morgan jerked the stopper out of the sink, Elsa's frown deepened. "That's what you said, Morgan. 'The Seaglass is the home I never thought I'd have.'"

"I know what I said!"

"So why are you letting him kick you out of it?"

"I'm not *letting* him, El," Morgan pleaded. "I just...I can't hang onto this place at the cost of Agnes getting the money she needs to move to a nice place in Florida. I was stupid and selfish even to try." She lowered her voice and looked out the kitchen window. "I panicked, I guess. I love it here, and I don't want to lose that."

Elsa moved a little closer. "What if he finds out about your power?" she murmured. "You can't seem to control yourself around him. What happens when you let it slip right in front of him?"

"Your team knows about you," Morgan grumbled.

"My team isn't an arrogant jerk who thinks in dollar signs and nothing else." Elsa fisted a hand on her hip.

"I will be fine." Morgan dried the pan and put it away. "Not that it's any excuse, but at least we know now where he gets his attitude problem."

"Yeah, I'd be grouchy too, if I grew up in that house," Elsa muttered. She countered Morgan's venomous look with another laugh. "It's true! We were lucky, Morgan. All things aside"—Elsa gave her a hug—"we were lucky to land at Hope Creek with people who love us."

"Yeah," Morgan said. She kissed Elsa's cheek.

"So what's your plan? Talk him into selling the

place to you, or take a job somewhere nearby?"

"You've met Trent. There's no reasoning with him, El."

Her sister's eyes lit. "Oh, I think there's *some* room for reasoning there." She gave Morgan's shoulder a playful poke. "You obviously haven't been paying much attention to the way he looks at you."

"That's called revulsion," Morgan said.

"Nope." Elsa shook her head, her pale-blond locks fluttering over her shoulders. "He looks at you like you're the last piece of chocolate cake in the pan, my dear deluded sister."

Infuriated, Morgan threw her dishtowel over the bar in front of the sink. It slipped, and she caught it before it fell to the floor. She threw it over the bar again, and it slipped again. With a groan, she crumpled the cloth in her fist. "If you're implying I'm going to use sexual attraction to try to—"

"So you are attracted!"

"—to seduce him into giving me the deed to the Seaglass Inn, you're—"

"Right," came Trent's voice.

Morgan jumped. The dishtowel flew into the air and landed on Trent's shoulder where he stood in the doorway.

His mouth twisted into a grimace. He pulled his cell phone away from his ear, and she realized he hadn't overheard, but her fluster wouldn't go away. "Just a second, Laura," he said into the phone. He plucked the dishtowel from his shoulder and held it out to Morgan with his fingertips. "Throw something heavier next time, if you're going for bludgeoning me."

Morgan snatched the towel away and slipped it—successfully, this time—over the bar. "What are you doing in my— Never mind. Coffee. I'll get it." Glaring at him, she pointed to the doorway. "*You* stay over there."

Trent's brows quirked upward. He glanced at Elsa, who merely smiled at them both. Morgan answered it with a scowl and pulled down the percolator.

He put the phone back to his ear. "Laura, I'm going to need to call you later." He paused, then added, "Not really a good time right now. Laura. Please?"

Morgan's mouth dropped open. Good Lord, the man was actually capable of saying the word—even if it appeared to take an act of Congress to get him to do so.

She heard Trent end his call. By the time she turned around, she found Elsa had left the kitchen. Morgan shook her head, staring at the phone still in his hand. "Do you ever disconnect yourself?"

He waved the sleek cell phone at her. "This is my lifeline to my business when I'm not in Boston." He slipped it into his pocket.

She wondered, with carefully sealed lips, whether "Laura" was part of that lifeline, then doubted it. That call was definitely not business. Irritable, she pulled out the sugar. "It may have escaped your notice, but we actually have beaches. And bike paths. And God forbid, sightseeing tours."

"I didn't come here for..." He stopped talking then, with his gaze on her as she pulled milk and coffee from the refrigerator. His hazel eyes locked on her face.

Heat washed through her. He'd removed the tie and undone the top button of his dress shirt. She stared at the hollow of his throat and found herself wondering if Laura ever planted her nose there and breathed in his cologne.

Sizzle.

Horrified, she hurried to the counter to set up the percolator. Her hands trembled. *No glow, thank God, thank God.*

He leaned against the cupboards by the doorjamb with his arms crossed. An odd look crossed his features, but it washed quickly away behind a frown. "I would have taken instant."

She grappled her power back into its restraints. "What's the rush?" she asked with affected composure. "New businesses to undermine?"

"No." He stalked into the kitchen, then sank onto a barstool. "For your information, there's a pile of work on my desk upstairs that I've been ignoring in order to help you. You're welcome."

She angled her head and stared at him until he returned her gaze. "You can't stand it when you don't get acknowledged for something, can you?"

When his expression clouded over, she realized how true it was. At once, she felt sorry for the jab. Growing up in his house must have been a thankless task by itself. Her life had been imperfect, but she had invariably had the love of her foster siblings.

How ironic that her slap-together family was more complete than his unbroken home.

He rose from the barstool, and she put a hand over his to stop him. "I'm sorry. Thank you."

A peculiar look crossed his face, the sort one got when another person said something in an unintelligible foreign language. His mouth hovered between a frown and something else that escaped definition, then he finally settled on a complete lack of expression. He gave a nod. "You're welcome," he said again.

She chewed at her lower lip, wondering whether she ought to say anything further, then ventured a look at him. "Why are your parents so..."

"'Belligerent' is usually the word I use in polite company," he added wryly.

She blushed and pushed a shifted flour canister back into its space, then turned to face him, feeling inexcusably nosy.

Trent sighed. "They used to be happy. They lived here when they were kids. Nice families, nice neighbors. Picket fences," he added with a smirk as he tilted his head toward the kitchen window. "They got married, moved to Boston. Had me. Got too busy to deal with a kid when business boomed." He hitched a shoulder then, as if his shirt had gone too tight. "I did all right. Stop looking at me like that."

She pulled his beer stein from the dish drain and set it on the counter. Their gazes met again for a few seconds, and she smiled a little. He looked away first. The ticking clock and the dim rumble of voices from people heading upstairs for the night permeated the silence. She paused to fill the percolator and set it running, then came back to the counter to find him still sitting there, stiff and serious. The light over the kitchen sink picked up the clean-shaven planes of his cheek and jaw. He must have run his hand through his hair at some point. He'd combed it for dinner, but the front stood up in mussed spikes.

Why do you keep coming into my kitchen if you dislike me so much? She rubbed her thumb along the edge of the sugar bowl. Gritty crystals of sugar ground along the pad of her thumb, sharply contrasted against the smooth porcelain. She wondered how his stubble might feel.

It was *so* time for another night swim.

"Go upstairs," she said before she realized she'd even opened her mouth. "I'll bring your coffee up when it's ready."

He stood, still looking at her as if he didn't mind doing so for the rest of the night. Her power jumped at its bonds. "Go," she repeated, as much a reminder as a need to get him out of the kitchen before her gift escaped her.

He left just in time.

When she looked down to her hand on the sugar

bowl, her fingertips began to glow.

The ring of water where his still-damp beer stein sat on the countertop answered it with a glow of its own.

Chapter Seven

Trent sat at his desk, crunching numbers and finishing up a report on his laptop. He'd called Laura back and made his excuses for their future broken date. He'd known he wouldn't be back to Boston by Mother's Day the instant the ultimatum left his mother's lips. They usually went to dinner—he, Laura, and both sets of parents—a pattern they had developed over the past few years. His father and Laura's went back about a decade through mutual business ventures. Everyone expected Trent and Laura to marry, a union as sound as the perfect corporate merger.

Trent couldn't imagine a match less likely. They were good acquaintances—even dates, when a black-tie function required it—but their relationship was all show and no spark.

Laura begged to differ, and the resulting argument might have taken an additional half-hour if he hadn't reminded her that she had a seven o'clock flight to Los Angeles the next morning. Thank God for small favors.

Trent saved his finished report and turned his attention to a proposed buyout John had e-mailed him. The figures from his secretary's report looked promising. He had the finances to turn the struggling facility into a lucrative little office unit right in the heart of Boston.

And there was no re-employment clause to hold things up until Kingdom Come.

His threat must have worked. John had gone over every possible wrinkle and ironed it out until the buyout was smooth as a freshly pressed tuxedo shirt. With a satisfied grin, Trent signed off on the proposal and sent a response e-mail to his lawyer.

Finally, for the first time in days, he'd gotten his rhythm back.

Morgan blew it by walking into the room.

The click of the opening door was no bother. Nor was the light step on the braided rug. But her scent whooshed in, a heady cool-water aroma that filled his nostrils and unraveled the neat-woven cord of his thoughts.

The smell of fresh coffee accompanied her, much less distracting, and he inhaled it as if it were the last tank of air on a deep-sea scuba dive. The gulps of tangy coffee-scent were no help in washing away her own, less obtrusive perfume. He tried in vain to close his senses to her.

What the hell had made him yammer on about his parents back there in the kitchen?

She placed a coaster on his desk and set the beer stein on it. "Getting anything done?"

"Not now, I'm not."

"All part of my master plan, you know." She started to withdraw her hand, and the smell of her perfume drifted past his nose again.

He forced his attention onto the stacks of folders on his desk. "Thanks."

"You're welcome," she said. She hesitated, then her lips curled in a dangerously intriguing smile. "We seem to be getting good at the minor pleasantries. Might we even move on to 'How are you?' at some point?"

Trent ignored the smile as he had tried to do with her scent, though he found it harder. "I'm buried, if you want to know."

"Sorry to hear that. I'll get out of your hair."

"You're not in my hair." An unsettling image rushed him of her running her fingers through his hair while he kissed her throat.

His ire shot to the fore, and he stuffed it in a mental junk-mail slot. He had loads of experience dealing with difficult clients. What was it about this woman that drove him so easily—and so damned frequently—past the limit of his patience?

Could be there's something else you're waiting for besides business closure, pal, his inner voice whispered. He glanced sidelong at Morgan to find her staring at the stack of papers on his desk. "What?" he snapped.

"I have some extra file folders downstairs, if you want them."

"Are you implying I'm disorganized?"

"I'm implying that the first good wind through those balcony doors is going to cost you two hours' worth of restacking that forest of paper on your desk."

"The doors are shut, as you can see, Miss Clifton."

She fixed him with that shocking-blue stare. "Suit yourself. I was trying to return the favor." She started for the door.

He swiveled around in his seat. "Wait, you're being nice. What's wrong?"

She swung back—not all the way, just enough to convey a weird indecision in her posture. "It's just...I can't...never mind."

"Too late. I'm minding," he said, engrossed with the way she brushed at a lock of her hair.

"Trent, I...I'm sorry about dinner." She back stepped toward the door.

Caught off guard, he rocked back in the old chair, whose legs creaked in protest. The sympathy in her eyes sent his hackles up. He let the chair thump down again and pushed a few papers toward the back of his desk. "What for?"

"We both know what for," she said. He didn't

look, but he knew she was staring at him. Seconds ticked past.

Why did she care? What did she want him to say? That during his childhood, he'd felt like an unwanted guest in his own house? That while his friends went on summer vacations to Yellowstone with their parents, he'd been expected to take internships at his father's firm because they were "good for him"? That he couldn't remember his mother ever saying she was proud of him?

And look at him now. On top of the world, a million women on his arm at social events, and enough money to buy a healthy slew of blue-chip stocks. And still whining about parental acceptance like a baby. He wished he'd kept quiet about the whole thing.

He thrust a few more papers into a sort-of neat stack. The list of jobs he'd found for her peeked out from under a quarterly report from his finance manager. He plucked it out of the pile and handed it toward her. "Dinner was fine. You want to worry about something, worry about which job you're interviewing for first."

The paper hung in the air a minute. Instead of snatching it in a fit of anger, as he'd expected—and hoped—she calmly drew it from his fingers. Curiosity hauled his gaze up to her face. No flushed cheeks, no sizzling anger in her eyes, no sign of rigidity in her posture. She studied the paper. Her gaze met his at last, and a javelin of regret punched through his midsection at the empathy on her face. She came toward him again, and he had to force himself not to edge backward until the chair banged the desk.

Bluff. Bluff. Bluff, his inner voice commanded. He sat up taller in the seat, imagining her as the owner of the five-star hotel he'd brokered last year. Tough as marble, but in the end, just as easy to crack as any deal he'd ever made. All it took was finesse—a patient exploration into which vein to chip at first.

Morgan paid absolutely no attention to his posturing. She slid a stack of his papers aside and pulled a single sheet from underneath them. At the top was her name, the address of the inn, and her e-mail.

Her résumé, already tailored to whichever position he chose from the list he'd thrust at her. When had she put it there?

"I'm still sorry," she said. She laid the job listing down on his laptop keyboard, and before he could say anything else, she quietly left the room.

****

The following morning, Morgan woke early and prepared her kitchen for the day's meals. Elsa and her team were leaving today. Morgan wished she were more like her sister, able to make a home out of wherever she landed, whenever she landed there. It would make giving up the Seaglass Inn so much easier.

She no longer felt that rush of anger toward Trent. Meeting his parents had made her wonder whether she were better off not remembering much about her own. Kincade, Elsa, and Ethan had been her family as far back as she could recall. A blessing, maybe.

Rain pattered the window over the sink. Morgan peered out at the iron-gray sky and the sheets of precipitation curling across the Sound. She decided not to influence them with her gift. A little rain would do Nantucket some good. Never mind that it went with her mood.

The power to manipulate water had always been something of a cosmic admonition to her. Whatever had given her the gift had also attached a mental warning label that anything she did with it would require a balance somewhere else in the world. She left the weather alone most of the time, to do what it needed—only nudging the storms away from Nantucket Island and safely out to sea when they were at their worst.

Except for that rainstorm Trent had brought on when they went to town. She smiled briefly. If it weren't so worrisome, it might have been funny that he drove her to the brink like that.

She filled the percolator and began mixing batter for crepes. If Elsa could carry "home" with her, maybe Morgan could too. Hope Creek had been home enough for her while she'd lived there.

Not inland. Never inland again. The rush of the sea was the pulse of Morgan's blood, the cry of seabirds and ringing of distant ship's bells the beating of her heart.

Somewhere down the coast, maybe, or up to Maine. She could do this.

Standing at the window, she struggled against the fist tightening around her throat. Her view of the little herb garden blurred, and then, inexplicably, she thought of the day she'd seen Trent standing out there, looking like a lost soul.

Were they really so different?

She couldn't—wouldn't—turn the Seaglass over to him in anything less than perfect condition. Agnes and Howard had poured their love into this place for more than half their lives. Morgan refused to allow Trent any reason to give Agnes less than full value for it. If she went, she would see Agnes well off first.

Almost unconscious of it, she twisted the tap and let it run over her fingertips. The cold water slid over her skin. Tiny shimmers sparkled along the ridges of her fingerprints, then fused together until her whole hand glowed under the faucet like a searchlight undersea. She cupped the water in her palm and watched it pool and bounce over her skin, then finally manipulated some into a shivering globe in her hand while the rest ran down the drain.

Like jelly, but wobblier, she'd told Elsa when they were younger. Elsa promptly splashed the water ball out of Morgan's hand with a gust of air and an impish grin. Things degraded into a messy but thoroughly satisfying water fight that left both girls laughing.

"How do you always know how to do what's right, El?" Morgan murmured. "How is it so easy for you to be happy?"

"No one has it easy, dearest," came Agnes's voice.

Morgan dropped the water ball into the sink with a slosh that doused her apron.

Agnes came up beside her and opened a cupboard to get a cup and saucer. She glanced at the water on Morgan's apron and gave a little smile. "Thinking hard?"

With a sigh, Morgan turned to the crepes. "I should have made steak and eggs. Something to send my sister and her team off right. I used to make her that for breakfast all the time, back in Montana."

"Your sister would eat dry toast as long as you made it." Agnes chuckled and tucked a lock of Morgan's hair back behind her ear. "I know this isn't about food. I wish I had been able to sell the inn to you."

Oh, how Morgan wished that, but she had used much of her savings to help keep Hope Creek running when she lived in Montana. If not for the room and board provided by her position as chef at the B&B, she might not have had enough to live on at all.

Kincade might have helped her. Would have helped her, if she told him of her troubles—but for the first time in many years, he was unburdened, blessed with a successful ranch and a good life. Cade deserved his happiness, and she wanted him to keep every cent for which he'd worked so hard all those years.

Agnes was still looking at her. Morgan turned to the mixing bowls on the counter and whisked the egg-and-spinach crepe filling. "Trent says there's a problem with the floor joist in the cellar. He's going to fix it."

"Oh?" Agnes responded. She sounded unconcerned, but Morgan felt the older woman's sharp gaze as if Agnes had poked her with one of the wooden mixing spoons.

Morgan whisked faster. "There are other things that need to be done here before you can close the sale and get the money to move south. I should help him out. I will...when I'm not cooking, I mean. I shouldn't have—I shouldn't have interfered, Agnes. I'm sorry. This is your livelihood...not mine."

Still, Agnes said nothing. Morgan dared a look to find Agnes hunting in the little crock on the counter for a packet of mint tea. Morgan hurried to distill a quantity of water as it arced from the tap into her kettle, allowing the impurities to drop into the sink and only pure water to fill the container. She dropped the filled kettle onto a hot burner and rushed it to a boil with her gift. The kettle hissed and then sputtered angrily.

Morgan cursed. She'd pressed it too hard—*punched it*, she and her siblings called it, though not on a scale that would drain her. She backed off her gift, and the kettle chattered grumpily, then started to whistle. Morgan lifted it from the burner and spun to fill Agnes's cup.

"What a shame you can't market that gift of yours openly," Agnes said. She gave another smile, undeserved. "No one puts food on a table faster than you, sweetheart." Morgan went back to mixing the crepe filling, but Agnes laid a soft hand over her own. "For the record," the older woman said, "I forgive you."

Tears rushed to Morgan's eyes and spilled down her cheeks before she could stop them. She dropped the whisk in the bowl and sniffled. "I've been so selfish," she whispered, unable to look Agnes in the eye.

The older woman set her cup down. She turned Morgan away from the counter and into a warm embrace. Patting Morgan's back, she said, "I know why you did what you did." Then she pressed a soft kiss to Morgan's cheek. "And I knew you'd do what's right, too."

Right? Morgan pulled away with a wan smile and wiped her tears with a damp cloth. She washed up again, avoiding Agnes's sympathetic gaze, then returned to her work. She wasn't even sure what was right anymore.

Trent entered the kitchen, punching numbers on his cell phone. He stopped halfway to the butcher block counter and frowned at them. "Why's it look like a funeral in here?"

It was. The funeral for the home Morgan had wanted since she got here. She scowled at the crepe batter because she couldn't look at him.

"Nothing a little breakfast won't cure," Agnes said. "How did you sleep, Mister Williams?"

He hesitated. Morgan suspected he was unaccustomed to people asking after his welfare. As if the issue were as rhetorical as the amenities they offered him at nice hotels and restaurants. "Fine. Thanks," he said at last.

"Wonderful. I'll set the table, Morgan," Agnes said. Her light footsteps faded from the kitchen.

Morgan picked up the bowl and turned to the stove to begin cooking. "Did you see Elsa and her team on your way down?"

"The tall one with the wild hairdo was already out in the hall. The other woman was just coming out of her room," Trent answered.

"Brian. Nina," Morgan corrected.

Morgan heard a barstool being drawn back. "Your sister has a good grasp of building design. She go to school for that?"

When had they spoken about building? Morgan kept her back turned and started the crepes cooking. "A couple of years of meteorology classes at a local college. Architecture's a...hobby," she said.

"Who plays around with architecture?" The musical rumble of laughter in his voice teased Morgan's imagination into thoughts of his rain-soaked chest and biceps.

Turning around for the crepe filling on the butcher block, she met his gaze at last. "Storm chasers see a lot of which buildings are left standing when a tornado passes through," she said crisply. "Some of it's just luck. The rest is rock-solid architecture. Which brings me to a point. You need help here."

His handsome features twisted into an almost-comical frown. "Did I miss the segue?"

"Dry rot?" she prompted. "The neighboring house has an old truck. We can borrow it to go to town for some lumber to resection that floor joist."

"I planned on having it done by a contractor."

"Who will, no doubt, do half the work and charge you twice the cost as you'd get by doing it with me." She blushed. *Should have picked a better turn of phrase.*

Trent's hazel eyes sharpened, and her feet stuck to the floor as if they'd been glued there with day-old oatmeal. He recognized her Freudian slip, all right. He didn't move, but something in his whole demeanor shifted from annoying interloper to alpha male on the hunt. His attention traveled from her eyes, to lips and cheeks that tingled with remembered stubble, then downward to her breasts.

Her apron couldn't shield her from that steam-hot stare, any more than it could stop her instant awareness of sensation. The silky feel of her bra against her skin. The brush of her shirt and apron over nipples gone ultra-sensitive under his scrutiny. The buzz of excitement low in her belly, and the pins-and-needles feeling of her gift rumbling against her mental restraints.

She stared at him, at that perfect mouth made for coaxing women into doing anything for him. That strong jaw, clean-shaven. Those amber eyes that trapped her like a helpless moth in their depths.

His nostrils flared. "Don't burn breakfast."

She whirled and shot to the stove so quickly that she bumped the bowl of crepe filling against the counter by the sink. Drips of egg splashed onto the stove. She ignored the mess and lowered the heat on her crepes while she poured the filling into its own pan. She couldn't blame the heat in her cheeks on the warmth of the stove, nor even on her embarrassment at feeling awkward in what should have been her element.

Nope. That was all him. She wouldn't be able to boil water by the time he finished with her.

Running on auto-pilot while all her senses tuned to the man sitting behind her, she turned the filling and cooked it to the required consistency. Her gift bubbled along her nerve endings. She carefully avoided touching anything damp with bare hands.

When was he going to get out of her kitchen, for heaven's sake? "Why don't you go to the dining room? The others are up by now."

His voice, when he spoke, was saturated with unmistakably male amusement. "I like the view here better."

She cursed under her breath, wishing she'd

worn khakis instead of the flowered skirt and blouse she'd chosen.

Back in Montana, she'd rarely had the chance to wear such feminine clothing. Jeans were the outfit of choice for ranch work, and Morgan had seen no reason to buy the flowing dresses she admired, just to see them languish in her closet. Any one of those holey, paint-stained pairs of jeans would have been preferable to the skirt now. She longed to rush out to the thrift shop for something loose and ugly.

She risked a look over her shoulder. "It's hard to cook a breakfast for eight with you...distracting me."

"Distracting you?" He rose from his seat and rounded the butcher block. Morgan spun back to her work and heard him come up behind her.

Right behind her.

She felt his body heat through the back of her blouse, though he hadn't touched her. His breath puffed across her neck where her ponytail left it bare. "I have lots better ways of distracting a person, Montana."

His husky voice skimmed her spine as if he'd run a fingertip down her back. Why, why, *why* had she said anything to him at all? Why hadn't she just kept her big mouth shut and let him sit there until breakfast was ready? Her body tingled all over—her gift, bouncing off her tenuous hold on it, and something much more primal, responding to his unspoken invitation. She started to hope that he'd quit this seesaw of flirt-hate with her, and stick to one...then thought better of it. She doubted she could handle any more "flirt" without doing something dumb. "I don't need a distraction."

"But you want one," he said in that same low tone, a pitch just perfect for inducing a woman to allow him anything he desired.

Was this how he'd succeeded so well in the business world? Had his sheer magnetism been the clincher in all those deals? Morgan could well imagine that any red-blooded woman who crossed his path must crumble under the coaxing, musical timbre of that voice. Thank heaven he hadn't turned that charm on her the first day.

"You were saying...?" he murmured from somewhere near her left ear.

She tried with increasing desperation to keep her mind on breakfast. "You're distracting me."

"About dry rot and replacement lumber?" he prompted. That amused tone again.

Business. Oh, thank heaven. "I can resection a floor joist well enough."

"And what will you be charging me for this service?" The amusement magnified.

"Your assistance."

He began laughing. "Morgan Clifton, chef and maintenance engineer."

"I don't care for your tone," she said loftily. "I helped rebuild a barn from the ground up when I lived at Hope Creek."

Silence for a moment, then he made a thoughtful noise. "Curiouser and curiouser."

"Alice?" she burst out, startled into meeting his gaze over her shoulder. When she saw the honey-warm look in his hazel eyes, she pulled her attention away to the stove again. "You're full of surprises, yourself." A bit more *Jabberwocky* than *Alice in Wonderland*, maybe.

"Books are good," he said with a sudden quiet. "They don't talk."

Morgan frowned. Books didn't hurt a person, either. How often had he wished as a child to trade his paper companions for one of flesh and blood? Someone who didn't condemn him as his parents seemed to do?

She lifted the first crepe onto an oven-warmed plate and filled it with a bit of the spinach mixture.

A second followed on its heels. She topped each entree with a sprinkling of dill and cheddar and wished she had a bigger crepe pan. The faster the breakfast preparations went, she faster she could get him out of her diminishing breathing space.

Trent edged around her and lifted the warm plates from the counter. He smiled, quickly, as if he knew what preoccupied her. "When you're done with your uffish thoughts, we'll be in the dining room."

She hesitated a moment too long. By the time she spun back to the kitchen doorway, Trent had already retreated.

Chapter Eight

Trent pushed away his empty breakfast plate and leaned back in his Windsor chair. It was going to be a long day, possibly the longest since his four-week merger of warring technology companies. After an uphill battle highlighted by a restaurant brawl between the former CEOs—and a resulting world-class migraine—Trent had closed the deal. He then retreated, exhausted, to his Boston condo and refused phone calls for a solid day.

A cakewalk compared to this dance with Morgan, and yet he couldn't resist it.

Why had he chosen a profession that included interpersonal contact? Why had he chosen a property that involved contact with *her*? She made him uncomfortable when she looked at him like that. Like a scrutiny from his parents, but in a much different way, and with a more unsettling effect. He was used to his parents. But Morgan... One look from her shot right past all the barriers he'd put up to stave off unwanted criticisms.

"Stuffed?" Elsa's quiet voice broke into his thoughts.

"Sure," he answered.

"She likes you."

"Excuse me?"

Sitting beside him, Elsa looked toward the kitchen, where Morgan had gone to refill the carafe of coffee. Elsa's team chattered with Agnes about prevailing weather conditions along the eastern seaboard, paying no attention to her and Trent. Elsa leaned closer to him and lowered her voice even further. "She'll die before she admits it, but she does. I've never seen anyone rile her up so fast."

Instead of spawning a rush of smugness, the comment irritated him. In a matter of days, Morgan Clifton had made herself more of a nuisance than anyone who'd been in his life for years. "A guy's gotta have some kind of claim to fame," he muttered.

Elsa said nothing more, but Trent sensed she wanted to. A second later, Brian produced a miniature computer and began discussing cloud formations. Agnes looked over his shoulder at the screen. Trent stopped listening until Agnes asked a question that caught Elsa's attention. Elsa rose from her seat and maneuvered to the opposite side of the table to drop into Morgan's empty chair.

Trent glanced around the table. They'd had to put an extra leaf in the table and pull chairs from another room. The only chair now available was the one beside him, a fact Morgan noticed right away when she returned. She glanced from the chair to Elsa, who remained buried in a discussion about the properties of storm clouds.

A faint line appeared between Morgan's brows. The idea of sitting beside him was clearly less appealing than a third-degree sunburn. She set the carafe in the middle of the table and, with grudgingly admirable grace, sat in the empty chair.

For a few awkward minutes, Trent let Elsa and her team fill the silence with a mini-lesson on cumulonimbus clouds. Nina explained something Trent didn't quite pay attention to, about why this or that change in air pressure was cause to run for shelter.

The more interesting point came when they broached the topic of tornadoes. Elsa launched right into the talk, while Morgan sat bolt upright and radiated discomfort like a sonar signal.

Odd. Confusing subject matter notwithstanding,

Trent could appreciate the knowledgeable way Elsa held forth about air pressures and wind currents. He wished he was that enthusiastic about...anything. But nothing Elsa said appeared to give anyone else in the room a reaction even close to the white-knuckled one he saw in Morgan. Trent half thought she would snap the handle off her delicate little cup and saucer.

Moved past reticence by the increasing press of curiosity, he asked, "You scared of them? Tornadoes?"

Her hand jerked. Some of her coffee splashed out of the cup and over its saucer onto the embroidered linen tablecloth. She mopped it up with a napkin. "No."

Her voice carried a crisp veneer, as if she believed talking would shatter the façade and give away some secret terror. Trent smiled, wanting to ease her discomfort—and not wanting to examine his motivation to do so too closely. "Do they have lots of tornadoes in Montana...Montana?"

She flashed him a rewarding smirk. "No, most of them are in Oklahoma and the surrounding areas. Right where my sister and her team like to hang out."

"I've got it covered, Morgan," Elsa said.

"Sure you do," Morgan answered, in such a sharp tone that Trent raised his eyebrows. She usually reserved that attitude for him.

The covert looks around the table tripled in an instant: Morgan to Elsa, Elsa to her team, even Agnes to Morgan. Trent's curiosity, piqued before, shot to DEFCON Someone's-Trying-To-Pull-A-Fast-One. "As much a fan as I am of subtext," he said, "how about all of you just say what you're not saying?"

"She's worried about me," Elsa said, "and she doesn't need to be. I'm strong enough."

"What are you gonna do, wrassle a tornado with your bare hands?" Trent cracked.

Instead of laughing as he'd expected, Elsa went dead serious. Her gaze found Morgan again. "I won't get hurt."

Desperation filled Morgan's face. Trent almost wanted to touch her hand—almost—but stayed frozen in place. "One slip when you're drained, Elsa..." Morgan faltered.

"I've never slipped."

"It only needs to happen once."

"Morgan...I love you, you know that. But stop *protecting* me. This is what I've chosen to do with my gi—"

If Elsa's sudden silence hadn't grabbed his attention, the terrified look on Morgan's face sure did. Double-checking his suspicions, he scanned the gathered diners. Every one of them wore expressions of shock. From somewhere in the inn, there came the *pop* of a settling floorboard.

Morgan shot out of the seat. "I have errands," she said. Hurt and fear pulsed underneath every syllable. "Call me when you get home, El." She picked up a pair of drained coffee cups and left the dining room.

Looking at her empty plate, Elsa nodded.

Nina began gathering dishes. "We should get going. Long drive back."

Agnes stood up with a too-sympathetic smile. "I'll get those, sweetheart. You go load up your truck."

Everyone scattered out of the room so fast, Trent wondered if he'd missed a shrieking fire alarm. He sat alone, staring across the table at an old china cupboard, for several minutes. The tramp of footsteps echoed through the house. Goodbyes echoed into the dining room. One by one, Elsa's team filed back through to bid him goodbye. Trent shook hands, preoccupied, relying on the automatic businessman to handle the pleasantries while he puzzled over the terror he'd seen on Morgan's face.

She knew Elsa was a storm chaser. The argument had more than the ring of a rehashed discussion. Not something to do with her sister's job, then, that worried Morgan. Not directly. Something more, something deeper.

Almost the exact look he'd seen on her face the night he caught her out swimming.

He had been around long enough in the business world to know when a person was trying to keep something big out of public knowledge. Curiouser and curiouser, for sure.

Elsa entered the dining room last. She smiled, looking like the incident that ended breakfast had never occurred. "It was nice meeting you, Trent. I know everyone says that, but really." She took his hand, shook it, but didn't release it. When he gave her a puzzled look, she leaned forward across the table. "Don't let them get to you. They just don't see you. But Morgan does."

"Elsa, c'mon!" called a voice Trent recognized as Brian's. "Bus is leaving, doll!"

Elsa grinned and released Trent's hand. "Goodbye." She spun, blond hair swinging, and hurried away.

Trent passed the rest of the day in his room, catching up on the business that had been piling up on his desk for half a week. Occasionally he heard Agnes humming as she went up and down stairs, but no knock came at the door.

Morgan didn't come up to his room once.

Needing to break the irritating silence, he logged in to a WiFi connection of the local radio broadcast and went back to his proposals.

The day warmed enough for him to open the balcony doors, and then close them again as the sun lowered in the sky. Words began swimming on the computer screen. He found himself paying more attention to the deejay, who'd been saying all afternoon that the unseasonably warm weather was bound to produce some storms.

Storms brought him around to Elsa, and then to her bothersome parting advice, which brought him right back to thinking of Morgan.

He leaned back in the desk chair, then realized he couldn't see the remaining papers on his desk without squinting in the gloom. He flicked on the lamp and saw that he'd cleared the space of nearly everything, but he found no satisfaction in it. Elsa's words haunted him. *They just don't see you. But Morgan does.*

What did she see? What would she expect to see? Why the hell did he care?

But Morgan does.

Trent rose from the seat and jabbed the power button on his computer. He stalked from the room and tramped downstairs, fully intending to leave the inn and walk all the way to town, as long as it got his mind off the Seaglass Inn and everything in it.

But the smell wafting from the kitchen stopped him like a set of concrete pylons.

Italian.

He sucked in the aromas of meat and sauce with unflinching admiration. How did a Montana girl living in Nantucket cook an Italian meal smelling like it came straight from the old country? Why would she want to hide such a talent in a little bed-and-breakfast that housed no more than ten people at a time?

She *was* hiding, he realized. Otherwise she'd move her skill to the largest, most prestigious restaurant she could find. She'd have gone with Agnes when the old lady moved south, and scared up a job at one of the many and much bigger bayside eateries in Florida.

Instead, Morgan Clifton had chosen a bolt-hole where as few strangers as possible could get at her. Why did she isolate herself and then fight so hard to stay here? Here, where the off-season population shrank to a fraction of its summer size? "Who are you?" he murmured.

Singing reached his ears—husky, slightly off-key, but no less intriguing for it. Trent caught the faint sounds of a radio and directed his footsteps to the kitchen.

Morgan whirled around in the middle of a crescendo and froze with a carton of fresh mushrooms in her hands. The round-eyed look on her face matched that of the owl on her snug brown T-shirt, which read "Sagerton Hootenanny Field Days." No apron this evening. She wore jeans, for a change.

Trent examined her outfit with a raised eyebrow. "I must have missed the memo on casual day?"

Her lips firmed. He admired the way she met his look, unflinching. "This is my night off. Agnes is house-sitting for Mrs. Mayweather while she sees her granddaughter in Boston." Morgan retreated to the stove and poured the sliced mushrooms into a skillet already sizzling with the smells of butter and garlic. Beside it bubbled a pan of frying meatballs. With her back to him, she added, "I thought you were out. You were gone all day."

"Been in my room working," he said, then grinned. "My absence was conspicuous?"

"Conspicuous in its peacefulness," she shot back, but he caught an intriguing gleam in her eye.

"Well, I'm conspicuously starving," he said. "Mind if I throw together a sandwich or something?" He approached the refrigerator.

She stopped him with a scowl and a large

serving fork pointed at his chest. "No one 'throws together' anything in this kitchen."

Answering her challenging glare with one of his own, he pushed the fork aside with a fingertip. "May I 'construct' a sandwich, then? 'Build' a sandwich? 'Assemble' it?"

The corner of her mouth twitched, then drew down as if she were trying not to laugh. "You have no concept of how to prepare good food, do you?"

"We had a cook," he said with a little too much defensiveness. "Not a great cook, but whatever he made didn't kill me, so I deemed it fine. When I got old enough to write my own ticket, I ate at restaurants. They haven't killed me, either." He left out that he actually appreciated her cooking, too busy with the way her faded T-shirt stretched around her curvaceous breasts.

Pause. Stare. Try not to stare. Where the hell was that stupid apron when she was supposed to be wearing it?

When he reached for the fridge again, she stopped him. "There's enough here for two. No construction necessary—I'll do it. Rather not have you demolish my kitchen."

"You don't think I can cook."

"I know you can't. Why else would a man eat at restaurants all the time?"

"I'm busy."

"Too busy. Cooking's not that hard. And women appreciate a man who isn't afraid to do it."

He angled his head. "Who said I needed the appreciation?"

Her cheeks went pink so fast that he couldn't resist the temptation. He swept across the space until her breath mingled with his. "How about you show me what I'm missing, Montana?" he murmured, enjoying the way her breath caught when her gaze went to his mouth. Deliberately, he ducked his head and brought her vision back in line with his eyes. "I'm not afraid to learn a few new tricks." He traced a finger along the seam of her jeans at the hip, and relished her little gasp. "I might even surprise you with the ones I already know."

****

Morgan held her breath. The cozy kitchen she had loved since her arrival on Nantucket suddenly became far too small a space to hold two people. Too small to hold *him*. She darted backward and whirled to the stove again, where she poured the sautéed mushroom mixture into the simmering sauce. She picked up another large fork and began turning meatballs so fast the oil spattered out of the pan and just missed her fingers. "Fine," she snapped. "Get the basil from the fridge. You can chop it for the sauce."

"I wouldn't know basil from broccoli," he answered, coming up behind her. His voice, low and intimate, spurred a wave of heat across her skin that rivaled that of the stove. "How about I turn these over?" He reached around her and eased the forks from her hands. She didn't resist. She had all she could do to avoid letting her gift slip under the power of that voice, that voice which coaxed her to unravel like the finest marsala wine.

Slipping away from him, she hurried to the refrigerator and selected a few handfuls of herbs for the sauce. Chopping them with brisk strokes, she watched him and tried not to be obvious about it.

He set the forks down, then began rolling up the sleeves of his dress shirt. As he washed his hands, his forearm muscles rippled. Mesmerized, she followed their sculpted contours up to powerful shoulders outlined under the crisp white fabric.

He returned to the stove, oblivious to her attention, and picked up the forks. Morgan stared at the profiles of his stubble-shaded cheek and strong nose. How had a man looking like that come from such sour, pinch-faced parents? She saw no evidence of his mother or father in his expressive eyes or—*Oh, all right,* she admitted to herself—that incredible, sensual mouth.

He filled the space between stove and butcher block so well, the kitchen seemed to have redesigned itself around him. And he looked too damn good standing there. He worked slower than she might have done, but with an air that suggested he met any task with a seriousness that got the job done, and got it done right. Did he apply that dedication to...other things?

He glanced up. When he saw her looking, he raised his chin. "What?"

She went back to her chopping with a vengeance. The basil and oregano never stood a chance.

"I thought you said 'chop it,' not 'pummel it into smithereens,'" he said. Finished with the meatballs, he laid the forks aside and wiped his hands on a dishcloth. He flashed a dimple that almost unraveled her. "I do know the difference."

Pow. Her gift slammed at her restraints as she looked at him. Again. Again. Good Lord, she needed help. She scraped the herbs into a small glass bowl and brought them to the stove, where the pot of meat sauce bubbled over a heat diffuser. She stirred the herbs in and wished fervently that they made heat diffusers for people. The boiling sensation in her body had settled into places she normally kept covered with at least two layers of clothing—clothing which felt desperately absent under his heated stare.

"Smells good," he said, leaning over the pot for a sniff. "What's in there besides tomatoes and grass clippings?"

"Basil and oregano," she huffed, only to find him grinning. The boyish look disarmed her, and she smiled back. "I buy fresh when it's in season. Local, if I can get it. This is home-canned sauce from Mrs. Mayweather's heirloom tomatoes, mixed with sweet Italian sausage and spare ribs. A little wine to flavor it."

He took another sniff. "Greek to me, right up until you said 'wine.'" He strode to the refrigerator and opened it. With a smile, he lifted a bottle of her favorite merlot from the bottom shelf. "This it?"

"Yes."

"Good." He opened a cupboard and withdrew two mugs, then poured some wine into each. As horrified as she was at his choice of drinking vessel, she almost laughed that he'd chosen something other than that damned beer stein. With a triumphant smile, he held one of the mugs out to her, then clinked it with his own. "To our one-night...truce." A lightning-flash of heat entered his eyes and disappeared just as fast.

Morgan stood motionless with suspended vertigo, as if she had crested the top of a tidal wave and clung there, waiting to plunge down the other side. Seconds passed, and under the bubbling of frying food, she swore she heard his breath quicken.

With his gaze still locked on hers, Trent tipped his mug back and drained the contents. He set the mug on her butcher block and curled an arm around her waist, so smoothly that she was in his embrace before she realized he'd even moved. "Wine's good with other things than food," he murmured, then bent to kiss her.

Her power exploded through her from the top of her head to each extremity. Adrenaline rushed after it. Fear. Excitement.

The merlot on his lips mingled with the more subtle taste of him, an indefinable something that drove her gift into a buzzing rampage. Horrified that he'd draw back and notice her skin, which had to be glowing, she grabbed his shirt and pulled him closer.

He made an appreciative noise and loosened his grasp to cup her backside in both hands, then dragged her against his body. The ridge of his erection jabbed into her belly. She gasped into his mouth and dropped her mug on the floor. Wine splashed the legs of her pants and she yelped.

"Leave it. I'll buy you new pants," he muttered. He threaded one hand through her hair, urged her head back, then kissed her throat. He pressed her back against the butcher block and arched against her. "But I like the skirts better."

"You would," she said with what breath she could manage.

His searing fingers swept under the waistband at the back of her jeans to stroke bare skin. "Of course I would. Too damn hard to get into pants. I want you, and I want you right now. I'm sick of trying to ignore it, Morgan." He nosed the collar of her T-shirt aside and nipped her neck.

"Ah—Trent," she whispered, wrinkling the front of his dress shirt in her fists. He nipped again, and she pulled so hard at the shirt she heard seams pop. With shaking fingers, she pried at the buttons.

He snatched the collar of his shirt and ripped it open. Buttons pinged on the floor. Wide-eyed, she forgot about her gift and stared openly at the blazing look of desire on his face.

He took her hands and flattened them against his breathtaking bare chest. She stifled a moan and spread her fingers over his pecs before he swooped in to kiss her again. "Hell with the shirt," he said, then thrust his tongue into her mouth.

Morgan reeled, giddy on the feel of his lips alone. Who needed wine? He kissed as thoroughly as he did everything else, filling her with his scent and taste and touch, but leaving her aching for the rest of him. He crouched and lifted her onto the butcher block. "Lean back," he said.

She did, arching her spine as her shoulder blades met the cool wood through her thin shirt. Trent pushed the hem up to her neck. He gave a groan that sounded like she was torturing him and smoothed his hands down her flat belly. Savoring the heat of his skin against hers, she closed her eyes. The scents of meat, sauce, and wine mingled in the air with the musk of his cologne. Her hair spilled over the far edge of the butcher block and she lifted her chin to let it slide back, exposing her neck and throat for him to kiss if he chose. When had she ever felt so wild, so wanton, so utterly worshipped?

His hands crossed her belly again, then slid upward to push her bra off her breasts, just enough to expose her nipples to the air. She held her breath, expecting his touch, his mouth.

Then he was gone.

Morgan started to sit up, to open her eyes. His palm came down on her belly again. "Stay there," he ordered, his voice husky, tense. She shivered with pleasure.

The slosh of the merlot in its bottle reached her. An instant before she would have opened her eyes again, his mouth closed on her nipple. The heat of his lips and tongue mingled with the chill of liquid. She moaned and clutched at the sleeves of his shirt, squirming, trying to pull him closer.

He closed his teeth on her nipple and molded his palms to her body. He swallowed, and then she sensed only the heat of his mouth on her. The suction of his mouth drove her into such a mad passion that she almost bucked off the counter. Her gift bounced around inside her in a trapped frenzy, faster and faster and faster until—

Her skin blazed all over. Shudders crashed

together down her spine. Pleasure fired through her and centered between her legs. Trent cupped her there in one strong hand, burning-hot through the fabric. Morgan gave a hoarse moan and went to pieces underneath him. Her joints loosened and she let her body go slack, stunned, her senses obliterated.

For a few seconds, she could only lay there panting. The world returned a little at a time. The rumble of laughter echoed from Trent's chest and vibrated against her fingertips.

Oh, God, her power. Had she...?

He arched over her and smiled, his eyes molten. "Told you wine was good with other things," he said. The grapes-and-roses merlot on his breath fanned across her face. "This one's an especially nice dessert wine."

"Dessert...?" she echoed, foggy-headed with relief and bliss. The smell of smoke tickled at her nose underneath the scent of wine. "Dessert. Dinner. Oh, shit, dinner!"

The smoke alarm shrieked an instant later. Trent launched off her toward the stove. He cranked the dials, then snatched at the smoking pan of meatballs. Oil splattered his hand and he swore loudly, dropping the pan into the sink with a crash. Still cursing, he wrenched the tap and ran water over his hand.

"Oh, God, Trent, are you all right?"

"Fine, I'm fine! Get the damned smoke alarm!" he snapped.

Morgan wrenched her bra and shirt down. She leaped onto a stool and twisted the smoke detector out of its base on the ceiling. The shriek stopped, leaving only the hiss of water running into the sink.

She hurried over, distressed, and reached for the tap. Her fault, all her fault. His hand, his wonderful hand that had just done such incredible things to

123

her and barely even touched her....

"I said I'm fine," he ground out. "Don't bother—"

She thrust her fingers into the stream and slowed the motion of the water molecules, super-cooling them until they ran like ice-water.

His eyes went wide and locked on her as if she'd just frozen him in place. Then, slowly, his gaze shifted to her hand, still under the running tap, where her fingers shimmered pearlescent under the stream of water.

Morgan closed her eyes, fighting her body's imperative to be violently sick.

It was all over.

Chapter Nine

Trent's feet did not move. Would not move. He kept his stare locked on Morgan's fingers—her glowing fingers—wondering if he were having a dream. Or a nightmare. Or *something*, for Christ's sake. Anything but what had just happened, what he couldn't get his senses to process.

The red patch of skin on the back of his hand began to fade. The heat seeped out of it as if it had never been. He wouldn't have believed it if the stinging hadn't stopped.

Then the cold replaced it. His hand went as numb as if he'd plunged it into a snowbank for half an hour. He gritted his teeth and yanked it out of the water. When he could avoid it no longer, he forced himself to look at her.

She hunched like a trapped mouse in front of the sink, with her hand still under the tap and her eyes screwed shut. So different from the woman he'd just...only seconds ago... He cursed under his breath and shut the tap off.

She opened her eyes. A few seconds passed before she looked at him. Her cheeks went red, and she drew her hands close to her body, trembling. The glow faded from her fingers. They stared at each other for a ceaseless minute.

Then she bolted.

"Whoa! Wait! What the—" He snatched at her arm and yanked his hand back at once, not wanting to touch her skin, then made a grab for the back of her shirt instead. "Morgan! Damn it!" He slammed into the edge of the butcher block and a utensil crock crashed onto the floor. She slipped out of his grip and ran.

Trent chased her out the door of the inn and onto the beach. She raced to the water and he stumbled after her. "Morgan! Fuck. Morgan!"

He caught her by the leg of her jeans and tripped her. She toppled headlong onto the sand and he dropped to one knee over her.

She rolled, raising her arms as if to shield her face. Gritting his teeth, he grabbed her wrists and forced her arms down to the sand. "What the hell was that?"

"Get off me, get off me, get off me!" she sobbed.

Shocked at the panic in her voice, he darted backward. She scrambled into a crouch and began inching toward the water. Staring at her tear-streaked face in the dimming sunset, he touched his hand and felt no evidence of the burn. "What'd you do to me?" he asked softly.

"Nothing, nothing, just go away, you can have the inn, I'll leave..." She shook so hard he thought he heard her teeth chatter.

He made up his mind and grabbed her hand. "I don't want to go away. I want to know what... Shit." He rubbed his face and tried again. "Thank you?"

She stopped struggling to retreat, but her trembling didn't cease. She kept her gaze on the sand.

Jesus. Uncharted waters, no kidding. He stared at her some more, then lowered his voice. "Come on. Let's go back inside."

She jerked at her hand again, still closed in his. He released her. "I promise—I promise I won't touch you," he added, wondering if even that was the right thing to say. To show he meant it, he stood up and stuffed his hands in his pockets.

She got to her feet, still watching him like she thought he'd pounce, and made a wide berth around him before starting back to the inn. He lagged behind, at a loss for what to say.

By the time he returned to the kitchen, she was already cleaning up the mess from their failed dinner. No singing. No animation. A hundred times more subdued than she'd been when he first walked in this evening. She paid him so little attention, he might as well have been a light fixture. Just the way things had been when he was young and still living with his parents.

With his gaze on the faucet, which was off, he edged into the kitchen, guilt-ridden for no good reason. He wished the whole evening had never happened. He wished he'd never smelled the food. He wished he'd never wondered about her.

He leaned against the wall by the doorway. Morgan crouched on the floor. She scraped up a pile of broken crockery onto a dustpan and stood up. The chunks of broken ceramic tilted and threatened to slide off the pan. She gave a watery yelp as if she were about to cry again.

Trent rushed forward and caught the mess against his waist and in his hands. A shard of crockery poked him in the belly and he flinched, but didn't let go. "I'm sorry. For—for whatever just happened. If I caused that."

She pulled the mess from his hands and tipped it into the wastebasket beside the wall phone. For a few seconds, she stood there with her shoulders slumped, and he realized she was hugging herself. "You didn't."

He started toward her, almost touched her, but remembered he'd promised not to. "What did?"

"Me," she said in a very small voice.

Her answer didn't surprise him, but it was no help with what to do next. Cautiously, not knowing what to expect, he approached her one step at a time. "I'm not gonna hurt you."

127

She whirled, and he backed off. "How do I know what you're going to do?" she demanded. "What *does* someone like you do when—"

"Someone like me? What am I like?"

"You—you just take whatever you want. You barge into someone's home, and you like what you see, so you shove them out of it and toss a little money after them. For all I know, you're trying to figure out how to make a buck off what you just saw." Bitterness cut through every word. "I'll save you the blackmail and leave."

Trent jerked back, as stung as if she'd slapped him across the face. He advanced again, anger pounding the blood through his veins, until he had backed her up against the wall. "I don't even know what I saw, and you've already got me building castles on your beach. I guess that's what you'd figure. Didn't you hear me thank you? Didn't you see me fixing goddamn stuff that isn't even mine to fix around here? You're fucking welcome."

He hated his tone even as the words left his mouth. Still groveling for appreciation like a whiny little brat, years later. Ridiculous.

He started to turn away, but Morgan gave a watery sniffle. He stopped. Tears trickled down her cheeks. She dropped the dustpan to wipe at them.

Trent reached out, slowly, to take her hand—the hand that had healed his burn before it got started. The words left his mouth even through his resentment. "I said I'm not gonna hurt you."

She glanced around the room like a trapped animal looking for escape. Her hand was cold and stiff as a glass paperweight. "How do I know that?" she snapped again.

"You don't see me dialing up the networks, do you? I'm not reaching for a carving knife." She didn't say anything, and he gave her a shake. "Christ, can I form an opinion before you crucify me?"

She tried again to pull her hand away, but this time he didn't let her go. Her eyes flashed with a little of the Morgan he recognized. "And what's your opinion?" she spat.

"I'll let you know when I have one," he snapped, then caught himself. He sighed and stepped back. "All I know is...you're definitely not what I thought you were."

"Neither are you," she said, and her tone made him look at her again. Her gaze was on his chest, left bare by the torn-open shirt. She avoided his eyes.

Frustration gurgled up through his nerves. "Look, I'm sick of being sorry for shit. I'm not sorry for"—he flung a hand at the kitchen—"for this. I'm not, 'cause I wanted it, and I was honest about that. No matter what I saw afterward, or whatever you did. And whatever you did..." He lowered his voice to a mutter. "Thank you." He jammed his hands in his pockets again and stalked out of the room.

****

Morgan stayed up most of the night cleaning the kitchen, taking her time, wishing she didn't hope so much that Trent would return.

What if he chose to make a spectacle of her? *Would* he do that? The Trent she thought she knew, the one she'd met while sneaking through his suitcase, wouldn't have hesitated.

But this was the same Trent who saw no problem with tormenting Spencer, her culinary nemesis. The same man who fixed a water problem that wasn't his, and carried a heavy whitewash bucket without being asked.

She scrubbed at the kitchen floor until her arms hurt, then tossed the brush into its pail. The kitchen gleamed like the events of the evening had never occurred.

Except that the utensil crock was gone, and she was starving, and her body pulsed with an ache that no amount of cleaning could eradicate.

How could a man so selfish on the surface be so unsparing with his passion? He had barely let her touch him. It had been all about her. Every touch, every kiss, every stroke of his beautiful, skilled hands.

She had been through her share of relationships, though they'd gotten steadily fewer and farther between as she grew older. She couldn't bring herself to chance that kind of closeness with someone, to risk the exposure of her gift and the safety of her family.

What would it be like, to be with someone who already knew she was an Elemental? Someone with an incredible body...and hands...and eyes....

She stood and brought the pail to the washroom off the kitchen. Brooding, she dumped the dirty water down the tub sink, then put the tools away.

Now that she had no distractions, the tears returned. Her brothers and sister had always thought her the practical one. The one who took her lot in stride, and remained unmoved by the judgmental opinions of others.

How wrong they were. She envied Kincade the happiness of a family who accepted him for who, and what, he was. Even Elsa's team knew of her power. How had Morgan's siblings ever found the strength to confess their gifts? How had they known who could be trusted with the secret?

Had they ever divulged it to someone so completely wrong?

With a frustrated groan, she hurried from the kitchen and climbed the stairs. She crept past his room, angry that she had hoped to see a light under his door and found none.

She reached her own room and closed the door. Tomorrow, she would look for a new job, somewhere far away, but she'd never call it home.

By the next morning, she had gotten maybe a scant hour of sleep. It was full light when she woke, and when she saw her clock she sat up with alarm. She never slept in so late.

She had left her window open, and voices drifted into the chilly room from outside. "I don't know, Diane. Wouldn't you rather stay at one of the newer places down the—"

"Look at it. It's so cute. Look at those tulips, Rodge, they're beautiful," said a woman.

Morgan scrambled out of bed and into a skirt and light sweater. Trent's remark regarding skirts came back to her, and she did her best to ignore it.

She rushed downstairs to the smells of coffee and baked goods. In the kitchen, she found the percolator already running.

Agnes, wearing Morgan's apron, set a fresh-baked batch of sticky rolls on the butcher block beside a plate already full of them. "Oh, good morning, sweetheart. Have you seen the spatula? The crock is missing from the counter, and I couldn't find where you'd moved it."

Morgan blushed. "I'm sorry I slept so late. I—"

"I broke it," Trent said, coming into the kitchen with a large paper bag. "Sorry, Agnes. You've got a couple coming to the door, by the way." He pushed the paper bag into Morgan's hands. "Good morning."

"M-Morning," she stuttered, then opened the bag to find something wrapped in tissue. She removed it and folded the paper back.

A glazed pottery crock with a lighthouse on the front.

Trent was already across the kitchen getting his beer stein from the cupboard. He filled it from the percolator and turned around. "Thank you," she said, more touched than she wanted to admit. "When did you have time to get this?"

He shrugged. "Stores opened early enough. I had

nothing else to do."

Which meant he must have slept as poorly as she. Had he been up all night thinking about her, too? About what they had been doing before the smoke alarm went off, or how she'd healed his burn with her power?

He stirred sugar and creamer into his coffee, then took a long swallow even though it must have burned his throat on the way down. His eyes were closed. Even his posture gave no hint to his thoughts. Morgan waited, uncertain.

He opened his eyes at last. She couldn't read his expression any more than his body language. After last night, how could he look at her like they'd never met? "Which one's the neighbor with the truck?" he asked.

"The gray cottage next door. Are you planning to fix—"

"The joist," he said. Nothing more. He started for the doorway. "Work to do."

"Not without breakfast, young man," Agnes interrupted. She pointed at the plate of sticky buns. A folded newspaper rested beside it.

Trent glanced at the food and hitched a shoulder. "Thanks." He took one of the pastries and stuck a corner of it between his teeth. He grabbed the paper in his free hand and waved it at them, then left the kitchen.

Morgan stared at the empty doorway with a surge of hurt. So that was how he planned to play it.

Pretending she barely existed.

****

Trent kicked his bedroom door shut and set his breakfast on the desk, then crossed the room to open the balcony doors. It promised to be mild today. He would have sat on the porch to eat, except he figured Morgan and Agnes would do the same. And he had work to do. Somewhere. He could scrounge something up to occupy him while he ate.

Something other than the image of Morgan laid out on the kitchen island like an offering. Something other than the catch of her breath when he touched her. Definitely something other than the way he'd wanted to plunge into her so deep he forgot everything else in his life.

He opened his laptop. Wrangling breakfast in one hand, he used the other to check his e-mail. Nothing that needed his attention there. No contracts, no teleconferences, not even a memo. He had purposely built his schedule for the month around the purchase of the Seaglass Inn. Anything else that had to be addressed, he'd already done the previous day in an effort to steer clear of Morgan.

There wasn't enough work in the world to distract him now. He'd thought if he tried hard enough, maybe he could ignore the whole thing. But it was impossible to ignore what they'd been doing to cause them to burn dinner. And what she'd done afterward.

He swore and pulled up the Internet, then paused, staring at the blinking cursor in the Search box without the faintest idea what to type. He had no words for whatever he'd seen—just the haunting image of her glowing hand and the look of horror on her face.

He jabbed the keys and typed *lumber yard Nantucket*.

A few options popped up. Trent picked the closest one and scribbled down the hours and location, then added a list of the materials he needed for the floor joist. He wolfed down the pastry and washed it down with half the stein of coffee, then reluctantly returned to the first floor.

He found Morgan in the kitchen, slipping her apron off. She paused when their gazes met, then went on as if she hadn't seen him.

The brush-off irritated him more than he wanted to admit, even though he'd done the same thing earlier. What the hell was he expected to say to her after she'd done something no human being should be able to do? "I have the list for the lumber yard. Are you coming or not?" he demanded.

She glanced around the kitchen as if looking for something to use as an excuse not to accompany him. His pride stung and he added, "I don't think the kitchen's going to have a meltdown in your one-hour absence."

She shot him a glare and began fussing with something on the butcher block.

He put his plate and the beer stein in the sink. "Look, you're the one who said you know all about carpentry. If you're too wrapped up in whatever you have going right now—"

"What do you even know about me?" she burst out, and he was surprised to hear a tremor in her voice. She wrenched on the tap and began washing his breakfast dishes, which somehow made him feel at fault for having dirtied them. "You're the one who's all wrapped up in your own world. When's the last time you bothered to look outside your own problems?"

He opened his mouth on a scathing reply that never came. Tears welled in her eyes, but she turned away as she noticed him looking.

He stared at her back for a while. Anything he said would spur a long, uncomfortable discussion about last night. Damn it, he was sick of feeling blame for his every action around here. No matter which direction he chose to go in with her, it got him grief.

The social obligations and financial returns of his job presented him with a steady stream of female pursuers, some available and some who wanted to be. Trent had started seeing Laura socially for that very reason. He found it easier to deter the horde when they thought he was involved with her. And hell, even without her, he could find enough other women to occupy him—with less bother than Morgan—for a few lifetimes.

Why did he let her get under his skin so much?

"Fine," he said at last. "See you later." He stalked out of the kitchen.

His Lexus stood in the driveway. He stared at its sleek lines and realized this morning's foray into town was the first time he'd driven it in four days. Why had he bothered to blow the money on ferrying it over?

Oh, right. This was supposed to have been a splurge, a celebration visit to close up what should have been a cake deal.

How wrong he'd been. The still-corked bottle of Dom remained where he'd put it on his dresser, taunting him with how *not* a cake deal this was.

He thought of the rusty bicycles in the garage and scoffed, then walked to the house next door. He hadn't seen its resident since arriving here and wondered if anyone would be home.

He rang the bell and waited. And waited. When he was about to give up, the door opened on a bearded old man in a wheelchair. "Yeh?"

Trent offered a smile and his hand, which the man shook after a moment of scrutiny. "I'm Trent Williams, sir. I'm buying the inn next door. The chef tells me you have a truck I might borrow or rent to make a trip into town."

"Pah. That girl don't need to rent from me. Keys are hanging up inside the door." He backed up into his hall and gestured to the wall. "Heard of you. Agnes said you was taking over the old place when she goes."

"Something like that." Trent ducked around the doorjamb long enough to glimpse an immaculately kept house, and plucked the keys from their hook. "Thanks. I'll be back with it in about an hour." He turned to leave.

"Hey."

Trent paused and looked back.

"I hear you're gonna relocate Miss Clifton. She ain't going far, is she?"

"Why do you ask?"

"Since my wife died, Miss Clifton's been bringing me dinners here and there. She's good company." The old man gave a brief smile, then raised his voice. "Anyway, you better tell her not to go without saying goodbye to old Gordon."

"Sure," Trent said, feeling like an outsider peeking into Morgan's life. For a woman who was—whatever she was—she had put down a lot of roots in this place. People cared about her.

Envy bolted through him. Caught off guard, he bade Gordon a distracted goodbye and hurried out the door.

The truck's back end had gone missing—Trent guessed a long time ago, by the make of the remaining parts. The bed had been replaced by a pressure-treated one joined together with carriage bolts. He gave one of the sides an experimental wiggle. It didn't move an inch.

When he started the truck, the radio tuned in to an oldies station that he turned off. Stick-shift. He couldn't remember the last time he'd driven a stick-shift anything. For a moment he considered asking Morgan along again, then discarded the idea. He didn't need her.

He drove into town, only stalling out once. Now that he didn't have Morgan's presence to distract him, he noticed more of the buildings' architecture and layout. Clearly a town built around its tourist industry, with a fondness for its nautical roots. Trent couldn't imagine what these people did in the off-season. Boston was busy, noisy, and in constant forward motion. What did the residents of Nantucket do in the middle of winter? Knit sweaters?

He found the lumber yard and parked the truck. With his list in hand, he entered the store and found what he needed.

Two men lingered by a stack of pine boards. Trent caught bits of their conversation while examining a board for any warping.

"—heard we were fixing for a blowout in a week or two," said a man in a red baseball cap.

"My nephew's a fisherman," said the other. "Says they've been watching the sky like hawks while they're out on the water. Storms might even come in earlier than reports are saying." The man laid a board on the wheeled cart beside them. "You know fishermen. Part sea-dog, part weatherman. Better tell your sister not to plan on that graduation party for her kid. Not outdoors, anyhow."

Trent laid a board on his own cart and pushed it toward the fastener aisle. His cell rang. He pulled it from his pocket. "Hello?"

"Hi, darling, I'm in Los Angeles," answered Laura. "I found the cutest condo. You should come see it."

"With what time?"

"Don't tell me you're still haggling over that old place in Nantucket. Your mother said it was a nightmare."

"My mother's not a real estate buyer." Trent angled the stubborn cart around a pole.

"Well, since you're snubbing me for your parents' Mother's Day dinner, I thought you might want to fly out here and spend next weekend with me. This place is too cute. I might buy it. I could use some professional advice on that," she added in a husky, suggestive singsong.

"Laura, I have some snags here that I need to address," he said. One snag in particular, with a weird thing about water, a stubborn streak that drove him batty, and lips he couldn't stop thinking about no matter what she was.

"Well, why don't I come see you this weekend instead? The condo can wait."

"Laura, now's not a great—"

"Oh, the painters are here. 'Bye, sweetheart." He heard the click of the receiver.

Hell. Trent stuffed his cell phone in his pocket, then wrangled the lumber cart through the store while he picked up the rest of his supplies. He should have left this crap to a carpenter. He should have been in Los Angeles, living it up with Laura while she spent her way through the City of Angels.

She was a damn sight less complicated, that was for sure.

Truth be told, he liked working with his hands. It gave him a tangible sense of accomplishment, as opposed to all the computerized wheeling and dealing he did in his office back home. He could see the result of his work right away when he built something. Early in his career, he had not only purchased real estate, but helped tear it down for resale of its parts. The labor provided a catharsis that workouts in his exclusive gym couldn't match.

He examined his hands, free of blisters and hardly callused. How long had it been since he worked like this?

On his way back to the inn, he left the truck's windows down. The wind gusted around the cab, smelling of salt and seaweed. Had he hoped too much that the happiness of his parents' childhood here wasn't some dreamed-up myth? Why did he want to hang onto this place, in spite of its need of updates and its razor-tongued chef?

When he pulled into the drive, he saw Agnes

cutting some tulips by the porch. She laid them in a basket on her arm. Beside her stood a young couple in polo shirts and khaki pants.

He got out of the truck and approached them. Agnes saw him coming and smiled. "Here he is. This is Trent Williams. He's buying the inn. Mister Williams, this is Roger and Diane Sanderson. They've just been married."

Trent thrust out his hand and shook each of theirs. "Congratulations." The word came out talk-show smooth, in a tone they could take any way they wanted. Married. He wouldn't have foisted that punishment on his worst enemies, if his parents were any indication of how things went after the I-dos. The gooey looks the couple gave each other mystified him. How long would that hold out?

"This is such a beautiful place, Mister Williams," said Diane. "I love the porch. Are you taking reservations for next season yet?"

"No," he said, fast enough that Agnes frowned. Roger's mouth opened, but nothing came out. Trent's business sensibilities gave him a swift kick, reminding him never to piss off a potential commercial contact. "I apologize, but I have work to do. Enjoy your stay."

Close shave, that. He left the couple and Agnes—looking after him with frank curiosity, he had no doubt—and brought his materials inside. Sooner or later, he would have to break the news that this building would be torn down and pieced off after the closure. He'd only done the joist work to prevent further problems on the property while he completed the sale and subsequent dismantling.

Morgan, thank God, was not present when he hauled everything to the basement. He found an old pair of work gloves in a dusty tool chest downstairs, then set to work with the same efficiency he strove for in everything else. By late afternoon, he had resectioned the soft part of the beam and removed the supports. Not once did Morgan make an appearance. When he found himself dwelling on that fact, he threw himself into his work with twice the determination. He didn't need her help, and didn't want her interference.

He swept his work area clean of debris, torn between the need to return to his normal life in Boston and the pull of unfinished business here. The image of her glowing hand kept haunting him. Avoiding her all day had done him no good.

Finished at last with his project, he turned around to go upstairs.

Morgan stood before him.

He jerked to a stop. Everything he'd tried shoving under the rug since this morning came back in force. His body ordered him forward, ordered him to touch her the way he'd been wanting to all day and trying to deny it. Her smell. The feel of her skin. The sounds she made when he kissed her lips, her throat, her breasts.

Total mistake to stay here. He should have called a retainer to finish this, days ago, and moved on to the rest of his life. He bit down on a burst of aggravation, scrambled, irresolute.

"I'm sorry," she said. She glanced over his shoulder.

"Don't worry about it," he replied. "I didn't need the help." He caught her scent in the stagnant cellar air. His body went on instant alert, reminding him he'd ignored its demands in favor of her last night. With a soft sigh, he started to turn away.

She took a step, and her scent wafted stronger past his nose. "I want to talk to you about what happened."

"There's nothing to talk about." He stepped around her, but couldn't shut out the look of hurt that flashed across her face. He resented the way he wanted to make it go away. Why did he keep torturing himself? What was it about her that made him stick, when he'd made a science out of excising complications from his life? What she'd done to the contract could have rendered this whole mess null, if only he hadn't been in such a rush to sign off on it. He clenched his fists, seething with impotent fury.

As he started up the stairs, he heard her tread on the steps behind him. "You're just going to keep walking away from me for the rest of this...sale, then, are you?" she demanded.

He neared the top step and turned to face her. "You know what, it was a mistake. A stupid, one-time mistake that shouldn't have happened in the first place, and won't happen again. And as for those back-charges on Agnes's rent, consider them your severance pay, because you should have been out of my life days ago."

Her eyes went wide. Even in the low lighting, he saw spots of high color on her cheeks. Guilt punched him. He thrust it stubbornly into some dark corner of his mind.

Morgan charged up the stairs past him, ramming his shoulder with her own. At the top, she faced him. "I'm not sure where you're going when you kick it, Trent Williams, but hell's too good for you."

Chapter Ten

Morgan rushed into her kitchen, fighting tears and hoping the inn's guests didn't catch her in such a state. How could he talk to her like that—to anyone like that? How could he be so callous, when he'd been so passionate and giving last night? How could two attitudes so vastly different even exist in the same person? She stared at the butcher block, shaking with equal parts pain and outrage. Her power buzzed, echoing her anguish.

Maybe it wasn't just her, she thought, looking at her hands. Maybe it was...this.

Stifling a sob, she turned to the refrigerator. The faster they went their separate ways, the better off the world would be. She would help Agnes finish packing the rest of the items in unused rooms and load them into Gordon's garage next door. He could forget, and she could...try.

Trent stalked into the kitchen. Caught by surprise, she whirled away so he wouldn't see her struggling against tears.

"You have no idea what goes into a property sale," he barked. "The time and expense, the paperwork, the haggling and dealing, the waiting...and that's without interfering know-it-alls tampering with the contracts." He stepped around the butcher block and closed in on her space, her sanctuary. His eyes blazed. "I bust my ass at my job *every day*, and I don't need you in my face telling me how to do it."

Her blood simmered. She bit back the tears on a welcome surge of teeth-grinding anger. "In *your* face? You came in here—to me—to continue this...attack. And keep your voice down. We have guests." She flung open the old refrigerator in search of dinner fixings.

"What makes you think you're any better than me?" he demanded. "When I bury myself, at least it's in something productive. You hide in your kitchen. You hide on this island. You're afraid of anybody finding out—"

"That I have a supernatural ability?" she murmured with a careful look at the doorway. She dropped a few packages of chicken on the butcher block, then closed the fridge. "What would you do, Mister Perfect? Put it up on a billboard and wait for the reporters to show up? Turn it into a marketing gimmick? Think maybe it would boost business?" She stared him down. "Do you ever *not* see numbers when you look at people?"

The corner of his lip curled. His nostrils flared, and the ticking of the kitchen clock punctuated his harsh breath. "What do you know about what I see? Get off your high horse, Morgan, and take a look at yourself. You're scared."

"So are you."

"What the hell would I be—"

"Me!" she snapped. The word echoed through the room. She blushed and lowered her voice, then closed the space between them. "Since walking out of here last night, you've done everything you possibly can to avoid me."

His fingers clenched—the fingers of the hand she'd healed. "If you think I'm scared of what you did—"

"Aren't you?"

"Would I still be standing here, yelling in your face, if that scared me?"

Panting with the effort to keep a lid on her tears, she said, "Maybe you're terrified of getting close to someone, and then finding out they don't like something about you." All the hurt of his rejection rushed through her body, and she used every ounce of it to fuel her fury. "You think this façade you put on is what people want to see. You can't even be your own person because you're so afraid of judgment." Her voice began trembling. She struggled to keep it level as she held up her hands, then let her power loose until her fingers glowed. "I've never tried to be perfect. There isn't a perfect. This is who I am. Do whatever you want with that fact—you will anyway—but at least I won't try not to *be* it."

He grabbed her by the arms with such force that she tried to leap backward, but his hold kept her in place. He leaned forward until his face was right in hers. "You want to talk about being your own person? Try doing it when all your life, people have shown you that person's not good enough for them. If you think you're going to start judging me too, you'd better think again." He hesitated, looking at her fingers. He had to feel the vibrations in her skin through his grasp. He held her hands up, forcing her to look at them. "And as for this, you're goddamn lucky to be something like this and have people who give a shit about you anyway." He let go.

Stunned, she remained motionless as he glared at her. Uncomfortable minutes slid past. She itched with the need to flee from the room, but he blocked the space so well it would be awkward to escape without having to approach him. Defeated and trapped, she blurted, "I have work to do here."

He went to the sink and washed his hands. She busied herself with opening the packages of chicken, grateful to have something to look at other than that troubled, fiery expression on his face. The look bothered her all the worse because he turned away from her, and she knew he was trying to hide it. She pressed her lips together, unwilling to feel even a microgram of sympathy toward him.

"I'll make you a deal," he said at last, without turning toward her. "You stiffed me on the floor joist, so you owe me one."

She laid the chicken on the cutting board with her mouth open on an indignant protest. *Well, he does make it easier to dislike him when he's like this.*

Before she could reply, he added, "Sticky window in the upstairs bathroom. Door could use some adjustment too." Again she tried to counter him. He turned at last and raised a hand. "I sent your résumé off to the job list I worked out for you. Now you help me."

She wanted to ask him exactly how helpful he thought it was to boot somebody out of their home, but she couldn't stomach the thought of another argument with him. "Okay. Then go to the wine festival with me next week."

His brow furrowed. "Is this one of your no-segue segues?"

"If we're trading favors, you can help me reestablish my networking with the local culinary businesses." And maybe she'd get him to start seeing Nantucket as a community, instead of a series of figures on his quarterly report.

A look of challenge entered his eyes. "All right. The bathroom first." He exited the kitchen with a stiff stride, leaving Morgan with the feeling that, for the first time since meeting him, she'd won one of their battles.

Maybe.

Over dinner, she discovered their guests had a passion for antiques. The Sandersons lived in Philadelphia, and had met during a summer antique show. They chose Nantucket for their honeymoon as a double-duty hunt for treasures they might bring back to the shop they'd opened back home. Morgan listened, distracted, trying to put on a good face for

145

the newlyweds.

"I know of at least two stores where you'll get some very nice finds at good prices," Agnes said. She looked at Morgan across the table. "Would you like to take them into town in the morning?"

"I'd love to," Morgan said with sudden warmth. One of her favorite tasks as a hostess was introducing visitors to the island's charms. A task that might well be lost on Trent, she thought, glancing at him. He sat at the end of the table nursing a beer over the remains of his chicken française. His gaze met hers over the rim of his pilsner glass, and turned as quickly away.

Well, at least he liked her food. And he'd abandoned the beer stein for the night.

He'd hardly paid any attention to her during the meal, and when he did speak, he was all business. Disappointed at the unapproachable, closed-off look on his face, she turned back to the newlyweds. As she watched the adoring way they stared at each other, Morgan struggled with a pang of wistfulness. Roger took his wife's hand and gave it a squeeze.

Smiling past the tightness in her throat, Morgan went to the sideboard to retrieve a plate of fresh chocolate-chip cookies. "If you're looking for case goods, I know a cute little shop that gets great finds," she told the couple. "Or, if textiles are your thing, I can show you to Agnes's secret weapon. Louise has been quilting since she was eight years old, and she saves the best antique fabrics in the back of her store. Appointment only, unless you're me."

Diane laughed. "I see you've done this before."

"Morgan's quite the tour guide," Agnes said. She chuckled. "When she first arrived, she made a habit of bicycling everywhere. Half the island knows her."

"What a beautiful place this is. The daffodils are just stunning."

"Oh, well, I'll be happy to pick you some for your room," Morgan said. "I stocked the garden with extras for that reason."

"You should see it when the hydrangeas are in full bloom," added Agnes. "A positive ocean of blue in almost everyone's yard. Nantucket's famous for them."

The delighted look on Diane's face almost made up for the total lack of expression on Trent's. Almost.

Morgan managed to get through dinner and the cleanup afterward without once speaking to Trent. Really, what could she possibly have seen in him that prompted her to do—what she did—with him last night? "I must be losing my mind," she muttered. By the time she finished the dishes, it had gotten late, and she let the quiet sink into her soul.

Then voices interrupted it.

Low murmurs came through the open window over the sink. She leaned forward to peer out into the garden. Trent stood facing away over the tub of herbs, with his shirtsleeves rolled up and his hands in the pockets of his dress pants—an unusually relaxed pose, for him. Beside him stood Roger, gesturing here and there as they spoke in the soft glow of the small floodlight. From the little Morgan could catch, they were talking about family. She strained to listen even as she chided herself for doing so.

Roger mentioned something about wanting lots of children. Trent answered in a tone too low to overhear. Another exchange, and then both men laughed. Morgan watched, fascinated, as the stiff line of Trent's shoulders relaxed into that easy magnetism she remembered from last night. Oh, he cracked that stony exterior, when he wanted to.

When he returned indoors, he saw Agnes and the Sandersons off to bed with a civility that would have been charming to anyone who didn't know what an unfeeling crank he could be.

Morgan wished *she* had never discovered what an unfeeling crank he could be.

Moody and disheartened, she clicked off the kitchen light and climbed the stairs toward her bedroom.

"What, no midnight swim? Water's got to be just shy of freezing," came Trent's voice. "Chance of losing limbs to frostbite. Sounds like good clean fun to me."

"Oh, so you're talking to me now?" She paused on the stairs. "For your information, I don't get cold in water."

"Why not?" he asked.

"I can heat it, at least in a small space around me. It's never any colder or warmer than I want it."

"Is that part of your...?" He pointed at her hands, clearly confused as to what he should call her power.

She nodded stiffly.

Rather than showing the distaste she expected of him, he surprised her with a thoughtful noise. "A human water heater. Interesting. Ever thought about hiring that out? You could be the next big thing in eco-friendly housing."

She shied away from his smile and encouraged the irritation brought on by his jokes at her expense. "You know, your on-the-fly switches from jerk to not-jerk are starting to make me dizzy."

"Accept a truce, will you? I'm going for not-jerk. Take it while the taking's good."

She hurried up the last of the steps to the upstairs landing. "Is that supposed to be your version of an apology? You can't flip people on and off like light switches," she snapped. "You can't say things like 'Get out, here's your severance pay,' and expect me to want..." She trailed off and stared at him, wondering how she could want more of last

148

night and still be so furious with him. Blushing, she hurried toward her room.

Footsteps sounded behind her, much closer than she would have thought, since he'd just been at the bottom of the stairs. When she turned around, she found him close enough to brush against her. "What?" she snapped.

"Look, I..." Something flickered across his face. His jaw clenched, and he dropped his gaze to the floor. He took a soft breath and muttered, "Sorry."

Morgan heard the distant tinkling of the wind chimes on the porch. Her cheeks burned. "What about Agnes?"

He tensed. "Never mind the money. This isn't about money."

She stared at him. He still hadn't met her gaze. They stood there, motionless, balancing on a tightrope of tension. The wrong words would tumble them down.

Morgan groped for something to say, stopped, and tried again. "I...I need to go."

He shifted even closer. "Morgan."

One word. Just one word—her name, and he rooted her there. He looked at her finally, and words caught in her throat at the unshuttered emotion in his eyes. He wanted her. Needed her, maybe without even realizing it. Maybe as much as she wanted and needed him. Maybe without ever intending it to be more than tonight, this moment, this breathless second.

And she couldn't say no.

****

He had expected her to back off. It would have been a relief if she had, absolving him neatly of any obligation to follow through on advances he made against his every rational thought. She'd been torturing him all day with her presence, her scent, the fascinating way she blushed whenever someone complimented her. Especially with the hurt on her face after he'd blundered through another attempt to push her away. He hated that look of pain worse than he hated the pain of having her near, when she saw him too clearly.

When he brushed against her, she didn't retreat. He struggled for mental order against this living, breathing scrambler of his senses. Impossible. The fact of her power, her criticism of him, the way she drove him out of his wits, the look in her eyes right now... It all tumbled together in her, a paradox that sent him running and then yanked him back to her again. Her fresh-water scent swirled around him, filling his head with fantasies of naked skin and smoking blue eyes. "God, what is that cologne?" he breathed, hovering over her lips.

Her shoulders tensed. "It's me."

He stilled and wrested his gaze from her mouth to her eyes. "Really? Another power?"

Sarcasm twisted her full, enthralling lips. "A side effect. I suppose you were going to tell me I should start a perfume line?"

Unable to resist touching her an instant longer, he slid his hands over her hips to press their bodies fully together. "I wouldn't share that smell with anybody."

Her mouth opened just a little—on more rebukes, he was sure. He snatched the advantage to slant his lips over hers, intending to scramble her the way she did him. But the trap snapped shut the moment their mouths met, and he never stood a chance.

A moan sounded in her throat, unwinding any last knot of resistance that tied him to firm ground. The demands of his body overpowered all reason. She was a siren, about to smash him into oblivion with needing her. Recklessness boiled through him. For the first time in his life, he threw all caution away, then let her wash over him in welcome abandon. He grazed her lips with his teeth. She whimpered and pulled at his shirt. He took her hand in his, then threaded their fingers together. "Come on."

"Where?"

He tugged her gently with him as he descended the stairs again. "The beach."

"What? I don't have my bathing s—"

He turned around long enough to plant another kiss on her lips, as much to silence her protest as to answer his own desire. "I don't, either." He towed her along, out the door and down the porch. The beach was deserted, and this late, all lights were off. Not even the moon lit the water tonight. Stars dusted the sky all the way to the horizon.

As soon as he reached the shoreline, he pulled her into his arms and kissed her again. Instead of putting out the fire inside him, as some distant part of him still hoped it would, each kiss only compounded the searing need to be with her. His heartbeat drummed in his chest, and he crushed her to him as if she could provide the air his lungs seemed to lack. He pulled impatiently at the buttons of his shirt. "Let's find out where this roller coaster is going, Montana," he whispered against her mouth.

She looked him straight in the eye and covered his hands with her own. Her slim fingers threaded under his to unfasten the buttons instead. When her hands slid inside his shirt to cover his bare chest, she tore a pained groan from his lips. Unable to wait, he pulled her blouse off over her head and let it flutter to the sand.

Ah, beautiful. Trent had seen his share of gorgeous women, but something in the combination of Morgan's lush curves, long, satiny waves of hair, and hungry expression made her one of the sexiest creatures he'd ever seen. He pulled her against him, then sucked in a breath of shock at how amazing her skin felt against his.

Dangerous, too, he realized. Holding her felt far too good. Good enough to make him keep wanting it. Wanting her.

Wanting *her*.

He started to step back, but she slid his shirt off, down his arms, to join hers on the sand. The stroke of her fingers along his skin set his nerve endings awash with fresh need. Abandoning retreat, he raised her arms and put them around his neck, then kissed her throat. Morgan raised her chin and raked her fingers through his hair. Her soft sigh fluttered across his ear and drowned any remaining hesitation. He sank to his knees, then stroked his hands upward along her legs until he felt the thin, lacy scrap of her panties. With the same forced patience, he drew them down. She stepped out of them, and he tossed them toward her shirt.

Morgan gazed down at him, trembling. Eagerness and indecision flooded her. His hands, his mouth, his very body—everything about him pulled her to pieces, and they had hardly begun. Warnings clanged within her in time with her heartbeat, *go-go-go*, but no matter how she wanted to escape to the water a scant ten feet away, she couldn't leave him. The heat in his eyes as he touched her scalded her to her soul, terrifying and exhilarating. How foolish she had been, thinking her life was perfect. She had never known she lacked this. Now, the thought of losing it pained her.

He stood again, running his hands back upward along her legs until her skirt bunched with them. When he cupped her backside, she jumped, and he dragged her hard against him. "Amphitrite," he murmured. "Isn't that the goddess of the sea?" Before she could express surprise at his knowledge of the Greek pantheon, he pressed a lingering kiss against her lips. The sensations of his mouth and manhood unwound her senses. "She's got nothing on you."

This man, this infuriating, entrancing, maddening man, had been made for loving a woman. She could easily imagine the scores of women who had fallen prey to his appeal.

Including herself.

With her last ounce of caution, she whispered, "What are we doing, Trent?"

"Isn't it obvious enough?" he said between kisses. He ground his hips against hers again, and the ridge of his erection nudged her. Even separated by his pants and her skirt, the pressure of it was enough to tear another moan from her. She couldn't speak, couldn't think.

"Let me make it a little more obvious, then," he said. He bent to kiss her breasts. One of his hands left her backside long enough to unzip his fly. He took one of her hands and guided it to his erection. He stiffened, growled, as her fingers closed around it, and his hips jerked against hers. "I want to be inside you," he added, "and I want it so bad it's killing me. Obvious enough now?"

Unable to stand it any longer, she pushed his pants down. He kicked them off into a crumpled heap, then drew her skirt up and lifted her against him. Morgan circled his waist with her ankles. He pressed against her center, and she heard her restless whimper answered with another low growl.

"Tell me you're on the pill. Something. Anything," he said. "'Cause I don't want to stop, Morgan."

She nodded quickly.

"Oh, thank God," he murmured. His mouth blazed against her throat.

He carried her toward the water as if she weighed nothing. They sloshed into the waves. As soon as the water hit her feet, her power burst through her in a blazing rush. She gasped at the consuming, tingling sensation, and then muffled a cry into his neck as he plunged into her.

He kissed her again, demanding now, grazing her lips and tongue with his teeth as he pulled her even tighter against him. She moaned and locked her ankles around his waist. "Do you have *any* idea how good you feel, Morgan?" he asked.

Lost in sensation, she let her power flow through her body. The water swirling around them heated enough to take away the icy chill.

Trent groaned. "I like this power of yours," he said, thrusting into her again. He waded deeper into the water, up to his waist. If not for his grasp and the exquisite feel of him inside her, Morgan felt she would have whooshed away on the current, never to be seen again.

He kissed her, stroking the curve of her lower back so lightly that she shuddered, desperate for more. He pulled her to him in time with another thrust, and another. "So damn beautiful," he muttered. He released her waist to trap one of her hands between them. He kissed each glowing fingertip, then pressed her palm to his chest. Beneath his water-slick skin, she felt his heat, the beating of his heart. Between that and the water swirling around them, Morgan thought she would go mad with sensual overload.

He thrust into her again, driving her even higher. "I was wrong," he said into her neck. He nipped at her skin. "We should have started this in a bed. We should have started it a lot sooner."

Morgan's body sang with power. Never had it surged through her so fully, so forcefully. The glow in her fingertips spread up her arms, tingled through her body down to her toes. Her skirt swished around them, tickling, teasing her already-

154

sensitized skin. "Trent," she whispered. "Trent..."

Her power exploded through her as she came over and over. Her mouth fell open in a soundless cry that she had no breath to utter. She shut her eyes against the flash of light that burst across her own skin.

A wave surged against her back, pressing her even closer against his body.

Trent pressed into her and thrust one last time, muffling a curse into her shoulder. He held her hard against his body. Raw gasps tore from his throat. He shuddered, then stood absolutely still.

He stayed that way so long she began to worry that she had hurt him, scared him, *something*. "Trent?" she whispered again when she could speak, herself.

His arms came up to cradle her back. At last, he raised his head. With his chest heaving, he stared at her, open-mouthed, as if he had never seen her in his life.

Humiliation swept through her. Tears pricked at her eyes. A mistake. She should have known. This had all been a horrible mistake. Choking off a cry, she tried to push away from him.

He jerked her back against him to kiss her again, deeply, ferociously, so passionately that even her drained power began to reawaken. His fingers threaded through her hair, tangling and trapping her until she had no desire to draw away.

He turned, still kissing her, still carrying her, still inside her, then sloshed to the beach. When he broke the kiss, she struggled to form words. "What are you doing?"

He laid her carefully on the sand.

She tried to catch his eye, to guess what must be going through his head, but he nuzzled the hollow between her breasts. His lips closed over one water-chilled nipple.

She gasped, and when his hand covered her other breast, she drove her fingers into the sand. "Keeping a good thing going," he answered. "We've still got a lot of night left."

Chapter Eleven

Trent woke in his own bed to infuriating sunlight. He draped an arm over his eyes to block it out. The motion helped thwart the daylight, but it didn't do a thing for the repeating memory of Morgan's half-naked, gorgeous body. Neither did it stall his mental picture of the way she threw her head back and exposed that sexy, slender throat when she reached orgasm after orgasm in his arms.

He had known she'd be passionate—known it from the first moment they traded barbs when he surprised her raiding his room. Every hostile word they tossed at one another had merely put off the inevitable collision of last night.

And, as with any collision, he now faced an aftermath of damage control.

Trent groaned and lifted his arms to press the heels of his hands against his eyelids, then dragged his fingers through his still-damp hair.

The water. The beach. Her room. Mistake after mistake, and yet he couldn't take his hands off her. He had left her at last in her bedroom, once she'd fallen asleep in the early hours of the morning. He never stayed with a woman overnight. He took them to bed, did everything right, and then slipped out while the getting was good. Before sex turned into something much more complicated than it ought to be.

He should never have let it happen with Morgan. Morgan, who had called him scared and who hated his guts and whose body and eyes and lips he couldn't get enough of last night. He'd thought he could lose himself in her. Drown all the other crap boiling around in his head in a wash of heated skin and raging hormones.

Well...not so much.

He cracked an eye open to search for the clock. Maybe a couple hours of sleep? He dragged himself up and sat on the edge of the bed to rub at the stubble on his chin.

He'd have to face her eventually. And he'd have to make it clear there would be no repeat performances. Parts of him lamented that severely. He shot to his feet and forced an image of her scowl into place over the ones of her heavy-lidded passion.

She hated him. She found fault with everything he did. She couldn't let an hour go by without digging at him for something.

But oh, God, the memory of how she whimpered when he touched her in the right places tortured him.

He had wanted to tell her last night...about the inn, about his plans to dismantle it. But he couldn't get the words out. It was so much easier to lose himself in her body, her voice, her eyes, than to admit to something he knew would hurt her even more.

And he'd only made it worse.

Muffling a groan, he stalked to his closet and tore the first thing he encountered off its hanger.

Jeans.

With a sneer, he tossed them down, then grabbed dress pants and a polo shirt instead.

He put it off as long as possible, but at last, there was nothing left to keep him in his room. He emerged with only a cursory look down the hall toward Morgan's room—the door was closed—then he descended to the first floor.

A furtive look into the kitchen confirmed Morgan was not within. He ducked inside with a huff of relief. It was still early. If he got his coffee and breakfast quick enough, he might be back in his room before he saw so much as a glimpse of her.

As he passed the butcher block, he snagged a croissant sitting there. Stuffing an end of the pastry into his mouth, he grabbed his beer stein, then searched in the old fridge for the instant coffee.

"Hello, Mister Williams."

At Agnes's voice, Trent jerked upright and smacked the top of his head on the freezer door. He stifled a particularly bad swear word on the end of the croissant before biting off a mouthful that would nicely prevent him from too much talk. Straightening up, he rubbed the top of his head. "Morning."

Agnes entered the kitchen. "I'm afraid I'm the only one here this morning," she said. "Would you like some breakfast?"

He raised an eyebrow at her on his way to the teakettle.

She nodded as if he'd spoken. "Morgan's gone."

Gone. The word socked him in the gut before he had a chance to think. What had they done? What had *he* done?

Agnes's eyes went wide, and he realized he must have looked alarmed. "No, no, sweetheart, to town," she said, patting his arm. "She took the Sandersons antiquing."

The nasty and wholly unwelcome grinding sensation in his belly dissipated, but if left behind a whopping lot of disgust. He choked down the bite of croissant. "What would be open this early?"

"She knows the shop owners very well, dear." Agnes beat him to the teakettle and filled it from the tap, then pulled down a teacup for herself. "She also mentioned the hardware store. Something about the bathroom window?"

The guilt he'd felt a second ago tried sneak

attacking him again. He was ready for it this time, and shunted it into a mental pigeonhole of Stuff To Ignore. Damn right, she should be taking the initiative to fix stuff around here. He didn't even own the place yet, and he was making repairs on it out of his own pocket. For what, he didn't know, except to keep it going until he could close on the technicalities and take it apart.

A sticky window's not that crucial, pal, said his inner nag. He ignored it with a firm reminder that working windows could be resold as easily as architectural molding and wide-plank flooring. He set his croissant on a napkin, then scooped some of the coffee into the bottom of his beer stein. "She say when she's coming back?" he asked.

"Oh, late this morning, I should think, depending on whether the Sandersons find something they like at the shops. Actually," Agnes said, settling on a barstool, "this is a good time for us to talk. Without any lookers-on."

His hackles went up at once. He stayed at the stove, listening to the water hiss in the kettle. What the hell was taking it so damn long to heat up this morning?

"You are doing a considerate thing for Morgan, finding her another job," said Agnes.

With no way to avoid her pep talk, Trent resigned himself to a few minutes of polite attention. Putting on his corporate face, he turned around. "I think I heard a 'but' in there."

Agnes smiled and folded her hands on the butcher block. "But...she'll want to come back to visit, even if you send her inland. What happens when she sees you've taken the Seaglass apart and sold off the pieces?"

His surprise almost caught him out, but he covered it fast. "You've been doing your homework on me."

"I looked into a couple of things," she admitted. "After you told me about relocating Morgan, I went back to my contract, and then to your Website."

His Website. The Website managed by the computer geeks in his office, who had way more time and cared more about Trent's online presence than he ever would. He'd visited it a couple of times. Nice, spiffy picture of a sleek office building and a couple of historic-looking houses. A list of the reclaimed building materials his company offered, and some contact information. Trent was too busy being physically present at property closures to care about that end of the business. "See anything enlightening?"

"I saw enough to realize your intentions for the inn after you're finished here. I haven't told Morgan." Agnes tilted her head. "I think you might want to."

He scuffed the toe of his dress shoe on the floor. "Look, Mrs. Preble, I'll do whatever I can to get Morgan a good job. I'll even check into housing, if she wants me to. But I don't think it's any of her business what I do with the property after it's mine."

"I don't believe business has anything to do with it, Mister Williams."

He turned around to scowl at the kettle. Damn thing heated up quick enough last time he'd been reduced to using instant coffee. This defeated the whole purpose of *instant*.

By the time the stupid piece of junk started to whistle, Agnes had joined him at the stove. She lifted the kettle from the burner with a hot pad, then serenely filled his beer stein with steaming water. With her eyes on her task, Agnes said, "She's going to be hurt."

His first impulse was to snap *I don't care*, but he fell back on his corporate diplomacy. "We all have to make a living, Agnes. This is how I make mine. I am going to find her a job, so she can continue to make hers. That's more than my company does for most people." When Agnes didn't reply, he looked up at her. "Why didn't she ever buy you out, anyway?"

"She has no money. She spent most of her savings to help her family back home. And when her brother sends her any, she always finds someone else who needs it more." Agnes gave a regretful sigh. "She's too kind for her own good."

Trent grunted. "Don't worry, it'll balance out. I've met plenty of people on the opposite end of the spectrum."

The older woman's gaze met his. The seriousness—and disappointment—in her eyes set his temper hissing like the teakettle. What did he owe these people anyway? He scooped some sugar into the stein, then added a splash of creamer. Without bothering to stir it in, he grabbed his croissant. "See you later."

He thumped upstairs to resume the work he should have been doing pretty much since he got here. The words on his screen swam before him. He hadn't realized how groggy he was after last night. Even the coffee didn't seem to be helping.

Worth it, whispered a voice in the back of his mind. He told it firmly to shut up.

Then he realized today was Saturday.

Laura.

"Shit," he whispered, fumbling for his cell phone. He flicked it on and speed-dialed her number.

"Hi, sweetie," Laura answered. Wind whistled in the background. "Nice timing. I just got off the ferry. I rented the cutest coupe, and I'm on my way down right now. Did you know the founder of Macy's was born here?"

Trent scrambled to absorb her rapid-fire chatter. "What, you're *here*?"

"Sure," she said, sounding hurt. "I did tell you

I'd be here this weekend. Today's the weekend, darling."

Trent pinched the bridge of his nose. "Laura, you know I like to see you, but this is a mess here, and—"

"When have I ever complained about your messes?" Laura's voice went sultry. "I like some of your messes. Your shirt on my floor is one of my personal favorites. It's been a while."

He pinched harder. Pain zipped from his nose over the top of head and down to the base of his skull, where it settled in as if it planned to stay the week.

Shit. What if Laura stayed past the weekend?

"Anyway," she said, "I should be there in ten or twenty. I have to make a stop. Want me to bring you some lunch? I'll bet the seafood here is good, at least."

"It's an inn, Laura. The food is provided."

"Oh," she said cheerfully. "I doubt it beats Masa's sushi. Be there soon. Kiss." The line went dead.

With a huge sigh, Trent disconnected the call and stuffed the phone in his shirt pocket. He tipped back in his chair and stared at the ceiling. "Awesome."

****

Morgan emerged from the Sandersons' rented taxi with an armload of packages and a grin she couldn't help feeling all the way to her toes.

Then she noticed the coupe in the driveway, parked behind Trent's Lexus. The inn was getting awfully packed with cars lately. She followed the Sandersons inside, answering their professions of gratitude with a distracted smile.

She helped Diane bring her purchases to the Sandersons' room, then returned to the kitchen, where she found Agnes pulling out the sandwich fixings Morgan had prepared before leaving that morning. "I'll finish that," she said.

"All right. How was shopping?"

"So much fun!" Morgan said with enthusiasm. "I miss doing that for our guests. Diane found a beautiful quilt for their baby's nursery."

Agnes beamed. "Is she expecting?"

"Not yet." Morgan giggled, then lowered her voice to a playful stage whisper. "But they don't want to wait to try." Her smile wobbled. She managed to rescue it, but it felt glued-on. She would never have that wonderful expectation of a warm, squirmy bundle of tiny hands and feet and nose. She'd have to content herself with Kincade's daughter and any children who might come to the inn before the close of its sale. She thought hopefully of the coupe in the driveway. "New guests?"

Agnes patted Morgan's arm as she passed by with a pitcher of tea. "Brace yourself, dear."

Puzzled, Morgan finished assembling the tray of sandwiches, added some fresh fruit, cheese, and crackers, then carried it to the dining room. She recognized the voices of the Sandersons and, with a pleasant thrill, Trent's chuckle. Then she heard the low, musical cadence of a woman's voice.

She emerged into the dining room with the tray. When she saw the woman sitting beside Trent—really close beside him—she forgot her manners and stared.

The newcomer might just have come from a Paris runway. Her wine-red slip dress complimented her blond hair and flawlessly tanned skin to perfection. Simple. Elegant. Gorgeous without trying. Morgan even envied the woman's long, graceful fingers, bare of jewelry as if they needed no embellishment.

Agnes saved her from social disaster. "Miss Barclay, this is our chef, Morgan Clifton. Morgan, this is a friend of Trent's family, Laura Barclay."

"Trent and I go back for years," Laura said with a lingering smile at him. She stroked his hand just enough to make it clear she considered him her territory. Trent didn't return the affectionate gesture, but neither did he draw away. When he saw Morgan looking, he gave a polite smile and nothing more.

She worked harder at keeping her smile this time. Gamely, she held out her hand to Laura. "It's a pleasure to meet you."

"Thanks. And you." Laura shook her hand, then Morgan sat down.

That was about the extent of Laura's attention for anyone but Trent for the rest of lunch. The woman's eyes roved Trent's face and body so often Morgan expected her to jump in his lap any minute. Trent concentrated on the conversation and his lunch, polite and professional to all. He might as well have been at a business merger. He looked at Morgan only when she added something to the discussion.

Was he really going to do this after their incredible night? Morgan felt an awful kinship with those birds who smashed into windowpanes because they never saw the barrier until it was too late.

Dignity. Dignity, she reminded herself, even as her pride wavered on the edge of a spectacular crash and burn. She knew better than to expect grand overtures from him, especially with onlookers present, but his indifference drove through what remained of her afterglow like a serrated knife.

She forced her body into a position of relaxed interest. Laura talked about jewelry. Her mother was a designer. Her father had retired early to devote his time to his golf swing, though he still dabbled in businesses through hired contacts. They traveled a lot.

The conversation got much more interesting when it turned to marriage. Diane and Roger told them, with loving looks that tugged at Morgan's heartstrings, of their own ceremony at an old stone church in Philadelphia. They favored tradition, and their large families had packed the venue to bursting.

"Oh, I want a destination wedding," said Laura when they asked her preference. "Aruba is the most incredible place on earth. I've been four times." She smiled at Trent so suggestively Morgan blushed. "Remember the first time we went? That little bar by the water?"

Trent answered that he did, then sucked down the rest of his tea as if he wanted to wash any further words back down his throat before they slipped out.

Roger looked back and forth between Trent and Laura, then diced up the last of Morgan's cheer with, "Are you engaged?"

Trent choked and grabbed for his napkin. Laura smiled.

Morgan's stomach swooped, then clenched as if it were about to violently reject every bite of lunch. As gracefully as possible, she rose from her seat and collected a few empty plates. "I'm so sorry. I need to get dinner marinating. Can I get anyone anything?"

When they declined, she hurried from the room and back to her kitchen, where it was at least marginally more possible to breathe.

But not for long. "We're not," said Trent behind her.

Morgan turned to face him. Awkward silence wound out over the next several seconds while she stared at him, staring at her. Collecting herself, she said, "You know, except for one tiny little detail, it's none of my business if you are. You... We..." She crushed a pang of hurt with vicious carelessness.

"No, never mind. What happened, happened."

His shoulders jerked, and he approached the butcher block. "Don't act like it doesn't bother you. If Laura and I were engaged, then what you and I did last night would piss you off." She tried not to look at him, but he sought her gaze. "Admit it. You think I played you. You went directly to the wrong conclusion about me, because that's the kind of person you think I am."

"I didn't think—*don't* think anything. The minute I get a 'think' in my head, you do something so insanely out of your character that whatever I think goes right down the drain." She looked at him, her insides curdling with a mess of attraction, repulsion, confusion, and frustration. "What are you, Trent Williams? Who are you?"

His brow furrowed. "This is all because Laura showed up? How does that change me?"

Morgan gave a humorless laugh. "She wants to eat you whole, and you don't act like you want to avoid it. It's just another one of the many ways you never say what you mean. Never *do* what you mean."

The insult on his face read clear as headlines. "Exactly what is that supposed to...mean?"

"In addition to the way you act as if you care about...people...and then immediately push them away?" She bit back her next words, knowing they would only end in an argument. Softer, she added, "Your parents drive you crazy. Why don't you ever tell them to stuff it?"

His eyes blazed like a lit fuse, and she knew she'd made a mistake. "What gives you the right to judge me? A little sex, and now you're my shrink?"

Something crashed behind him. Trent spun around and Morgan looked past him.

Laura stood in the doorway with empty hands held out. At her feet was a broken wine glass, rapidly spreading a puddle of merlot on the linoleum. Her cheeks had flushed, and probably not from the wine.

Oh, wonderful. Trying for calm, Morgan asked, "Are you all right? Don't worry about the glass. I'll clean it up." She shot Trent a glare as she went for the dustpan and hand broom. "I'm sure you two have a lot to talk about. The garden's free."

Trent glared back. Morgan ignored it, humiliated and angry for herself, and embarrassed for Laura, who clearly thought she and Trent had an understanding that Trent had not tried to disprove. And now he'd dragged Morgan into the mess. She bent and brushed the broken glass into the dustpan. "Seems like I'm cleaning up a lot of messes in here lately," she muttered, more for Trent's ears than Laura's, and with emphasis on *messes*.

"I'm sorry about the glass," Laura said. Her voice caught, and Morgan felt even worse. "I'll be outside, Trent."

When she left, Morgan heard Trent's footfalls behind her. "Thanks for throwing me under the bus."

She gave a harsh laugh. "You did that all by yourself. When I..." Her cheeks burned. "I expect a man not to be already involved with someone."

"I'm not," he snapped. He bent beside her, and began picking larger pieces of glass from the floor where they had tumbled away. He tossed them on the dustpan.

"Go *away*," she snarled, trying with increasing desperation not to give in to tears. Not in front of him. "She's waiting."

He snatched her hands. A few fragments of glass trickled back onto the floor. Wine droplets fell on the thigh of his slacks. He ignored both. "What's the matter with you?" he demanded. "We had an amazing night last night. Now, it's 'See you around, sport'?"

"If you wanted anything more than that, you might want to make it clear to Miss Barclay. You might have wanted to make it clear *before* anything happened with us."

He swore half under his breath and got to his feet, pulling her with him. The dustpan of glass just missed an untidy return to the floor. "If I wanted to mess around, headache-free, it sure as hell wouldn't be with you."

She pulled her wrist out of his hand and dumped the glass in the trash. "If I'm so much trouble, I invite you to leave the kitchen," she said with mocking politeness.

"Can we just stop sniping at each other for a few minutes?"

She shook the last of the glass into the trash, then put the dustpan down. Once again, she realized her mistake too late. It gave him the excuse to take her by the arms again without fear of dumping the glass on the floor. She lunged for the pan, but he jerked her back to him.

"Listen good, Montana, because I'm not going to repeat myself," he said. His voice was low, filled with anger and the edge of a growl. The tone sent a flurry of unwanted shivers through her, reminders of the way he'd sounded last night. Possessive, demanding, single-minded in his task of giving her pleasure.

He gave her another shake. "I wanted what we did last night, or I wouldn't have done it. Laura's a friend. A good friend. But I'm not marrying her. I'm not marrying anyone as long as I live." His lip curled, and he dropped her arms. "My parents are enough bad example of that." He backed away as if he thought touching her further might burn him, but his eyes still blazed. "Don't worry, it won't happen again."

When he left the room, retreating as he always did in the wake of a confrontation with her, Morgan found no comfort in it.

It won't happen again.

She tried not to acknowledge it, but the more she resisted, the more she realized the promise disappointed her.

Chapter Twelve

Trent entered the inn's backyard with the sinking feeling that the longer he battled with Morgan, the more of them he seemed to lose. Soon, he'd be on permanent damage control. Losing anything nettled him. Morgan plagued him like an increasing swarm of locusts that found his pride the tastiest snack this side of Egypt.

Laura stood at the edge of the garden, by a picket fence bordered with daffodils and tulips— identified only because Laura had always favored cut flowers from those blooms. *Irony, thy name is Seaglass. Nuisance, thy name is Morgan Clifton.*

Laura faced the sea with her arms crossed and her hair fluttering in the breeze. In her dress, perfectly cut to show off what Trent had always thought her nicest feature, she looked completely out of place. He cleared his throat.

She turned around, and he caught her wiping at her eyes. "I should know better," she said. "You never were one for being tied down to me. I only ever saw what I wanted to see."

Real regret poured through him. Laura had always been supportive of his career, encouraging, not too pushy. She listened when he ranted about his parents' string-pulling. They had fun here and there. He hadn't realized she took him so seriously. He tried a smile. "What can I say that will make me less of an asshole?"

She gave a soft laugh. "You've got your work cut out for you."

He approached her and took her hands. "I am

171

sorry, Laura."

She shook her head with what looked like a rueful smirk. "You're *sort of* sorry," she said, but there was no sting in her tone. "It's my fault for thinking you wanted something permanent. We even talked about it when you went away to college, if I remember. You weren't interested then." She met his gaze. "And you're not now. Not with me."

"Not with anyone," he assured her.

She smiled then, that infuriating, knowing smile women got when they thought they were one-up on a man. "She's pretty."

"And definitely not with her," he added forcefully. "I have been known to make mistakes." He tilted his head. "For which I sometimes apologize."

She nodded. "I forgive you. You're a bastard, but I forgive you. We've been friends too long." Laura sniffed. Before he could balk at the unfamiliarity of the word "friend" as applied to him, she added, "Which reminds me—*friend*. Since you're in an apologetic mood, you can take me to the Nantucket Wine Festival. Daddy's thinking about purchasing a vineyard."

Her, too? What was it with this function? He'd only just gotten over the worry that he'd have to contend with Laura versus the complicated mess of his—whatever—with Morgan. "A vineyard. What on earth are you talking about?"

"Daddy and I spoke about it when I told him I was coming to visit you and your...project...so I got a ticket. He likes wine. Mother likes wine. They don't know anything about growing grapes, but that's what hiring out is for. They just want a nice summer place. I'm going to stick around a bit longer. Check things out, make contacts."

He played his desperate last card. "This thing sells out, Laura. Fast."

"Yes, I know. But Daddy knows the people who run the yacht club that's hosting it this year. It's kismet."

Not the sort of kismet he'd have hoped for. He pictured escorting Laura and Morgan around the wine festival, with not-too-pretty results. Was it too late to swear off women and live like a hermit somewhere in Tibet? He glanced toward the kitchen window, then back to Laura, hoping she would magically change her mind.

Nope. Real life didn't work like that and never had. Anything he wanted, he had to get the hard way.

But he couldn't say no to her. Laura was just as much a pawn of her parents' meddling as he was of his. Why *had* they never told their parents to stuff it?

She seemed to read where his thoughts were going. "Trent...your parents... They want you to be happy. You know that, right?"

"Since when are you talking to my parents about me?"

"I had dinner with them a few weeks ago." She brushed a lock of hair behind her ear. "I think they're starting to realize how much of you they've been missing, and maybe they don't know how to tell you that." She exhaled on a soft chuckle. "I guess they're getting the Trent Williams wake-up call, too."

Trent doubted that, but he decided to leave the subject for later. "All right. Morgan wants to go to this wine festival, too." At Laura's frown, he added, "We talked about it already, and I can't back out. We have a deal."

Laura gave him a sardonic smile. "Is that what you call it these days?"

"I deserve that shot, I admit that. One shot," he warned with a narrow-eyed look.

173

"Oh, I get more than that," Laura said. "Who else is going to keep you humble?"

When they got back inside, coffee and some sort of cookies were in full swing in the dining room. Morgan was absent. Working on dinner, Agnes told him when she found him looking at her empty seat.

Annoyed that the old lady had caught him searching for Morgan, Trent stared at the tiny coffee cup at his place setting. With an inward sigh, he filled it from the carafe with the two sips he could get in it. How many times would he have to refill it to equate the amount he could get in the beer stein? He stared at the ridiculously delicate cup and decided he'd rather chew glass than go to the kitchen.

How in the name of everything sacred was he expected to foxtrot around Morgan for the rest of this sale? How could he be expected to keep his hands off her when the fresh-water smell of her lingered in the air of this place, taunting him? He had always been able to walk away after spending the evening with a gorgeous woman...but Morgan had tormented his thoughts as soon as he left her in her room last night. Not because of her body, although it was breathtaking. Not even because of that power, that amazing, impossible, fascinating power to make water do what she asked of it.

No. The thing that kept him coming back—usually swinging—was the way she challenged every word out of his mouth and every move he made. The way she accused him of doing the expected thing, rather than what he wanted.

What the hell did she know about what he wanted?

What did *he* know about it?

He tapped his thumb on the tablecloth, wanting to run upstairs and check for responses to his e-mails regarding Morgan's re-employment.

"Trent? Cat got your tongue?" Agnes asked.

"Yeah," he muttered, still focused on the coffee in his cup. He hadn't put any sugar or creamer in it. He pulled the sugar bowl toward his cup and struggled to bring his attention back to the gathered company. "Sorry, what?"

Agnes beamed with such a perfect example of that knowing-female smile that Trent looked toward Roger, hoping for some male solidarity. No luck with that. Roger stared at his new wife with a sappy, adoring expression. *Good Christ, get me out of here,* Trent pleaded. He dumped cream and sugar into his cup, not really caring how much he added of either, then pushed to his feet. "I've got a few calls to make." He glanced at Laura, who seemed content to chatter with the newlyweds. "All right here?"

"Sure," she said easily.

Lucky her. Laura had always had that social gift of gabbing with anyone, regardless of her mood or the occasion. Trent had it himself when necessary, but the more time he spent here, the more he wanted to be back in Boston *not* talking with people who thought marriage was the greatest thing ever conceived. Things made sense in Boston. Deals went smoothly—more smoothly, anyway—and the only meddler in his life was his mother.

He tromped up the creaky stairs and heard a shifting noise coming from the bathroom. He approached the open door and looked inside.

Morgan was at the window, raising and lowering it. The window slid easily on its track. "What are you doing?"

"Addressing your to-do list," she said without looking at him. "I did the hard part. The door's your problem." She gathered up the rusty toolbox from the cellar and wheeled around to the doorway. She stopped when she realized Trent blocked it. "Excuse me."

Her scent washed around him, and he sucked it in before he could stop himself. The words came out likewise unchecked. "What's your hurry, Montana?"

She blew out a harsh breath. "Are you back to Point A on your yo-yo string, then?"

Trent, who hadn't intended to block her way before, now braced his arms against either side of the jamb. "I've got enough critics in my life," he informed her.

"I'd be a lot less critical if you had one consistent setting."

"Maybe your problem is that you spend all your time around appliances that do what you tell them without talking back," he snapped. "You have your carefully-controlled little environment, where no one can get close to you and then leave you, once they find out you're different."

Her gaze shot up, wide-eyed and injured. Trent arched back in surprise, but didn't budge from the doorway. The look on her face shot past all his barbs and boardroom armor, into a spot long-hidden even from himself. Something unwelcome and indefensible punched through him and left a hole that wouldn't go away. He couldn't even be angry about it. The hurt on her face blew his hostility to smithereens before it got started. "That's it, isn't it?" he asked softly. "What happened to your parents, Morgan?"

Tears filled her eyes. She blinked and lifted her chin, staying right in his face, and he had to admire her for it. "They left me. On the doorstep at Social Services, when I was five."

Trent opened his mouth, but for minute he couldn't find anything to say. Dumped like a sack of kittens. He lowered his arms to take one of her hands in his. "Did you have your power then?"

She broke his gaze and shook her head stiffly. "That happened later. A chemical accident at a mine when we were young. Cade, and Elsa, and Ethan, and me. There was a river, and I remember this...this huge boom..." She scowled and jerked her hand from his to push at his chest. "Get out of my way."

"No." He blocked the door again, unable to believe that someone could toss her in the street like that. His parents were never going to win any awards, but they'd given him a roof over his head. An education. A chance. The ache starting in his chest burrowed deeper. "Why'd you leave your ranch? Why come here?"

"Because my foster brother deserves to have the peace he worked so hard to get. Nobody bothers me here. Nobody *used* to."

He stared at her, watched her fight to keep from crying. "So, what? Your power is another reason for someone to leave you? That why you don't tell people about it?"

She lifted her gaze to his. "Would *you* stick around?"

"I'm still standing here, aren't I?"

Neither of them moved or spoke for several awkward seconds. He made to brush with his fingertip at an escaped tear sliding down her cheek, but hesitated. What could he say that would make things any better? He, whose life—even minus the superpowers—was as screwed-up as hers?

Why did people allow others so much power to hurt them? They needed to be born with emotional flak jackets, just to protect themselves from each other. Trent dropped his hand to his side, then stepped back, allowing her the room to leave.

Instead of taking the offered retreat, she glanced at the door, against which he'd braced his foot. "If you have a spare fifteen minutes, we can fix this right now."

"I thought you said it was my—" He cut himself

off when she frowned. *Olive branch, idiot. Grab it.* "Let me get a look at it." He eased her aside to examine the door's hinges. What he'd thought at first glance to be a problem with a sloping floor was only a matter of bent hinges. "I think I saw some hardware in the basement. We can replace this, easy."

She didn't respond, and when he looked, he found her studying him with a funny look that floated somewhere between a smile and tears. "That's nice. The 'we.'"

He didn't know what to say to that, so he added, "Many hands, light work, blah, blah, blah. Got a hammer in that toolbox?"

Together, they worked on the door, Morgan holding it while Trent replaced the hinges. She was quiet, but she radiated a warmth that bothered him. Unused to gratitude, and downright put off by a show of affection toward him, he remained silent. How affectionate would she feel when she learned he'd be scavenging this building in a few weeks?

When he finished setting the last screw, he stood up. He hadn't needed her to hold the door any longer, so she'd moved to the sink. Now, he found her twirling what looked like a ball of clear gel in her hand. "What's that?"

"Water."

He looked closer and saw her palm glowing in the creases. Too curious to avoid it, he moved closer to poke at the ball. His finger sloshed right through it to touch the skin of her palm. When he withdrew his hand, the liquid shivered back into its ball shape. "Huh. That's weird."

She eyed him. The look on her face slid a little more toward a smile this time. "Weird, am I?" She tossed the water ball at him. It splashed against his chest and soaked his shirt.

Grinning back, he turned on the sink and

178

scooped a handful of water at her. She let out a rewarding squeal, then shoved him aside. She thrust her glowing hand toward the stream of water, then flicked it toward him. The water followed her swipe and shot at his midsection.

Trent leaped back, laughing. The water splashed to the tiled floor. "Cheater!" He leaped toward the shower and wrenched the tap on, ready to aim the shower head at her.

Giggling, Morgan rushed him. They collided at the edge of the tub. He tripped backward and flung his arms around her. They tumbled against the wall of the shower, and water poured down on their heads.

Warmth filled the hole in his chest, and he soaked it up with bittersweet greed. When had he last laughed like this? When had he *ever* done so?

She looked up, soaked, smiling, and bright-eyed, with her arms around his waist.

He shook his head ruefully. He hadn't been able to say no to her since he got to the inn. He wondered if it were even possible to do so. He exhaled, part laugh, part sigh. "I give up."

"That's because you're no match for my water-fight skills."

No longer laughing, he stroked a lock of wet hair back off her cheek. "I give up fighting you, Montana. You win."

When she gaped at him, he flung his arms wide. Only half-joking, he said, "Wine festival. Whitewashing. Fixing doors. Whatever it is. You win. Take advantage now, because I don't say it often."

She blinked and wiped dripping water out of her eyes. "You're not relocating me?"

The hopeful look on her face burned through his good humor. In its place came the familiar crush of guilt. He sighed again. "I have to, now. People are

179

waiting for me to close on this. But it doesn't mean I can't help you in other ways." He rubbed at his chin. Suddenly, the weight on his chest was too much to stand anymore. He had to do this. Had to come clean.

He sucked in a deep breath and let the words fall away like the anchor they were, knowing he'd sink along with them. "I don't just buy, Montana. I sell. This place is worth a fortune in old architecture."

Her mouth dropped open. Visible pain flashed through her whole body as if he'd just yanked her heart out and stomped on it. "You're *tearing down my home*?"

He didn't even get the chance to reply. She shoved backward, stumbling over the edge of the tub. When he reached to steady her, she pushed his arm away and fled the room.

He climbed out of the tub, wiping water from his eyes, and tried to follow, but his cell rang. He yanked it from his damp pocket. "Hello!"

"Trent?" His father.

Trent marshaled his temper at once. "Yes, sir."

"We've arrived back in Boston," said Leland. An awkward silence followed, all the more puzzling because Leland had never in Trent's memory done anything awkward. "I want to talk to you about this inn you're buying."

Dripping, Trent yanked open the now-plumb door to scan the hallway. Morgan was already gone. "Dad, now's not a... Why the sudden interest?" He thought back to what Laura had said about his parents, and stalled out for anything else to say.

"Never mind, it can wait. Don't worry about Mother's Day. Stay there and mind your work."

Trent had planned on that, but hearing his father's agreement prompted him to pull the cell away from his ear to check that it was, in fact,

Leland Williams calling him. "Dad? You sure?"

"Just stay there," Leland said more gruffly.

That tone, Trent recognized. "Yes, sir," he said again. "I'll...call you."

Leland bade him goodbye in his usual businesslike manner and hung up. Trent stared at the Call Ended notice on the screen and wondered if he'd missed some crucial part of the conversation.

Nothing had gone right or made sense since he opened the Clipper Room door at this inn. And under the category of not making sense, first on the list was the realization that he didn't want to tear down Morgan's home at all.

****

Morgan managed not to speak to Trent for a full day—not difficult, since he spent most of his time barricaded in his room or out with Laura.

Laura was a surprise unto herself. She knew so many things about such a huge variety of topics that Morgan found herself once again regretful that she'd never been to college. Before leaving Sagerton, the farthest she'd ever gone from home was a five-hour drive to a cattle auction. And then, once she'd made up her mind to go, she'd come straight here to the ocean. How much living had she missed in between?

"I wouldn't regret it too much," Laura said when Morgan confessed her wistfulness. Morgan, Diane, and Laura sat outside at a café the next afternoon, having stopped for lunch in the midst of a girls'-day-out trip to town. Laura sat back in her chair and crossed her long legs. "Fate put you right where you need to be. Your cooking is better than some of those fancy restaurants in Boston. And most of the ones here, if you want the truth."

Morgan blushed and tried to deny it. She hadn't expected friendliness from Laura to start with. Hearing her praise Morgan's cooking bordered on the surreal.

"Don't undercut yourself," Laura insisted. "You should have been presenting at the wine festival." She lifted her wine glass for a sip, then studied Morgan with disconcerting focus. "You're wondering why I'm being nice to you."

Morgan's blush magnified into a four-alarm fire on her cheeks. She dared a look at Diane, who watched the exchange with a look of concern.

Uncrossing her legs, Laura set her glass down. She gave Morgan a smile. "Pay attention, because you're going to need this: the first thing to know as a businesswoman is when to cut your losses. The second thing is to recognize talent when you see it. And you have talent. You don't need to have a college degree to have that." She leaned forward. "And not just a talent in cooking, by the way. Whatever butt-busting you're giving him, it's working. Keep on him, sweetie."

Morgan didn't know what to say, but a warm little spot started in her midsection that had nothing to do with the half-glass of wine she'd had with lunch. She wanted to believe Laura saw a difference in Trent from the cold-hearted number-cruncher he'd been when he arrived...but no one changed that fast. Certainly not in response to a small-town chef with an oddball Elemental gift.

Laura relaxed into her chair once more, as easy in her demeanor as Morgan was confused. To Diane, Laura said, "Now. Where did you get that fabulous quilt you showed me? I want one just like it for my bed."

Talk turned to antiques, and then to the wine festival, an annual event that brought food and drink aficionados to Nantucket from all over the world. Morgan had presented her first year here to favorable response, which helped bring business to the Seaglass.

Too late this year to throw her proverbial hat

into the ring. But what if, next year, she made one of her signature dishes for the festival?

No. That was behind her now, and none of the businesses here on the island currently needed a chef. Trent would receive a reply to her résumé any day now. She would most likely have to resign herself to employment inland. That, or she'd have to return to Hope Creek with her tail between her legs. Kincade and Allyson would welcome her back, but Morgan would never get over the bruised pride of failing at her own dreams. Nor would she be happy, so far from the ocean.

She ran her finger along the filigreed handle of her fork. Picturing herself back in Montana, she felt a rush of annoyance with herself. She had never backed down before, even when Hope Creek was failing and it looked like she'd be on the street again. If her biological parents had ever given her anything of value, it was the courage to stand on her own two feet.

Whatever life threw at her, she would face it head-on. She owed her dreams that much.

When she, Diane, and Laura returned to the inn, Trent was stalking the driveway with his ever-present cell phone to his ear. "No, no. I want the truck here tomorrow, or I go elsewhere with my business. I already checked with the manager, and he okayed it. What's the problem here?"

Morgan remembered his admission that he planned to demolish the inn and sell off its parts. Imagining all the pieces of her memories here scattered to the winds, she tried to skirt around him.

He clapped a hand on her shoulder as she passed. Insulted, she whirled on him, only to find him still arguing into his stupid phone. The conversation went on another few minutes, until it sounded like Trent had won whatever battle he'd been waging with the caller. She fumed and thought fondly of pitching him off a boat into the middle of the ocean. Then maybe watching while he was devoured by sharks. And taking pictures so she could relive it later.

He hung up and lifted his hand from her shoulder. "There'll be a truck here in the morning. We'll need space in the driveway. Do you think the neighbor would mind us using his driveway for our cars?"

"What? Receive a reply to my résumé already? Must be time to start demolition."

Laura and Diane passed them on their way inside. Diane passed her a sympathetic smile, while Laura gave Morgan what she could have sworn was a way-to-go wink.

How strange people were. Some of them were nothing like their first impressions. But Trent... Still irate, she started to follow the women indoors.

"I'm not demolishing it," he said. "I'm fixing it."

She stopped in mid-stride, then thought absurdly that she ought to visit the doctor soon and have her ears checked. She turned around.

Trent shoved his phone into his pocket. "And yes. I got replies to your résumé...from all three employers. They want to interview you."

Morgan turned around to stare at the inn. The lines of the old building blurred. So this was it, then.

Wait.

She blinked away her tears and turned back. "Fixing it?"

He nodded. "I'm still going to resell it. I wouldn't know what to do with a bed-and-breakfast." He approached her with a strange look on his face, one that from anyone else, she might have thought of as an apology. "I'll sell it intact," he said. "Okay?" When she didn't answer—couldn't answer—he added, "Look, I still need to make some money off this sale, or it's bad for the rest of my business. But I can do this much for you."

She swallowed. Nothing had changed. He still intended to close the inn, sell it off, and ship her away to some rootless existence far from the water. Away from...

Did he not understand her at all?

"Look, I just spent half an hour on the phone with this guy, arguing my way out of a lot of money because of how much you love this place." He watched her for another minute, clearly expecting a response she wasn't prepared to give, then finally flung his hands in the air. "I can't win with you. Nothing I say or do is going to make the least bit of difference to you, is it?"

"What would you like me to say?" she burst out. "Thanks for the favor? Congratulations? I'm sorry, but I'm not pre-programmed!"

He kicked at a stone, and it tumbled across the driveway to rest in the tulips bordering the fence. "I'm doing what I can. I don't expect a damned laurel wreath, but you could at least not look at me like you're..." He blew a harsh breath and walked away toward the inn.

Disappointed, she finished for him. Just the way his parents looked at him. Through her indignation seeped a discomfiting feeling of guilt.

He had listened to her. He'd seen her upset when he told her of his intentions for the inn. He had changed his mind about dismantling it, an action she'd have sworn was both expensive and against his business judgment.

Maybe he'd simply changed, himself. Or maybe they had.

Chapter Thirteen

Mother's Day passed less eventfully than Trent had expected. He'd called his mother, driven by obligation and the knowledge that if he let the day go by without some sort of acknowledgment, he'd get nothing but grief about it later. Maureen took the opportunity to inform him that his presence wasn't important anyway, and that she was going to spend the weekend at a spa. But after that, he heard her voice catch in something that sounded suspiciously like she was hurt. When Trent asked what his father planned to do, his mother didn't answer.

He hung up the phone with the beginnings of a headache. He had enough to do wrangling his reactions to Morgan, let alone adding his mother into the mix. The day he figured Maureen Williams out was probably set on some ancient calendar to coincide with Armageddon.

The Sandersons bade them goodbye and returned to Philadelphia, taking with them their unsettling example of marital happiness. Was that even possible past a honeymoon?

Morgan hardly spoke to Trent over the next several days, particularly after she contacted her potential employers to set up interviews. Her silence alternately relieved and frustrated him. His mood, when he considered her, changed about as frequently and unpredictably as the wind.

And speaking of wind. This was the first morning of the Nantucket Wine Festival, and he wondered how the tent and expos would hold up if it got much gustier.

He emerged from his room at the inn, pulling on a gray suit jacket. Agnes met him on the landing.

She smiled as she surveyed his attire. "Very nice, Mister Williams, very nice. You're going to cause quite a stir among the ladies at the festival this week."

He smiled back, and the warmth he felt in it surprised him. "I wish you'd decided to come." A further surprise, he realized, since he meant it.

"I've got my own schedule the next few days, dear. Don't mind me, I'm well occupied." She patted the breast pocket of his suit. "I have something for you, by the way." She held up a folded scrap of cloth.

Curious, he took it. A blue silk handkerchief, with a lighthouse stitched in white on one corner, and *Seaglass Inn* beside it in fancy script. "What's this?"

"We used to have a sign out front of the inn. That was our logo. Howard and I went to the festival every year, and he'd wear that in his pocket for luck."

"I don't need luck," Trent said automatically.

"Oh, everyone needs a little luck." She took the handkerchief from him, then tucked it into his pocket. "There, now. Have fun."

Fun. Sure. Right up there with the Spanish Inquisition.

He drove Morgan and Laura to the festival, the opening ceremony of which was held at one of Nantucket's yacht clubs. He had grown up sailing, and the sight of the boats moored in the harbor tugged at something in his chest.

He missed the water. Out there, nobody cared who you were or how you got that way. Everything depended on the timeless rhythm of wind and wave. If he'd been more of a romantic, Trent might have figured the sea was in his blood. But living with Leland and Maureen had sucked any such romantic notions out of him with merciless precision. Cold, hard numbers were the only spoken language in the Williams household.

But even that, if Laura were to be believed, was changing. Was anything sensible anymore?

They arrived to a crowd already browsing the tent and mingling with other wine and food aficionados. Tasteful music from an acoustic guitar floated across the grounds. Everyone shielded their drinks and appetizers from the fitful wind.

Trent breathed easier. This, he could do. Schmoozing, making himself memorable at a function, building business...easy.

Not so easy gauging Morgan's mood. She spoke freely with Laura. As she mingled with the guests, she chatted and talked shop with an ease and composure that made the businessman in him absurdly proud of her. He watched her move among the guests with straight-backed poise. Always when she wasn't looking, and always with a swell of admiration and approval. And always tearing his gaze away with a pang of gloom once she turned her attention to him.

She didn't need his approval. And strangely, he admired that even more.

To him, she was polite but reserved, as if he were just another vintner or wine enthusiast. She wore a dusty-blue dress that hugged her figure in all the right places, then flared gracefully out around her calves. More than one man followed her with his eyes as she glided among the crowd.

Trent stared, too, remembering their night on the beach and the things she'd said. Half of him wanted to go up to her and apologize for turning her out of her home. He'd never even had a concept of "home" until coming here. Seeing the way Morgan interacted with Agnes, with Elsa, even with strangers, made him wonder for the first time if this was what having real roots might have been like. Even her harping about his beer stein had developed a homey ring to it.

The other half of him hated that, in spite of his every effort to the contrary, he was once again reduced to being sorry for his actions not measuring up to someone's standard. If he ever had children—which he certainly would not—he'd let them be what they were, and not what he wanted to impose on them.

Feeling like a bone tugged between two equally belligerent hounds, he tipped back the rest of his champagne without bothering to appreciate its crisp, layered flavor.

"Excuse me," said a man close by.

Trent looked up to find a well-dressed man standing at his elbow. The man held a glass of champagne, swirling it while he looked across the lawn. "I couldn't help noticing the lady you're with."

Prickles rushed along the back of his neck—the same sensation he endured when he was about to lose a deal to a competitor. "What, Miss Clifton?" he asked sharply.

The man took the snap without any sign of discomposure, which was more than Trent could say for himself. Looking toward the tents, the stranger said, "I was referring to the lady in yellow, actually. I'd like to invite you all to my home for a late wine tasting."

Idiot, Trent cursed himself. He let his ruffled feathers re-settle, scanned the crowd, then found Laura talking with a trio of men whom they had met on their arrival. She seemed to be holding her own, no doubt picking their brains for the best vineyards currently for sale across the country. The men watched Laura raptly as she spoke. Trent figured, with a private smile, that they were as interested in her as in the conversation. *Another bunch bites the dust.*

He looked back at the man standing beside him. Tailored suit. Neat black hair, with a touch of gray at his temples. Comfortable posture. The stranger paused to take in the bouquet of the champagne before he sipped it.

Trent held out his hand. "Trent Williams. The lady in yellow is Laura Barclay." The two shook hands, and Trent added, "You might want to hurry. Looks like she's developing a following, Mister..."

"Schena. Dominick Schena." The man gestured to Morgan with his wine glass. "Morgan Clifton?"

"Yes." The prickle returned, with friends.

"Yes, I remember her. Wonderful smoked salmon. Is she not among the presenters this year?"

"No, the Seaglass Inn is being sold."

"Sold? That's a shame. She's a gifted chef. Not leaving the island, is she?"

Less cheerfully, Trent replied, "It's looking that way." He downed the remainder of his champagne and thumbed the glass. "I've bought the inn."

Hell. He'd been pissed off since Morgan's interference with the sale contract. But over the past few days, he'd found satisfaction in simple building repairs that hadn't been present in the boardroom for a long time. He watched Morgan as she talked to a group of people with more animation than he'd felt in his most intense business meetings. Her smile glowed. She laughed, and strangely, his chest ached at the sight of it.

She loved this place. She'd made ties here, in spite of a supernatural power that should have isolated her from the rest of humanity, almost the same way he had isolated himself.

Except he'd done it voluntarily. Of all the names in his address book, all the business contacts he'd cultivated over the years, how many would come running when he needed them most? How many did he know well enough to do the same for them?

Had he wasted half his life running on the wrong treadmill?

Schena broke into his thoughts by moving across his line of vision toward Laura and her knot of admirers. "Well, congratulations on your purchase," the man said. "Good luck to you. I hope to see you all this evening. I'll give Miss...?" His voice rose in what sounded like a hope for confirmation that Laura was, in fact, unattached.

Trent plastered on a smile. "Miss Barclay," he said.

"Miss Barclay," Dominick repeated. "I'll give her the details. It will be a small party, but I promise you, the wines are memorable."

"Happy hunting," said Trent.

When Schena left, Trent searched again for Morgan, only to find her missing. He turned in a circle.

There. She stood just inside the tent...with Spencer. Her hair had begun to loosen from its clip, and it whisked her cheeks in the wind. On her face was an expression of extreme dislike.

Not good. Trent abandoned his empty champagne glass to a nearby server, then strode toward Morgan. A few raindrops pattered the shoulders of his suit coat. Festival-goers hurried toward the tent to escape the worsening weather.

Spencer rounded on him as soon as he got close enough. His haughty expression changed to something more subversive. "Hello again, Mister..."

"Williams." Trent didn't extend his hand for the bite he was sure to get, by the look on the chef's face. Morgan's cheeks had flushed crimson, and she eyed the chef as though she wished him drowned.

Spencer ignored her. "I hope you're finding the selection of food here more palatable than my crab salad and lobster have been," he added with his usual absence of sincerity.

Knowing the chef hadn't had any part in preparing any of the festival's food, Trent said, "Delicious. The crab, especially."

Morgan's gaze flicked toward him, and a *ping* of warmth burst in his chest. Seized by impulse, he added, "We've been invited to a Mister Schena's. Care to go?"

"Schena? *Dominick* Schena?" Spencer goggled as if someone had yanked a truckload of reclaimed barn board out from under him just as the bid closed.

Wondering what his problem was, Trent looked to Morgan. She glanced at Spencer with a gleam in her eyes that made it clear the chef's discomposure had made her evening. Trent struggled not to crow aloud at the delight on her face.

"He's one of the foremost winemakers on the East Coast," she explained. "A big advocate of preserving the Sound's natural areas. His parties are wait-listed...when he opens his house to them. He engages a chef for some of his dinners, and more than one has launched his career just on that."

"Or *her* career," Trent added. "Shall we be off?" He gave her a smile and his arm.

Grinning, Morgan took it. "Goodbye, Spencer."

They left the chef in the dust as the rain began falling harder. More people rushed toward the tent, but Trent turned his face upward and soaked in the drench with a smile.

He turned the smile on Morgan to find her beaming at him. "Thank you," she said. Her eyes shone. She stared at him like he was Hercules. And for once, he felt like it.

"You're welcome," he answered, with that ache in his chest again. Funny how he didn't care about his Italian suit getting ruined. One smile from her had paid for it lock, stock, and wine barrel.

****

"I am sorry about the cramped conditions," Dominick said as his chauffeur drove them down the shoreline. Rain drummed the windshield of the limousine. "I ought to have brought the bigger car."

Bigger? Morgan stared around the roomy back seat. He had served them drinks from a tiny bar tucked into the corner. She, Trent, and Laura sat back in plushy, butter-soft leather seats. She could have done gymnastics in here. Winemaking must have been better to Dominick Schena than she'd realized.

As she watched him, the man glanced frequently to Laura, who sat beside him. Laura stared at him at least as often, and the length of silence while she did so led Morgan to suspect she wasn't interested only in Schena's vineyards.

The sky through the windshield lit in a flash. Everyone had barely uttered an exclamation before Morgan heard the crash of thunder. The rain increased into a constant hiss on the windows. Through the open partition, she saw the chauffeur turn up the wipers. The *thwip-thwip* of the blades filled a pause in the conversation before thunder rumbled again.

"Don't worry, we'll be out of it soon," Dominick said. "My house isn't much farther. You are all very welcome to accommodate yourselves there overnight, if you wish. Please don't feel you'd be imposing on me."

Almost as he said it, the chauffeur turned down a long driveway. Through the watery rush of rain down her window, she made out a sprawling house hugging the property. Warm light glowed from large windows facing the shoreline.

The chauffeur opened the back door and held an open umbrella for Dominick. The man handed it instead to Laura. When he gestured for Morgan to join her under it, she shook her head and thanked him. Trent waved him off also. Dominick escorted Laura ahead of them.

Halfway up the long stone staircase leading from the carriage house, the storm began a full assault. Rain fell stinging on Morgan's bare skin. Wincing, she hurried along faster.

Cloth swept over her. She looked up in surprise to find Trent adjusting his suit jacket over her shoulders. His arm came around her back, and a warmth sped through Morgan that almost drove away the unmoderated chill of the rain.

How...thoughtful.

She stared at him as they climbed the steps, but he had turned his attention to the footing. His dress shirt had soaked through, and now clung to his body. Water dripped down his cheek from hair gone spiky with the wet.

Morgan's thoughts went instantly back to their incredible night on the beach. The image crowded out her resentment about being relocated inland.

He had changed his mind about piecing off the inn, no doubt at considerable cost to himself. She had assumed he was as cold-hearted to the world as his parents were to him. Had she been wrong about him from the beginning? Was there a crack in that businessman armor after all?

Lightning flashed again, and a deafening boom of thunder followed it. The rain poured down still harder.

The rain.

Oh, selfish. Selfish! She glanced over the lawn to the shore. Waves battered the sand and spewed froth into the air. The sky glowered, darker and darker, brightened only when lightning pierced the clouds. A storm like this would only end in a mess for the residents of Nantucket. And there went the wine festival, too.

"Trent," she whispered. The wind tore her words

away. She tugged at his sleeve until his attention came back to her. "I can temper this. The storm...with my power."

He stared at her like she'd gone out of her mind. "You think you're going to affect *this*?"

"Shh!" She pulled on his sleeve again, and they fell behind Dominick and Laura, who had reached the door. "I've done it before...influenced the weather. I did it with you, when we rode the bikes to town. You made me angry, and..." She gestured toward the churning clouds.

He hesitated mid-stride. His arm slipped closer around her back, and he bent close to her ear as they walked up the steps. "Uh-uh. This is no place for theatrics, Montana," he muttered over the thunder.

Insult pounded through her. "Theatrics!" she whispered, but they had reached the house.

Dominick opened the door to a bright, spacious contemporary interior. "I'll get a fire started. I'm so sorry about the wet-through." When he offered to find them dry clothing, they declined.

He showed them to the bathroom, where Morgan dried most of the water from her skin. It did little for her power, which tickled at her nerve endings as if it sensed the upset of the ocean outside...and the further upset within about Trent. She'd always prided herself on her judgment of people. It pained her to admit it, but she'd been wrong from the beginning. Trent was by no means as cold as he wanted the world to think.

She returned to the living area. A stone fireplace rose up to the ceiling in the corner of the room, and white couches stood in a half-circle around it. Over the mantel hung a large flat-screen television. Through the windows on three sides of the room, Morgan saw the storm blanketing the ocean. Lightning flared again and again.

"I'm not here nearly as often as I'd like to be,"

195

Dominick admitted as he started a gas fire snapping in the fireplace. "My vineyard is in New Jersey, and I've been working on opening another in Napa Valley." He picked up a remote from the glass coffee table and clicked it. The television flickered on, and low music from some streaming radio station filled the room. "Sit. Enjoy yourselves, please. I'll see about some refreshments."

Morgan studied Dominick. She had known the man was successful, but this was *successful*. She looked for Trent, and found him standing at the window looking outside. Laura sat on the couch, admiring an album of photos.

Trent glanced at her as she approached him. "Getting worse out there," he murmured.

"Yes," she said dryly.

He smirked at her. "There's no point stopping this," he whispered. "It's too big. Look at it out there." Even as he thrust a finger toward the storm outside, thunder shook the windows.

He stayed silent so long after that, Morgan thought the conversation was over. She lingered, watching lightning strike the water. Her power jumped in sympathy, and from the corner of her eye she caught a flash of light from her hands. Alarmed, she crossed her arms and jammed her hands under her armpits.

Trent glanced at her, stepped toward her, then halted. "You okay?"

"Fine," she said.

"Trent, Morgan, look," Laura said.

Morgan turned in time to see Laura pluck the remote from the coffee table. A red band was scrolling across the bottom of the music station's screen. Laura pressed a button on the remote and it switched to a television program.

"Let me," Morgan said. She switched the station to local news.

A reporter stood in downtown Nantucket with a raincoat and microphone. Behind her, streetlights flickered. A storefront window had been smashed through by a fallen tree. With dismay, Morgan recognized the Lightkeeper.

The images flicked through rain pouring off the tent at the wine festival, and guests quickly retreating to the relative safety of the yacht club. Gutters filled with rushing water. A building with half its shingles missing flashed across the screen. Then they were back to the reporter, who struggled to keep the hood of her raincoat on, then finally gave up and urged her cameraman to seek shelter with her in the news van.

Elsa was right. The storms had arrived, and they were as bad as predicted.

Oh, good Lord. What was she doing here, enjoying herself, with *this* going on?

Trent and Laura were occupied with the newscast. Morgan slipped out of the room toward the front door.

Trent's suit coat hung on a hall tree. She pulled it down and thrust her arms through the sleeves. Through the hall, she glimpsed Dominick returning to the living room with a tray. Quickly, before he could see her, she ducked out the door.

Chapter Fourteen

Trent stared at all the red and yellow obliterating eastern Massachusetts on the newscast's radar display. Another location shot showed a tree that had crushed the roof of someone's car, and then crashed through the roof of the building nearby. Trent squinted at the screen, at the demolished bed of tulips that had once bordered the building. His heartbeat went into overdrive.

His car. The Seaglass Inn.

Agnes.

He turned around as Schena entered the room with a tray of drinks. "Morgan?" Trent called. *"Morgan?"*

No answer. Schena and Laura stared at him, then looked around the room with alarm on their faces.

"Shit," Trent whispered. "Dominick, I need a car."

In minutes, he had pulled a borrowed Jeep from the garage and parked it along the shoreline. A frantic search on foot brought him to Morgan, hunched against the rain in the shallows on the beach. "Get out of there! Are you nuts?" He jerked her to her feet and pulled her back from the surging water.

She turned around, outrage on her face, and shoved dripping hair out of her eyes. She opened her mouth, no doubt to hurl accusations at him.

"There's no time to argue!" he shouted over the wind and crashing waves. "The Seaglass is damaged. Agnes could be hurt."

Her expression changed at once to a look of terror so sharp his gut seized in response. He grabbed her hand and pulled her toward the Jeep. Wordlessly, she ran with him.

From there, Trent broke at least three laws, and severely bent five others, getting back to the Seaglass Inn. The wipers, even at their highest speed, couldn't slick away the rain before more poured down. They skidded around corners so fast, he almost hydroplaned the vehicle. Beside him, Morgan gripped the seat, grim-faced. "We'll get there, we'll get there," he said, trying to ignore the racing of his own heart and concentrate on the treacherous road.

When they arrived at the inn, the driveway was choked with rescue vehicles and goggling bystanders. Trent couldn't even see what remained of his car, nor the inn's damage. He tossed his cell in the console and jumped from the Jeep almost as soon as he'd parked it at the side of the road. "Agnes? Agnes!"

A firefighter warded him off as he approached the yellow hazard barriers set up at the end of the driveway. "This isn't safe, sir. You can't come through here."

"The hell I can't," Trent snapped. "Agnes!"

A flash of dusty blue streaked past in his peripheral vision. Morgan raced toward the inn's door.

Trent leaped over the barrier in front of him and rushed toward her. He grabbed her around the waist and lifted her off her feet. She kicked at him, nailing him in the shin so hard he saw stars. "Agnes!" The fear in her scream turned his stomach. More firefighters crowded around them. One pulled Morgan from his arms, and he found himself clutching at air, wanting to hold onto her and keep that fear at bay.

One of the firefighters grabbed his shoulder. "There's no one in there, sir. Who are you looking for?"

Trent struggled to find his composure, a calm he could find in the most intense of meetings, but one that had now deserted him. "The inn's owner, Agnes Preble. We left her here when we went to the wine festival." Rain poured down into his eyes. He pulled Morgan closer, away from the barrier. "Does Agnes have a cell phone?"

"No," Morgan moaned. "I mean she did, I gave her one...but she never used it, never charged it. She said she didn't need it."

"Let's go next door," he said. "We'll check on Gordon, see if he knows anything."

They hurried to Gordon's cottage. No one answered when they knocked or rang the bell. Morgan produced a key, and they let themselves in.

A quick search proved no one was home, but on the kitchen table, they found a brochure for a boat tour of the Sound.

Dated today, and starting three hours ago.

Beside it sat a pair of teacups, and a wrapped coffee cake on one of the plates from Morgan's kitchen. Morgan gave a muffled cry. "Trent, they're out on the water. In this."

She turned to him, and the panic in her eyes plowed through him like a bulldozer. "All right, don't worry," he said. "We'll make some calls, get the Coast Guard on it. They might even be bringing the boat in already. Hell, maybe it's sitting at the dock." He stalked across the kitchen and started jerking open the drawers in search of a phone book. Nothing. Nothing. Nothing. He whispered a curse, then finally found the book in the drawer under the microwave.

He yanked it out and slapped it on the counter. "See? Like I said, don't worry." He managed to make his voice sound as calm as the words, but the squeeze of his gut surprised him. The thought of something bad happening to Agnes bothered him much more than he'd thought possible. She cared about people. She didn't deserve... No. Action, not worry.

He picked up the kitchen phone and punched the numbers while staring at a photo on the fridge of Morgan, Agnes, and Gordon in what looked like Gordon's side yard. He couldn't even have said what he told the lady who answered. A jumble of questions, a tangle of answers. Something about the boat schedule, and who he thought was on it. No, *knew* was on it, because the gut feeling he'd always had when he was right about a business transaction was now jabbing him frenetically to do something. Agnes was in trouble, and besides the fact that he now realized he cared about the elderly woman in return, the worry in Morgan echoed in him like a ringing chime.

But when he turned around, Morgan was gone. He rushed through the rest of his phone call, then slammed the handset down. "Morgan?" He ran through the house, up the stairs, back down again. His gut started screaming.

On his second run through the living room, he noticed the sliding door to the deck was open. The curtains whipped into the room with the cold, misty scent of rainwater.

I can temper this, she'd said. He'd seen her manipulate water. A tiny faucet-flow of it. Not a giant, heaving ocean full. And her power worked better, she'd said, when she was touching the water.

She'd be *in* it.

His gut dropped out of him entirely. He bolted to the door and screamed her name. Rain pummeled his face.

Footprints led down to the shore, already

dissolving in the downpour. He flung the door shut behind him, then raced down the beach, scanning the water with a ripping pain in his chest. His heart hammered at his ribs. He shouted her name again.

Then, like a seal gracefully rising from the turbulent surf, Morgan appeared. She stood in the water up to her chest, and every visible part of her shimmered with a pearlescent glow. The light spilling off her skin illuminated the sea for yards around her, defying the growing darkness of the storm and oncoming night. Even the rain spilling down around her took on a glow of its own.

Though the waves surged past her left and right, the surface around her settled, lapping at her shoulders as if she were in a wading pool. The calm spread outward in a circle from her body, arching farther and farther across the ocean's surface. Far off, no more than a dim shape against the storm, a boat pitched in the waves and struggled toward shore.

Agnes.

He held his breath, afraid to call to Morgan, more afraid not to. For the first time in his life, he couldn't think, couldn't act. The cool-headed businessman had deserted him.

Could she do it? Could she tame this monster? Lightning flashed across the boiling sky, and terror flashed through him.

She'd be electrocuted before she got the chance.

He bolted toward the water, needing to get his arms safely around her and pull her back from this insane attempt. He plowed into the waves. Panic forced the words out of him over the boom of thunder and rush of waves. "What are you doing? Get back on the beach!"

The light around her flickered as she turned. He saw the curve of her face, the surprise in her eyes. He powered toward her through deeper water with desperation slicing open his heart. All those hours in the gym, and they were no use. For every foot he swam, the current dragged him back two more. Pain tore through his chest. He couldn't do it, it was no good, *he* was no good. Not without her.

He stretched toward her with everything he had. Almost, almost, almost.

Morgan gave a shout. The glow around her snuffed like a burned-out lightbulb. The tide dragged at his feet, and then she went under.

Morgan. Oh, God, Morgan. His heart bucked wildly, cut off from life-giving air even before a huge wave swept over his head.

****

Tumbling over in the water, Morgan scrambled to hang onto her senses and the elusive inner spark of her power. Her gift slipped away, uncatchable, capricious. Her throat burned with swallowed brine. Panic pounded at her and she flailed her arms, trying to find the surface. *Don't lose it, don't lose it,* rang the chant in her head, as much for her gift as to stave off the terror threatening to crush the breath from her lungs. The current pulled at her. The ends of her hair rushed shoreward, then a wave spun her around, and she lost all sense of direction.

The tide was sweeping her out.

Oh, God, she'd been so foolish. How had she thought she could tame this storm? Who was she, to try to control it? Now it was too late, and her power so out of reach...like the two people she loved best in the world. Despair washed through her, flooded every crevice, and pushed her power even farther away.

Why had a roof and four walls mattered so much to her? Home would never be bricks and timber and shingles. It would never be what was important. Life. Air in her lungs. People she cared for, close around her. Those things mattered. *Agnes. Trent.*

I'm so sorry. Everything I have is nothing without you.

Strong fingers grasped her arm, slid, grasped harder.

Trent.

Morgan almost cried out with relief. She strained toward him. Her fingers swept along fabric, and then the current jerked her away from him.

She broke the surface and gulped air. The beach lay so horribly far away. Rain poured into her eyes. "Trent! Trent!" Desperate seconds ticked past.

He surfaced, already yards away but closer to shore. "Morgan! Your power. Concentrate!" Thunder boomed.

"I can't!" she cried, even now trying to catch the inner fizz that told her the power was there. It skipped away again and again.

Trent plowed through a wave toward her, pushed along by the current. "You can! I know you can!" His hand found hers and closed over it. He pulled her closer to him, their bodies pitching in the water, and his other hand pushed her water-slick hair back. The confidence on his face stunned her. "Come on, Montana. Let's get out of this."

And in the midst of that tranquility in his eyes, Morgan found her power. It poured through her nerve endings and filled her skin, warming her against the frigid water. Her body glowed. The turbulent water around them glowed. Her gift raced back and forth through her, stronger than she'd ever known it.

This was home. *He* was home.

Grinning—was it crazy that she was grinning?—she said, "Hold onto me!"

He nodded and held her hand more firmly. Morgan seized the threads of her power, then punched it.

A lighthouse-beacon flood of light poured

outward from her skin across the water. The leaping waves slowed. Spinning around in the ocean, Morgan directed the waves to settle far out in the Sound. She pushed the storm-tossed currents out, out, out to sea, a human water break against the tide. The tour boat, silhouetted against the darkening sky, began to hold its own. *You're safe now, Agnes.*

The power bounding through her awed and humbled her. She sensed the water shifting, sensed it sliding around her, around the boat, around Trent. Confident now, she pushed harder against the current's resistance. The rage of the sea subsided into deeper waters. Thunder rumbled, now passing away from the Sound. She let her power go now, certain it would return if she needed it. The glow faded from her skin but left her smiling.

Trent whooped, then planted a loud, wet kiss on her cheek. They bobbed in the water as he tugged her closer. "Knew you could do it," he murmured. He cupped her face in both hands and kissed her lips.

Warmth poured through her. She reveled in it, reveled in being with him and knowing she belonged there. Even with the love of her foster family, her life had always been a puzzle with missing pieces. Now, it was complete.

Well, almost complete. She longed for children. Two, three, ten...it didn't matter. As long as they were Trent's. Beaming, she kissed him back.

A searchlight passed over them. "Hello!" called a voice.

In the glare of floodlights, Morgan spied a few rescue workers on the beach. "We're all right," she called. "We're coming in."

When they got to shore, a firefighter pulled a thermal blanket around her. "Are you both okay?"

They nodded. Trent took a blanket and pulled it around his own shoulders.

The rescue team insisted on giving them a thorough checkup before letting either of them loose. "You sure you're all right, ma'am?" one of the firefighters asked over the waning patter of the rain. "What were you doing in that water? Is someone else out there?"

She shook her head. "Just us."

They finished with the rescue team and hurried back to the inn. When Morgan saw the extent of the damage, her heart, floating only minutes ago, dove into the pit of her belly. The corner of the roof had smashed in, taking out a guest room and the sitting room below it. The sitting room's graceful leaded-glass window lay in shards all over the lawn. Broken glass glittered, mocking, in the lights of the fire engines circling the property.

Trent retrieved his cell phone from the Jeep and began making calls. She didn't even hear what he said. Words and images jumbled together. She turned in a circle, dazed and heartsick and impatient for Agnes's return.

Gordon's house had survived the storm's onslaught. Across the street, others hadn't been so lucky. The gutters had fallen from little bungalow on the corner and crushed the hydrangea bushes in front. One side of the cape across the way had lost much of its shingle siding, which now lay scattered in the yard like broken teeth. What did the town look like? Was anyone hurt? Morgan rushed back to Trent, aching for answers.

He ended his call, then glanced at the inn's damage. His hazel eyes were dark in the glow of rescue vehicle headlights. His damp hair had matted to his forehead. He had what looked like a bruise over his cheekbone, but his concern was all for her. "You going to be okay?"

She could hardly think to answer. Everything crowded together on her tongue. Exhausted, but unable to stop moving, she hurried back to the shore. Trent followed, silent, even as the rain stopped and the clouds began to part on stars.

He came up beside her on the beach and squinted into the Sound. "The boat's coming in. Look."

Sure enough, the tour boat was now pulling steadily toward the harbor. Morgan swallowed back a cry of relief. Trent must have sensed it, because he leaned close to her ear. "You're still crazy, Morgan. But you're brave as hell. We're going to make this right, don't worry."

She stared at him, wondering. A few weeks ago, she would never have imagined him comforting her. For a long minute, he held her stare. She read a hunger in his eyes. A need for something more than sex. A need she recognized as if, for once, they spoke the same language. Then he shuttered it away and was gone, back to the inn.

****

Trent spent the next three hours on his phone. First with Laura, to let her know they were fine. She and Schena were likewise unhurt. The worst of the storm hadn't hit their side of the island. Schena offered to bring her back in the morning, and Laura accepted. After hearing the admiration for Dominick in Laura's tone—even infatuation—Trent agreed. Schena was a well-known, respectable man by all accounts. No sense dragging Laura back to this mess now, anyway.

At least someone would be happy tonight.

Half the time, he wanted to chuck it all and head back to Boston. The other half, he remained at Morgan's side as if he'd been fused there. Every time he thought of leaving, he remembered the look of fear on her face and the answering terror in his heart. Even now, with everyone alive and the only damage done to replaceable objects, he felt her

207

distress like a nausea brought on by bad shellfish.

She had almost died. After everything that had happened between them, he'd expected that to bother him. The extent to which it bothered him, bothered him more.

What the hell right did she have to affect him so much?

He didn't want to care. The ups and downs of their...whatever-it-was...were worse than a stock market soar and crash, and far less predictable. Another damn reason he should just go.

But the mess here demanded a clearer head than Morgan's, and for once, both sides of him refused to budge. His business sensibilities recoiled at the idea of leaving any job unfinished, especially one that would run smoother with his personal involvement. He needed to be here. He was good at doing what had to be done, and with a more level head in times of crisis than most.

More insistent, though, was the flat refusal that bubbled up inside him when he thought of putting any distance between himself and Morgan. He felt like the frayed rope in a nasty tug-of-war, pulled out of recognizable shape by the need to be in two places. Yank. Boston. Yank. Morgan. Yank. Boston. Any minute, he'd snap.

Agnes returned to the inn unhurt, but Gordon had suffered a few bumps to the head during their disastrous sea trip. "I'll stay next door to take care of him," she said. "He has plenty of extra space for all of us."

"No reason I can't stay here," said Trent, surveying the broken window of the sitting room.

"Oh, Trent, don't. It's a mess," Agnes protested.

"Better if I'm here," he told her. "I'll get on the phone with the insurance company. Write something up. Make some more calls, be here when they come to look at it." And then make the dreaded call to his parents, who would only chew him out if he didn't. That would go way, way down the list, after everyone else he could think of. They'd have a field day when they found out he'd invested his money in what was now damaged goods. And with the sale of the property still pending.

And he wasn't going to dismantle it, so there would be no profits coming after the closure to offset this mess.

Just great.

He turned to Agnes, looking her over as casually as possible to be sure she wasn't hurt, without being too obvious about it. "No big deal, Agnes. I'll do the legwork. You worry about Gordon."

He said it offhand, a throwaway comment he might make to any business associate in a similar situation. But the approval on the older woman's face forced him to turn away, hitching his shoulders under a shirt that suddenly seemed to have shrunk two sizes.

No respite there, either. Morgan beamed at him from her place at one of the hazard barriers. A burst of warmth flashed through him. He stifled it and dropped his gaze to the broken glass on the lawn, only half-listening as Agnes gave a statement to the fire department.

He didn't want Morgan's appreciation. Didn't want how it made him feel like he was balancing on a giant ball, just waiting to crash down when he made the wrong move. He sure as hell didn't welcome the way he liked it so much. That road had always led to more looks of disappointment when he didn't live up to something, and he'd had enough of that to choke a horse. This was a matter of business, a problem that had to be fixed. Not a play for admiration. She was alive, and that was enough. It had to be enough.

The idea that it might not be enough scared the

hell out of him.

When the inn was pronounced structurally safe to enter, Agnes retrieved a few belongings and bustled off next door to help Gordon. Trent and Morgan took stock of the inn's damage. The front corner rooms looked bad, but he eyed the exposed rafters and load-bearing walls with relief. Nothing a strong back and some carpentry skills couldn't handle. Damn shame about that leaded glass, though. No one made details like that anymore.

He could probably find a replacement. One of his old college mates knew a guy with a great salvage yard—

Morgan's sniffle jerked him out of his planning like a master lobsterman plucking a full trap from the seafloor. He turned to find her crouching over a mess of blue-and-white porcelain shards on the sitting room's braided rug. A crushed cardboard box lay beside them, half-packed with newspaper-wrapped objects. When Morgan touched it, he heard the ominous clink of broken dishware. So much for that packing effort.

She lifted a broken teacup from the rug, then stood and turned in a tearful circle. She fingered the cup's shattered edge. "This belonged to Agnes's grandmother." Her breath hitched, and a few tears tracked down her cheek.

Trent recognized sentimental value, in the clinical sense. People attached absurd amounts of importance to the strangest things. He'd made his living off that premise. Scarred barn wood often commanded more money at auction than brand-new, pristine hardwood. Buyers went nuts for all the nail holes and gouges. Character, they called it.

He tugged the cup from her hand and set it on a television stand. The upset on her face pushed him past his reluctance. "It's just stuff, Morgan."

Her gaze came up again, wide-eyed and deep

blue and so sorrowful it hurt to look. "Some of these things have been in her family for generations. This inn is full of collected memories."

"She's alive. *You're* alive. That's more important than teacups." Unable to help himself, he cradled her cheek. She was forever making him do things he didn't want to do. Even the act of being near her, when his life would be so much less complicated if he were miles, yards, feet away.

"I know that," she said softly. Her voice caught. "But this place...Agnes's things, her livelihood..." She leaned into his touch.

Even his hand betrayed him to her. He stroked her soft skin and let her cool-water scent wash all the other troubles out of his head. "Come on," he murmured. "Let's board this up and call it a night. We can't do much until morning anyway."

She said little while he found some wood scraps from his work on the floor joists, and a few sheets of plywood that had been stored in the cellar. He nailed them up with a distant recognition that he ought to save them if possible after this. The local price of lumber would be going up, if other parts of New England had sustained this sort of damage.

This kind of structure work would have devoured any nest egg Agnes might have saved for her move south. Trent understood then why Morgan worried so much about Agnes's means during retirement. The old lady would probably be living on ramen noodles and canned tuna as it was.

While he worked, Morgan cleaned up the broken knick-knacks and made a visual survey of the rest of the inn. She found him as he tacked up tarp in the guest room, and gave a brief report. Nothing but the two rooms seemed to have suffered much of the onslaught. Lucky, that.

He finished driving in the last nail—lumber prices be damned, he'd need a few more sheets of ply and some new studs after all—then turned around to find Morgan hugging herself and shivering. He realized then they still wore the clothes from their "swim." He hadn't noticed, too busy with the warming physical labor of patchwork. Even her power to moderate water temperatures must reach its limit at some point. "Why don't you go change? I'll seal up this room so we don't lose too much heat tonight. Sitting room's already done—"

Instead of doing so, she approached him with her hands outstretched and a look in her eyes as irresistible as it was indefinable.

Trent backed off a step. "I'm sweaty."

"I don't care." She walked into his arms.

Pulled in by the gravity-force of her eyes, Trent kissed her and tasted the faint salt of tears and seawater that lingered on her lips. She pressed close to him, holding onto his shirt as though he might be able to anchor her in place. "You all right?"

"I don't want to think, Trent," she said. The catch in her voice startled him. "I don't want to think anymore about a roof over my head, or who I am, or where I belong. Just kiss me, and keep kissing me." She turned her face up to his, all full lips and long lashes.

Faced with a temptation like that, he couldn't refuse. He dropped his hammer, and it landed with a thud on the old toolbox. He reached to cup her face in his palm, then hesitated as he noticed the grime and work-roughened skin of his hand.

Before he could pull away, she took his hand and pressed it to her cheek. Her lids flickered shut, and those hypnotizing lips curled into a smile that released the breath trapped in his chest. How and when had everything his body did become so intertwined with her?

He kissed her again, and her scent, her softness, the sound of her breath, all melted into him to swim through his blood. *I don't want to need you,* he thought. But as she plunged her fingers through the hair at the back of his head to pull him closer, he knew she'd ensnared him beyond all hope. He had no power to deny the drive to touch her. Her mass of mahogany hair. Her lush, soft curves. That oh-so-velvety skin at the nape of her neck, where his touch brought forth a sigh from her lips that disassembled all reason.

He lifted her against him, already moving upstairs. Her long legs wound around his waist. The siren wrapping herself around her prey—and he, no longer willing to fight it.

Up the stairs he carried her. Kicked open the bathroom door. Steered her to the tub. Kissed her in a desperate bid to silence the need now screaming through him. He couldn't stop it, couldn't refuse it, couldn't even hesitate a minute to consider it. Hell, he practically shook with it.

Morgan tugged at his shirt. "Off, off, take it off," she whispered.

He wrestled with the buttons on his shirt, then tore the last two in a frantic rush to touch her again. He flung the shirt to the rag rug beside the tub in a damp, quickly-ignored heap. The rest of his clothes followed, and then she was in his arms again.

He dragged his lips along the hollow between her neck and shoulder, drinking her in. Her whimper brought shudders pouring down his spine. He molded himself to her body, unable to get enough of her. The pressure of her belly against his erection burst through him like a dynamite blast. He groaned and clutched at the skirt of her dress, greedy with hunger. "You, too," he said, sliding the hem up her long, long legs.

She shucked off the material and tossed it down beside his shirt. No waiting, no teasing. Just a gorgeous, unobstructed view of the sexiest body on earth. He filled his senses with her, and still, he needed more. Would it ever be enough?

She turned on the shower head and beckoned him into the tub. One corner of those kill-for lips turned upward. "You said you were sweaty."

He didn't need telling twice. Trent stepped into the shower and pinned her to the tiled wall with his body. She jumped, and he slid his arms around her to warm her. He let his hands linger on her curvy hips, then gave an appreciative growl. "Real sweaty," he agreed. "We're going to be in here a while."

Chapter Fifteen

After that first collision with the cold wall of the shower, everything in Morgan's senses was awash with heat. Hot water, hot skin, hot mouth. Her own body blazed in response to the stream of the shower on her skin. She trembled under Trent's hands, curled possessively around her hips and breasts. He bent close to whisper everything he wanted to do to her, his lips brushing her ear. His words burned a path through her straight to every nerve ending.

When his rigid erection slipped between her thighs, she moaned and arched toward him.

He stepped back with a satisfied-cat gleam in his eyes. "Not yet, Montana," he muttered against her lips. His mouth never left hers as he tipped the shower head farther downward. "Turn around."

She did so. Trent circled his hands around her body to pull her back against the slick, muscular wall of him. He tucked his chin into her shoulder and kissed the ultra-sensitive skin at the base of her neck. The suction of his lips sent delicious quivers rushing every which way through her skin, only to converge again between her legs, where she ached for him almost past bearing. "Please," she gasped out, reaching back to touch him.

Instead of allowing it, he pushed closer against her. His erection slid between her thighs again, inaccessible to her hands, but its pressure a sweet agony so close to where she needed him.

He cupped her breasts and lifted them. The shower spray pelted her skin. Her nipples tingled, and she backed against him with a shudder. When he flicked the sensitive tips with his thumbs, she gave a soft, startled "Oh!"

"Mmmm, that's good." The seduction in his tone pulsed through her body. He rocked his hips, sliding harder against her. "What about this?" The fingers of one hand slipped around her hip and between her legs to stroke her in slow, deliberate little circles. "Let it go, Morgan," he whispered.

Her world reduced to that boiling-hot point of pleasure. With a gasp, she threw her head back and arched in his skilled embrace. Her power burst its bonds and raced through her, throwing the shower into a light so fluorescent she had to shut her eyes. Every droplet of water hitting her skin seemed to fizzle on contact, and her heartbeat thudded as though it meant to pound her apart.

Trent groaned into her shoulder. He thrust again, his belly hard against her backside, his erection hard against her womanhood. "That's it," he murmured. "So gorgeous." He stroked her faster. "I could live on the sight of you like this."

Even the sensation of the water whirled away. The heat of his hand poured into her, blasted through her, tore a long cry from her lips. She came so hard her knees buckled.

Trent thrust deep into her with a cry of his own. She stumbled forward a step, but he held on, his arm still around her, and braced her against him. "I've got you, honey," he said, his voice rough with desire, and yet somehow so tender she wanted to cry.

He rocked against her, slow and gentle. Her power started bubbling again like oil on a hot skillet. Water coursed down her skin, leaving glowing trails that fused together until her entire body shimmered again. "Trent," she gasped.

"I could get used to this," he said, holding her close as he thrust still deeper. He splayed his fingers over her breasts and pulled her back against him.

"Knowing when you're about to come."

She reached back and grasped his hips, urging him on, faster and faster. The groundswell of power within her surged upward. Morgan shuddered and fell back against him with a cry. Trent gave a choked-off groan and followed her as the wave of her power crashed down.

Shaking, Morgan braced a hand against the shower wall. For several moments, only the hiss of the shower spray and the sound of their breath filled the air. Then, with a long, satisfied sigh, she leaned back and savored the feel of him against her body. "I think I could get used to this, too."

When she turned around, she found him staring at her. Just staring. Water trickled down his cheek, down his chest. His stare never left her face. Dismay oozed into her lovely afterglow. "What's wrong?"

He gave a soft laugh, barely a breath. "Why is it that I can't do a damn thing right in the rest of my life, but when I'm with you, it's always so good?" He trailed a finger down the curve of her shoulder to her breast, and followed the motion with his gaze. "Even when we get pissed at each other, it's good, Morgan." He barked a laugh. "The whole damn island's fallen apart around our ears, and all I can think about tonight is, 'Holy shit, I'm *happy*.'" When he looked up again, his expression had gone quieter than she'd ever seen it. His eyes went so soft she ached. "I want that. I want more of that."

She froze, hardly breathing, hardly believing her ears. In his eyes was the Trent she'd always hoped was there, the one who would never consider throwing someone out of their home. She couldn't find her voice.

He reached around her and shut off the shower. "Come on," he said, taking her hand. He stepped out of the shower, tugging her after with a smile. "Let's keep a good thing going."

****

In the dim, gray light of morning, Trent had a hard time finding the words that had been on his mind all night—even after Morgan fell asleep in his arms. He hadn't slept at all. One-handed, he reached up to rub at his eyes, which felt as if the entire contents of the beach had been poured into them.

If he said what he wanted to say, would it just come back to bite him like everything else did, eventually?

Did it matter all that much? They had almost died yesterday. Anything that happened from this point on paled in comparison to that stark fact.

He was alive, he reminded himself. She was alive. They had now.

And now was...

Perfect.

For several minutes, he remained still and absorbed that—the alien, wonderful feeling of lying there, doing nothing, and enjoying it.

Had he ever before just *stopped*?

Morgan cuddled into the hollow of his arm, her hair spread in a glorious dark cloud on his chest. She'd stayed with him. He couldn't have let her go if he'd wanted. For the first time in his life, he didn't feel the driving need to get up and rush to his computer to start work on his next big corporate acquisition.

But there was important work to do today.

He eased out from under her. No need to wake her. This wouldn't take long. At least, the first part wouldn't.

He padded across his room to the dresser, where he found his cell phone lying on top of a legal pad. He picked up the phone, and then a folded sheaf of papers, which he stuffed in the back pocket of his jeans. *Keep moving, Williams. Don't lose momentum now.*

He turned his phone on and pressed a speed dial button on his way to the walk-in closet, where he would be less likely to disturb Morgan's sleep with his conversation. "John? Yeah, I know it's early. It's important, or I wouldn't be calling. I need you to do something for me. There's a few extra donuts in it for you." He explained briefly what he needed.

John thought he was nuts, but he didn't fight Trent much. After the contract fiasco, he doubted John would fight him if he expressed a wish to show up naked at their next country club golf tourney.

He finished his phone call, then tore the closet apart looking for a pair of jeans. Dress pants. Dress pants. Dress pants.

With a shrug, he pulled out the jeans he'd worn the night he found out his parents were coming to visit the inn. The night he and Morgan had almost made love in the kitchen. The night he learned of her power.

It seemed so long ago.

Standing in the closet doorway, he studied her sleeping form. What an amazing ability. Would he ever have had the courage to possess such a power, hide it, and still risk its exposure to help others?

What had he ever risked at all?

Could he find that kind of nerve to start risking everything now?

He rubbed a hand over his stubbled face and through his mussed hair. "Want a thing done, get it done," he murmured to himself. A quote his father had often repeated to him during Trent's—briefly—less-hurried youth. One that had always hovered behind him like a harpy, dogging any lagging footstep.

But now, in a weird way, and without all that stress-inducing bullshit, it made perfect sense.

That word again: perfect. If it kept showing up like that, he might have to start believing in its existence. He slipped a polo shirt over his head and padded out of the room.

Breakfast.

In the kitchen, he switched on lights and began hunting through the cupboards for pans. He could manage an omelet and some coffee. With a grin, he pulled down the beer stein. After this, he ought to have the thing bronzed.

His cell rang. While he heated the skillet, he jabbed a button and tucked it between his ear and shoulder. "Yeah?"

"Trent. Are you all right?" Laura asked.

"Yeah." He laughed quietly. This morning, he was about as "all right" as he'd ever felt in his life. "Why wouldn't I be?"

"They're showing pictures of all the damage on the news this morning. The inn's a mess—I'm looking at it right now."

"Already boarded up. How did you and Schena get along last night?" he added with unaccustomed cheer.

She paused, and he could almost hear the speculation in her silence. "Wonderfully," she said at last. "I think I might get used to the wine business. He's bringing me back to the inn after we eat breakfast, but he wants to fly me out to Napa next month." Her tone softened. "It's nice to hear you happy."

He smiled. That about summed up their entire friendship. He'd been lucky to have her for an ally without even realizing it. "You're something, Laura," he said with admiration.

"Yeah." She chuckled. "Don't you forget it, either."

Funny how Morgan had changed his perception of his life. She had brought the good stuff into focus as easily as an eye doctor switching test lenses. He wasn't even sure when the switch happened—just that he never wanted to see the end of it. "I've got some cleanup work to do," he said. "See you soon."

When she hung up, he dropped his phone on the counter. His parents would probably call soon. He'd texted his father last night, and he'd been waiting ever since for the anticipated outburst of worry and reprimand. Trent had mentioned his plans in as few words as possible, succinct and unapologetic. Whatever his parents did about it was their own damned business. He wasn't changing his mind for them anymore.

Halfway through cooking breakfast, he noticed Morgan in the kitchen doorway. He let his appreciative gaze travel down her snug T-shirt and jeans to the work-beaten sneakers on her feet. "Thought you'd want to sleep in," he said.

She tied her hair into a ponytail and sauntered into the kitchen wearing the smile he'd come to think of as a visual magnet. "I hope you're not just throwing that together," she said.

"Wouldn't dream of it. We might need a forklift to get this thing out of the pan. I made enough for two." Skillet in hand, he turned to the butcher block, where he'd already laid out two plates, the beer stein, and a coffee cup for her. As he cut the omelet and laid half on her plate, a residual flash of concern assailed him. The same one he used to feel when he brought a crayon-and-construction-paper card home to his parents and wondered if they'd like it. The card never made it to the refrigerator door.

The look of delight on her face blew any doubts out of the water. She laid her smile on him, and it was worth all the six-figure deals he'd ever made. How did she do that? "Smells great," she said. She plopped onto a barstool and lifted her fork.

He pulled up another barstool to the opposite side of the butcher block and tried for a casual air, when he really wanted to jump up and yell, *Yes!* Was it really this easy to make someone happy?

He picked up his fork and sliced off a corner of his omelet. "Coming from you, I'll take that as high praise." He studied her face as she ate, watched each nuance of her hands, absorbed the minute flicker of her long lashes. He held his breath for several seconds before trusting himself to say anything. "I've got business to take care of today. Starting with you."

She looked up. Trent pulled the folded papers out of his back pocket. "What's that?" she asked.

"The contract for the Seaglass. Stipulation is, I can't close the sale until I find you a job, and I've finally got one for you. I just need your signature agreeing to the appointment."

The look of dismay and confusion on her face sent him into impatient restlessness. "Just read it, read it. Last page."

She took the papers as though they might bite her, then turned to the last sheet in the stack. "My signature line's still blank underneath."

He gave her his sternest expression. "Well, come on. You can't expect me to get the contract all greasy while I'm cooking, do you? Besides, I didn't have time to write *Seaglass Inn Owner-Operator* and still keep the omelet from burning." He shoved a forkful into his mouth. He lifted an eyebrow and gave her a haughty look. "Eggs cook too fast."

For a minute, she just stared, wide-eyed. "I can't afford to buy the inn."

"I didn't ask what you can afford. Just add your job title and sign it, Montana."

The suspicion in her eyes almost made him laugh. "Not until I know how much I'm going to owe you."

Sitting up straight, he finished chewing his bite of omelet. "All right. I'll put it in writing, if you want. The cost," he said, lifting his beer stein, "is that you never bug me for drinking out of this thing again." He dropped his scowl and replaced it with the grin he'd been holding back since she arrived in the kitchen.

With a shriek and flutter of papers, she shot out of her seat and flew around the butcher block. She flung herself at him so hard he tumbled off the barstool. They slammed against the refrigerator, and she kissed him with such ferocious abandon that he almost carried her back upstairs.

Laughing, he said, "That's a 'yes,' then?"

She nodded, eyes bright and ponytail bouncing.

"Good." He settled his hands on her hips. "Because between you and me, we've got a lot of work to do."

****

Morgan had never expected Trent to give the Seaglass Inn to her. She floated on that surreal joy— a home, all her own, a place she had always belonged and never realized it until being there. The feeling carried her through the rest of breakfast and the return of Laura and Agnes to the inn. When she told Agnes, the older woman merely gave her a knowing smile and said all the best china was still stored in the dining room hutch.

She wanted to pinch herself. Was this how Kincade had felt when Allyson walked into his life? How did he not burst with all that feeling?

For the next half-hour, the four of them finished cleaning up the storm damage. Laura insisted on helping. Morgan told Laura all her favorite recipes for pairing with the local wines. She watched with indescribable happiness as Agnes regaled Trent with anecdotes about the old inn.

But nothing surprised her more than the sight of a white Mercedes-Benz easing up to the curb at the bottom of the driveway. The gleaming luxury car was as out of place in the still-littered street as a

Ritz-Carlton on the moon. Morgan gaped at it until she spied Trent, who stiffened with an armload of broken tree branches on his way to the wheelbarrow.

As far away as he stood, she noticed the clenching of his jaw and the grim look in his eyes, and she realized his parents were in that car. He looked if he expected yet again to disappoint them, and was now resigned to hearing how. She fisted her hands, ready to rebuke them if they even let one word of reproach past their lips. Did they even know their own son?

His parents emerged from the vehicle—first Maureen, in khaki slacks, a sweater, and lightweight twill coat...and then Leland, wearing a polo shirt, short jacket, and jeans.

Trent came up beside Morgan. His expression went from dour to disbelieving. "I've never seen them wear stuff that normal."

Even without the look of shock on Trent's face, Morgan realized the expression of open worry in his mother's eyes was a first. "Mom. Dad. What are you doing here?" Trent asked.

Maureen hurried to him. "Are you all right? We saw the pictures on the news, and we thought—"

"He's fine, Maureen," his father said. "You can see for yourself the boy's fine." Leland turned on the heel of his pristine sneaker and surveyed the inn. His gaze lingered on Trent's patchwork, and then the pile of lumber stacked neatly at the edge of the driveway. "John Lattimer called me...at five o'clock this morning."

Trent heaved a sigh and opened his mouth.

"Never mind your 'Why is he telling you about my confidential business,' boy," Leland interrupted. "He's been a friend of the family for years. He was right to call me and tell me you want to sell off half your holdings."

Morgan blinked. Opened her own mouth.

Couldn't get words out if she'd pried them with a crowbar.

Leland turned his stare on her. "Didn't tell you that, I suppose? Trent never did like to share his business transactions. He's liquidating assets and putting money into this place, then donating the rest to restore any damaged historic buildings on the island."

Morgan's heart squeezed. She whipped around to look at Trent, who ran a hand through his hair. "Dad, I wasn't going to tell her yet."

Maureen, who had been wringing her hands, gave a little yelp and threw herself at Trent. She seized him in a hug that crushed an "Oof!" out of him.

"I was so worried about you," his mother said. "I wouldn't have forgiven myself if...I've been such an awful—" The rest of her words dissolved into a loud sniffle, and she stroked his cheek. "What an amazing, brilliant, wonderful son I have...and I could have lost you without telling you that. And when I heard what you were doing for the people on Nantucket... I'm so...*so* sorry," she whispered. "I hope you'll forgive me... Forgive us."

"Mom, it's okay," Trent said. He patted her back with such heartbreaking awkwardness that hot tears spilled down Morgan's cheeks.

Leland looked at Maureen, and Morgan watched in wonder as the man smiled at his wife. Clearly, Trent's parents had done some talking since their last visit to the island. Had they changed, or merely opened their eyes?

Leland gestured to Morgan with a raised eyebrow. "I think you might want to start explaining some things to her, boy." He slid his hands into his jacket pockets and studied Trent. His gaze warmed. "Your grandfather's tool box is in my trunk. What do you need?"

Trent looked like he'd been handed the moon. For a few seconds, he just stood there as if he were trying to decide whether Leland had really spoken at all. Morgan watched as the frosty businessman peeled away layer by layer, until it left a man who had tried so hard for years to please his parents, without knowing what he wanted for himself.

Maybe he'd been searching all his life for home, too.

"I could use an extra pair of hands," Trent said softly. "Come on, Dad. I'll show you." Father and son strolled toward the inn.

Maureen stood beside Morgan, sniffling and dabbing tears from her cheeks with a silk handkerchief. "I've been so silly for so many years. He's a good boy," she murmured. "A good boy."

"A good man," Morgan corrected.

Trent's mother sniffled again and nodded. "I think I'm going to like you, Miss Clifton." She clasped Morgan's hand with a smile.

They worked throughout the day. Morgan made them breakfast, lunch, and dinner...supplemented with Trent's bottle of Dom Pérignon. The sound of happy chatter filled the inn and filled her heart: Trent and Leland discussing structural repairs and historic buildings, she and Laura sharing recipes and future event plans for the inn, and Maureen and Agnes laughing about old travel stories.

This was what made a home. Morgan floated on that contentment for the rest of the evening. She thought about all the years ahead of her, bringing people together under this roof for good food and company. At the end of the night, everyone shared a bottle of Dominick Schena's best wine. When Agnes, Laura, and Trent's parents retired for the night, Morgan carried the glasses to the kitchen and set them on the counter. She leaned against the butcher block and smiled, soaking in the knowledge that this place belonged to her now, as much as she had always belonged to it.

The phone rang. She snatched it from its cradle before the noise could wake anyone. "Hello?"

"Miss Clifton?"

Trent's voice.

She turned around, searching for him. "Where are you?"

"I'd like to make a reservation to stay at the Seaglass Inn."

She moved to the window over the sink, but couldn't see him out in the garden, either. "Okay," she said, then smiled. "For how long?"

His voice echoed behind her, as well as through the phone. "The rest of my life works for me. How about you?"

She whirled around to find him in the kitchen doorway with a grin on his face and his cell phone to his ear. He stuffed the phone in his pocket and came toward her.

Morgan hung up the phone. Her heart began pounding as he reached into his other pocket. "I texted my dad this morning, before you got up," Trent said. "I told him I want to move my business base here, start doing some construction on the side. Maybe branch out in a new direction. After all," he added, pulling his fist from his pocket, "why not keep this good thing going forever?"

He opened his palm to reveal a velvet box containing a breathtaking diamond-and-sapphire ring. Morgan clapped her hands over her mouth. The ring blurred in a rush of tears.

"Don't start crying now. You do, and your power will kick in, and then it's all over from there." Trent chuckled. "What do you say, Montana?"

With her breath hitching, she nodded.

"That's a 'yes,' then?"

She raised her gaze to his to find him grinning.

Beaming back, she leaped at him and threw her arms around his neck. "You're wrong, Trent. This isn't a good thing. It's a *great* thing."

A word about the author...

Nicki Greenwood graduated SUNY Morrisville with a degree in Natural Resources. She found her passion in writing stories of romantic adventure, and combines that with her love of the environment. Her works have won several awards, including the Rebecca Eddy Memorial Contest. Her first book, *EARTH*, debuted in 2010 through The Wild Rose Press.

Nicki lives in upstate New York with her husband, son, and assorted pets. When she's not writing, she enjoys the arts, gardening, interior decorating, and trips to the local Renaissance Faire.

Visit Nicki at: http://www.nickigreenwood.com

www.ingramcontent.com/pod-product-compliance
Lightning Source LLC
Chambersburg PA
CBHW070925180626
46817CB00003B/1199

* 9 7 8 1 6 0 1 5 4 9 7 8 5 *